# Heiress

# Of

# Comrie

## A Scottish Romance

# By Kara S. McKenzie

*"Thou art all fair, my love; there is no spot in thee.*
*Song of Solomon 4:7 KJV*

# *Dedication*

To my sister for her song, to my sweet friend, Barb, and my Aunt Verna and late Uncle Herm for supplying me with Scottish ancestry information, and for those who will pardon any descrepencies in my attempts to create an accurate portrayal of the time period.

# *Heiress Of Comrie*

A Scottish Romance

## *By Kara S. McKenzie*

*"Thou art all fair, my love; there is no spot in thee.*
*Song of Solomon 4:7 KJV*

# Chapter 1

*Note: There is a dictionary included in the back of this book for some of the language variations.

Ismay withdrew her foot from a puddle she'd stepped in which had pooled on the edge of Crieff's cobblestone streets. "Hech ay!" She whispered under her breath. "I'm quite sure a kelpie's been causing mischief the day long!" She crossed herself at the thought of one of those wickit water demons afoot.

Och! It was 1810, and she was twenty now, another year older. And here she was still afeart of tricks cast upon her, brought on by all those auld Celtic tales she'd haird so often around the fires at night as a wee bairn. "No, it couldn't be kelpies, but maybe something else."

Though her rain-soaked, buckled shoe irked her sorely, she supposed it was no worse than what had happened moments afore. The homespun gray skirt and blue plaid scarf, she'd so carefully chosen on this particular day, were ruined from a muddy onslaught of a carriage wheel.

She reached up and shoved a wet strand of hair away from her face. She wiped the smudges from her mud-spattered face with her hand. She supposed she'd smeared the grit on her cheeks rather than wiped it clean.

She shook her hands. This ill-kindit day was turning out tae be the ruin of iverything!

She was a muddy mess. Now how would she convince some vendor or shop owner tae take her seriously, as clarty as she was, not fit for seeing? Efter this, any auld Scot would turn a blind eye tae her and consider her a scunner.

She breathed a sigh. Not that she'd had any luck earlier that day wi' the townfolk here. But, surely there would be one person in Crieff who might offer her wark. She couldn't imagine there not being one wee job for her tae take on during Michaelmas, the largest cattle sale of the year.

She shivered as she tightened her scarf securely around her shoulders.

If she did not get the money soon, she wasn't sure what she'd do. She'd seen the look of the tairible tax man who'd visited only last week wi' his hatesome speech and his hand stretched out. If only her faither's cattle were still in her possession!

Her cheeks fired with heat. Trying tae steal her heirship from her is what that ill-kindit man was attempting tae do, but she wasn't without a watherful fight and wouldn't let go of her rightful holdings that easily. She was speeritie and not without vigor. That scoonrel, as ill-kindit as he was, would have the ridiculous coins she owed him. The hatesome man should have given her a wee bit more time tae come up wi' the burdenous amount, at least a month or two tae grieve her losses.

A tear settled in her eye, but she straightened and held it back. She'd no time for crying about what might have been.

She turned suddenly when the bold, bonnie sound of a highlander's pipes in the distance plucked at her heart. Its melody ran through her blood at the sound of it growing steadily louder. Oh! They were comin' 'round the corner, the Crieff musicians wi' the red and green plaid!

The music brought back memories of her childhood.

She recalled making her way down this very same path on cattle days wi' a skip and a beat while chasing the comforting, hearty sound. She'd been proud tae be a Scot through and through and shed a tear when they'd passed her.

2

Naught had changed since then as she still couldn't keep these tears from stealing onto her cheeks.

She stepped back onto the street without regard to her surroundings magnetized by the bagpipe's strong melody. Her heart fluttered.

"Whoa, Lass! Do you wish tae be run over!"

Ismay put out her hand to hold back the horses which were on a path headed for her. Her frilled bonnet fell to the ground into the mud.

Indeed! What more swickerie could that auld kelpie be up tae? That water demon should go back tae his loch.

Ismay crossed herself again.

She took a firm hold of the bridle of one of the horses. It had been bearing down on her, and she held it still. "Oo aye! There's a braw mare. You must not be anxious sweetie." She cooed softly to the large animal though it was nearly three times her size.

"Indeed!" A woman's shrill voice rang out from a seat next to the man. "A clarty gypsy, and a muddy mess she is." The woman stared down her nose at Ismay with a look of disdain. "You take your hands from the horse, tinker! I'll not have ye touching what doesn't belong tae you."

She turned to the man with a haughty air. "They'll pilk off wi' your last shullin if ye daena watch them."

Ismay picked up her hat. She let out a sound as she eyed the unwelcome pair. Pilk off wi'? Clarty gypsy? The woman was rude tae say such wickit things about the tinkers. Her foggy childhood memories of the traveling wagon people were pleasant enough. They were certainly not as the woman had made them out tae be.

Ismay straightened as she held her bonnet in her hand. She looked the woman in the eye. "I'm an heiress, and I've a parcel of land in Comrie and a heartsome home of dark whinstone tae prove it!"

3

Dark strands of damp hair fell loosely over her shoulder. She pushed them back. She brushed at the mud on her skirt and cheek.

The man in the wagon seat had been studying Ismay beneath dark brows that were tilted inward. His jaw had been set firmly in place until Ismay spoke, then his mouth suddenly curved up on one side. An amused grin spread over his face. "An heiress you say?"

Ismay's large blue eyes widened as she stared back at him. "Tis true! I do have land. You might not believe it, but it's as right as the good book of oor Lord and Savior."

She backed away from the horse.

The man smiled but didn't answer her.

"She's a clarty tinker. Look at that mud and filth." The woman reached up and tucked a strand of sleek, coppery hair behind her ear. Her large, pouty lips opened slightly, and her dark brown eyes narrowed as they roved over Ismay's clothing. "Heiress! Indeed!"

"And you're not a lady but a low-born wutch, instead!" Ismay stared at the woman and wagged a finger at her.

"Indeed!" The woman got up.

"Grizel." The man turned to the woman and tugged on her sleeve. "This blether of tongue is not mannerly. The lass' dreich situation is not of her own doing. There's no need tae dispute the matter."

"Dreich?" Ismay stepped to higher ground and lifted her chin as she spoke. "I told ye that I'm an heiress, and I'm not in any ill-aft position."

The man held firmly to the horse's reins. A look of interest spread over his face, but he said nothing.

"You daena believe me, sir, but I tell ye the truth."

The horse shook its head and let out a snort.

The red-haired woman stared at Ismay darkly. "Ian, I believe you're right. This wee tinker isn't worth oor time.

Let's not sit here in the way and listen tae the waif rander on as she does. Oor business is on the other side of toun."

Ismay gave the woman an annoyed look.

The man sighed. He turned and spoke quietly. "Move aside, love. My horse is itching tae go on. Another blaud might be comin' again shortly, and you'll need tae find your way back tae your family afore your caught in it."

He smiled and tipped his head.

Ismay stepped aside from the horse. She smoothed out her skirt and stood upright beside the cart. She mumbled under her breath. "There is no one tae go back tae. No family."

She watched as the man gently shook his reins and clucked to his team of horses. The wagon lurched forward and rolled past Ismay.

Ismay put her hands on her hips as she watched the cart disappear down the street.

A drizzle of rain clouded her face as she turned back around.

The last of the town's folk had retired to their homes. The bagpipers had left as shops closed, and animals were penned in for the night.

The streets were suddenly quiet.

A wagon that held a tinker and his wife, with two daughters, and a passel of youngsters rumbled past.

Ismay noted their ragged clothing. Even though their skirts and scarves were worn, the family was on all accounts clean, and their hair was brushed and cared for. Clarty? It wasn't true!

The daughters appeared to be about her age.

Both sisters sat on the back of the wagon and dangled their legs from the platform from which they sat.

Ismay stared at them long and hard. Their dark hair fell in ringlets, and they both had large, almond-shaped eyes the color of coal. She couldn't quite place it, but there was something streengly familiar about their looks and actions.

The older one folded her hands in her lap and stared in the direction of the highland hills as her sister chatted merrily at her side.

They both looked her way as they rounded a bend in the road. Ismay thought one of them might have raised her hand to point, but she wasn't sure of it.

A sudden longing filled her heart as the cart drove out of sight. She was alone in Crieff, on the southern edge of the Highlands, acres from her home. It was a poor place for a young woman to be after the sun went down.

The town was suddenly very secret and hushed. Other than the lowing of the drover's cattle and a few open taverns with muffled laughter, little else stirred.

With the recent death of her parents, and the absence of Ailsa, her closest friend, Ismay suddenly felt very alone.

Tears fell onto her cheeks, and she wiped them away. There'd been much tae consider since her life had been so abruptly altered in such a short time. Mourning the devastating loss of a loved one, while making attempts tae settle the troublesome matters of an estate, hadn't been an easy task.

She took a path and walked down a wooded hill to the bank of a river. Dark fir trees cloistered the homes around the quiet settlement while a waning sun carved a path for her to walk on as she headed farther out of town. A robin tweeted a lonely song from the branches of a Yew tree.

She threw the hood of her arisaid, or cloak, over her head. The changeable Scottish air caused her to shiver.

She smiled. Her faither had often said the weather was neither braw nor bad, but that it was the choice of clothes that mattered. Dear faither.

She sighed as questions circulated in her mind while she stood in the street alone. How was she tae manage the estate now, or draw an honest wage in Crieff? Who might she find wark wi'? And where might she sleep? She'd no money nor friends tae take her in.

As the sun sunk lower, and the air cooled, she met the silence of the forest trail as she wove her way out of town, farther from the rough-handed cattle drovers and shady toun folk of the night.

*****

Roslyn swung her feet beneath her family's traveling cart to the sound of the wheels thundering against the ruts of the rocky path. She looked up when her mother climbed out of the cloth opening of their covered wagon holding a wee bairn in her arms.

Shona, Roslyn's younger sister, was next to Roslyn on the baseboard at the back of the wagon.

Their mother's face was strained, and her cheeks were flushed. "I was kinda hoping one of you might look efter the wee ones for me. I'm so awful tired."

Shona smiled and nodded. "I'll watch over them, mama. Come and stay out here wi' Roslyn. You take a rest."

"Thank ye, dearie. I know it would lift my spirits tae have time of my own."

Shona got up and crawled into the wagon.

Roslyn waited as their mother took a place beside her.

The horse's hooves pounded against a wooden bridge over the River Earn amidst the rushing sound of the swift ford below them.

Roslyn stared at the low banks that sloped gently to the water as they passed. Varieties of sparsly spaced trees lined the edge of it.

A swan dipped its feet into the water and lowered itself in. It moved in a direction away from the rumbling wheels of the wagon.

Roslyn reached out and touched her tiny sister's cheek. "She's a sweet one, oor wee bairn. She has a bonnie face."

"Aye, that she does." Her mother smiled.

There was a brief silence as they stared into the dark behind the cart. The full moon had risen higher in the sky shedding light over the trail.

Her mother looked at the baby again. "I've been thinking. It won't be long, and you'll be wanting tae marry a traveling man, Roslyn. You'll be caring for your own youngsters. You're oor eldest daughter. Your faither and I hope tae find ye a braw lad wi' a worthy wagon who'll treat ye well. It'll bring your papa and I joy tae see ye well settled."

"Oo ay, mama." Roslyn smiled. "I've heard this afore."

"So you'll be of a mind for it when we find a good man for you."

Her mother reached out and touched the edge of Roslyn's newly cropped hair. "Rose, dearie. It'll need tae grow now. What were ye thinking?"

Roslyn's brown eyes twinkled as she shook out the curls on her head. "I had tae do it, mama, tae play the pairt of Robin of Locksley the way it should be duin." She drew back an imaginary bowstring and grinned.

"Wheesht, Roslyn!" Her mother gave her an exasperated look. "A lass of marrying age must take these notions from her head. Your days of merrymaking need tae come tae an end. What man will have ye when ye do such fullish things?"

"I hope a man wi' some blythesome humor. Ye take too much tae heart." Roslyn smiled when a braw poem entered her mind. "I daena know if you'll like this one, mama." She recited it aloud.

"Wheels o' churning yestermorn.
Papa fiddles 'round the fire.
Dark-haired lass recites a poem,
awaitin' what transpires.

Off tae a greener hillock top
a wanderin' wi' a bit o' luck.
Seekin' space and time tae roam
vowin' tae settle in a home."

Her mother's brow rose. "Oh, Rose, I daena know where your thoughts go at times, but I am glad ye come back tae us when the day is said and duin. And it is almost time for ye tae settle wi' a young traveling lad, a tinker's son. We'll set ye up well, though he must own a wagon and at least one horse."

Roslyn didn't answer. There was no sense arguing her position as tae what 'settled well'' meant. Her mama and papa's thoughts weren't a saicret, yet they were quite different from her own.

Her heart skipped a beat as their cart passed a simple thatched cottage set on a hill. Cattle grazed within a fenced portion of the land.

A youngster carried a bucket to the house and went inside while another child looked out over the land from the porch where he stood.

Hech ay! Roslyn sighed dreamily. Tae own a home wi' roots, solid walls without wheels and live off the land! What a blissin these folk had.

From the time she'd been a wee one, she'd known little but the life of farin from town tae town, selling wares and hunkerin around a fire telling stories. She couldn't say it was a poor life as it was quite lively at times, but only a wee bit like the dreams she harbored in her heart.

She tucked a curl behind her ear. Too much traveling, mostly in her mind. Though the wheels beside her kept turning.

"What is it, Roslyn? Where are your thoughts taking ye this time, lass?" Her mother tugged on her arm. "Come now, child."

She lifted the babe in her arms and handed the youngster to Roslyn. "Here, take the bairn. Your thoughts should be wi' your family. The places ye go tae will take you from what's right and real. There's no sense in 'em."

Roslyn lifted the child into her arms. She smiled at the baby's sweet face as her mother went inside the wagon.

"Tottie bairn," she whispered. "What is right and real, tae me, is quite different from the roaming and peddling on the road iveryday here. I'd want tae set down roots someday and live in a house where I've time tae think."

She sighed as the wheels rolled gently into the darkness. Another day of the tinker's life had churned its way to an end. They'd be stopping shortly to set up camp.

*****

Ismay let out a slow breath as she pondered where she'd sleep this night. If a blaud came, in all its fury, she'd need a place to stay where she'd be dry.

She shivered. The thought of finding a shelter in the streets, or in the country, wi' no money for a bed at an inn, or for food, was unnerving. And she'd no tinker's wagon, nor family tae take her in. She knew no one.

She sighed. In this town, she was no better off than an orphant. How she longed for her home!

10

But home was four long miles west in the highlands. She couldn't leave Crieff now, at least not afore she'd found a way tae make money so that she might save her property.

There had tae be a wind-beaten, vacant barn she could bed down in for the night, maybe further out of town, where no one would see. It would be good tae be near a loch where she might wash the mud from her clothing.

She veered away from the dark corners off the road and from small mounds tae keep from running into a trowe, one of those naughty, wee, ugly creatures who came out at night. It wasn't likely she'd see one, but she'd rather not take any chances and steer clear of the places she'd haird they might be found.

She crossed herself and sent a prayer tae the heavens tae ward off the ill trickit trouble-makers.

She turned from the wooded darkness. Would there be a safe place for her tae sleep?

*****

Down the road, just outside of Crieff, Ismay spotted the very place she'd hoped for, a quiet, darkened stable a distance from the main house. It appeared the owner had turned in early for the night.

She snuck inside and crept to the end of the row of stalls. It was dark, and the horses were only slightly restless. A couple of them snorted as she passed, but most were quiet and still.

She shivered as she burrowed deeper into a mound of fresh hay in one of the empty stables. Her stomach growled, and a slight dizziness overtook her.

It wasn't exactly what she'd envisioned earlier as there was no loch in sight, and the barn was full to the brim with horses, but it would have to suffice.

She pulled her cloak tighter around her. At least the building provided shelter from the rain and a welcome relief from what might have been, though the smell of the stable overpowered her senses.

She covered her nose with her scarf and coughed lightly. Just a wee bit pithy! It might be a longer night than she fairst expected.

The horses quieted after her entrance.

Ismay smiled at the thought of her faither who had taught her the way of sweet-talking the furr-beasts in the stable.

It hadn't taken the animals in this place long to calm as a result of her gentle manner. The horses seemed to pay no mind to her sharing their rudimentary shelter with them.

Ismay swallowed drily. The silence of the night was deafening and difficult to bear.

Much had happened very quickly since her life had taken the ill-faured turn it had, and she'd been stripped of all she'd held dear in only a few short months. Things had fallen into such disrepair in so short a while. Time had not been a friend tae her lately.

Her intention was tae keep the home, she loved so dearly, in her own safe hands. But what might she do now when it seemed that all hope was lost?

If the cattle drovers had allowed it, she'd have gone wi' them on the morn's morn in the blink of an eye. She had grit and wasn't a timorsome, sickly lass. She would've warked for the necessary coins as heartily as any of those men, and she knew it, because she'd duin as much at her own home. Her faither had never spared her hardship.

She loosed her tightened fist and stared into the darkness of the stall. But those men would never consider a wee lass such as herself for their perilous wark. It was a rugged lot of them that took the animals south. And if truth be told, she'd most likely not pull her own weight in the face of such testing even though her heart would be tough as a bull's horn.

She sighed. More than once that day, tears had dropped from her eyes as she brought to mind the misfortunes that had befallen her in the past week, and even now they spilled onto her cheeks.

She wiped them away in efforts to put her woes behind her.

She looked upward and drew the folds of her cloak tighter around her.

She figured she should pray, but lately felt she hadn't the heart for it. How might she talk tae the Almighty Lord when she harbored the resentment she did toward Him inside her?

She turned when one of the animals stirred. Another let out a whinny and stomped its hoof on the hard dirt floor.

She looked up again. It seemed God so tairibly forsaken her. But why? What had been His purpose?

She sighed and pushed Him out of her mind.

She spoke quietly to herself. "Oo ay, my earthly faither…why would ye do this? Why have ye allowed these things tae happen, and what am I tae do? If losing mother wasn't enough, you had tae go and leave me wi' such streenge words I did not understand. There's no sense in this collieshangle."

She wiped the tears away again that fell steadily onto her cheeks.

She whispered to herself. "And there'll be naught left of you, faither…or of mother, if I lose my home."

She curled up against the wall shivering. Maybe in the morn's morn things would be different. Maybe then she'd find the wark she'd came tae Crieff in search of.

\*\*\*\*\*

Ismay slept little. She tossed and turned in the hay with thoughts of being on her way soon. Though the shelter was still dark, there'd be stable hands tae contend wi' afore long. The murky cover of night was her protection, yet in a few hours the sun of the misty morn would be comin' up over the horizon.

She looked around the stable. The moon shone beams of light through tiny, open cavities in the wall.

A wee horse next tae her dipped its head over a short gate. Its chocolate brown eyes fixated on her.

Ismay got up and brushed hay from her hair.

She went over to the animal and reached out to pet its sleek, silky neck. "Do ye have a name, bitty one? Will ye keep my saicret and not let anyone know that I'm here?"

She smiled. "At least I'll be leaving shortly as there's no doubt your maister will be out soon. I wouldn't want him tae see me."

She looked down the many rows of stalls full of first-rate horseflesh. The animals were exceptionally groomed in choice condition. Most were likely bought and cultivated for sale and would fetch a fine price. The owner was by no means underprivileged and uncommon in walth, maybe not tae the status of a laird, but a bonnet laird and a gentleman for sure.

She sat back down and drew her cloak over her shoulders.

The same couldn't be said for her, poor as a wee bairn sewer rat. She had less than a shullin tae her name and hadn't had a scrap of food for days.

Och! How she yearned for a bowl of gruel or one smaw tattie tae fill her aching innards. If anyone would have given her a day's wark, she would have willingly labored without a lick of trouble, and she'd have taken on the task wi' pride and warked round the clock for her food.

She looked back at the horse. What might this one be worth?

Oo ay! If only she were rich like this family had tae have been. The sale of one of these noble breeds, here in this shed, would surely cover the taxes for her home and a merry amount of broth. The cost of one wee furr beast would allow her tae hold onto all she owned precious wi' one deal in the making.

There were more horses in this stable than she'd thought possible. She supposed if even one of these sleek animals were tae go astray, it wouldn't cause a smaw binkie tae the owner's holdings.

She shivered as she stared at the bridle hanging on the end of the stall on an iron hook. She looked down the row of horses to the darkened doorway at the end of the stable. Then she turned back to the horse beside her.

It was true. One horse would pay for any debt she owed. It would be all it would take.

Her heart pounded as she suddenly put her hand to her mouth. Och! What an errant thought had just now come into her mind! She shook her head.

Her empty stomach growled, and her heart lurched in her chest. Oo! No! Tae steal one of these horses? This ill-deedie thought pervading her mind wasn't worthy at all. The Lord would want her tae turn the other way from such a sinful plan.

She lifted her fingers to cover her face and peeked through them as she stared at the sleek, quiet beasts in the dark. The stall was black as night, and the maister's house was still.

What made her want tae turn from the Lord's still, soft voice? Why did she suddenly wish tae forget God's ways at this moment even when she knew what was best tae do?

A fire burned inside her. It was right tae follow His direction, yet it would seem so sample tae take measures into her own hands, tae save the heirship. It would only be this once.

She stared futilely into the darkness and swallowed dryly holding back tears.

Her own faith was weak, and she'd been left penniless wi' no thought as tae how she might rectify the situation. Did the Lord not understand how desperate she was as she'd watched her estate crumbling from her very grasp?

Ismay's eyes widened in the silence of the stable. Her breath was unsteady in her chest. But for the sake of her faither's land? Pilking off wi' a horse? Could she do such a tairible thing?

She crossed herself. It was against what she believed was right and true.

She turned onto her side in the hay and let out a deep sigh. But for a wee bowl of broth in her emple stomach and the peace of mind she'd gain if she paid her debt tae that swick of a tax man? Maybe it wouldn'tbe so bad.

She glanced at the animal.

How might taking one wee horse possibly cause injury tae this wealthy man when he had a galore of them? Could it be so tairible for him, when she was stairvin and on the brink of losing her heirship?

She'd never have tae do it again, and someday she could make restitution for this dark deed when she was able.

She sighed as Bible verses raced through her mind.

Wheesht! Be gone! Without this money there'd be no way to sustain herself and no one tae assist her.

I'll pay it back in time. I'll find a way. I'll give back what I owe tae the owner.

She got up and took the bridle as her heart thumped unmerciously in her chest. Her hands dampened with sweat.

If she went promptly in the shadows of the night, the owner woudna know of the missing horse for hours. She'd take a wee one, at the end of the row, and be in the Highlands in a skip and a wink efter the sale of the horse.

She stared at the leather strap in her hands long and hard. Truly, could she do such a thing? It would be wickit.

She lifted her hand to put the bridle back but then recalled what she'd lose if she did not do it.

She groaned. "Lord, ye must forgive me. I canna lose my own faither's home." A tear struck her eye. "I've no one now."

She gulped as she struck a path toward the end stall moving quietly in the darkness.

She drew closer to the horse she'd chosen and whispered in its ear. "There's a wee one, a braw wee lassie you are." She slipped the bridle over the horse's head and unlatched the gate. "Come wee pony. Daena be afeart. I've got ye. I'll find ye a braw home wi' a drover soon."

She climbed onto the pony's back and quietly led the animal toward Crieff in the shadows of the road. Her heart skipped beats at the thought of the owner finding her wi' the small beast.

As soon she was able, she'd slip out of town afore anybody knew better of it.

*****

# *Chapter 2*

The day brightened with the dawn. Roslyn got up and tiptoed away from her family's wagon. She was careful not to wake her brothers or sisters so her mother could sleep longer.

She took a path that led away from their cart and stopped occasionally to close her eyes and breathe in deeply. Freedom tae think! Quiet and solitude. No crackling fire, nor creaking of their small, traveling wagon. No wee bairn's cry, nor heavy breaths of sleep to pervade her thoughts.

A rare glimpse of sunlight streamed down onto her as she eyed the green valley below the hillocks through layers of thick fog. The glen's gently sloping sides had the look of areas carved out by glaciers in times past.

The cool air encircled her, and she wound her scarf around her bare shoulders. The hair she'd cut did have a purpose for mornings such as this. She shivered.

From a distance, the town of Crieff claimed its territory, walled in by patches of purple fields of heather and dark evergreens. Stone fences ran along the road zig-zagging between the patterned mix of colors in the fields.

Roslyn hummed a lively tune as bonnie words found their way into her thoughts. She'd a fondness for the power of language and how she could arrange it subtly like brush strokes on a canvas.

On this day, she pieced together small phrases from pretty hues of the hillocks and glens. She composed a poem as she walked.

Emerald lace points
in evergreen rows
sweepin' the tempest sky

as dusty, wooly clouds
spindrift past
God's handiwork at rest.


When her mind was occupied as such, often her other senses were diminished and sometimes altogether retired as was the case this early morn. She skipped along happily rearranging verses as she stared at the distant landscape.

She failed to notice the sound of pounding hooves of a horse coming down the road and the caustic scent from dust whipping into the air as the sleek, gray animal reared up and whinnied in her path.

"Whoa!" A braw man in a full Scottish kilt called out. "Get out of the way!" His look was one of astonishment.

Roslyn leaped aside of the animal's fierce hooves before almost being knocked to the ground.

The man settled the horse and quickly dismounted. He looked concerned. "Are ye hurt, lass? Are ye injured?"

Roslyn stepped back as her brown eyes widened. "Hech ay!" She drew in a breath. The man was a brawly one, quite unmatched in Roslyn's eyes. Dark brown curls fell wildly over his ears. There was a roguish, unkempt look about him, and he might have come straight from one of her tales of forest outlaws.

Her lips parted while he waited for an answer.

"Miss?"

"I'm quite well." She put her hand to her chest to still her breaths. "Oh, please. Daena look so pained." She pointed to the treeline in the distance. "The dark evergreens in the valley were more than likely tae blame."

The man gave her a curious look. "Those trees? But it was my horse that almost injured you."

"No, I must apologize." Roslyn smiled. Then she laughed at his serious expression. "I often lose sight of what's around me. My mind was on the evergreens, and I took my eyes from the road."

"You're not injured?"

"Not at all. There's no harm duin." She lifted a hand to her short, dark curls and brushed pieces from her eyes that had fallen into her face.

"Well, I hope not," he replied. "I'd not wish tae cause ye distress."

"If anything, your quick words brought me tae my senses. Otherwise I might not have seen ye coming." Roslyn brushed dust from her dress. Her eyes sparkled as she watched him. "I was lost in my thoughts again. My dear mother and faither tell me all the time tae keep my mind on the world around me."

He studied her quietly with a smile. "Well, the fog is thick. I suppose you couldn't see through it."

Roslyn came to stand next to him. "It is true." She nodded hesitantly and smiled.

"I'm Callum Crawford." He reached out and took her hand giving it a hearty shake. He grinned.

Roslyn stared at him. That smile! He might have been from an auld Celtic tale! She could write about a face like his.

She quickly let go and blushed. She sighed. Where were her thoughts?

"You daena live here?" Callum looked around.

"My papa's wagon's down the road. He's a tinker. I'm Roslyn Day." She pulled on a curl as she watched him.

"And out early in the morn, Roslyn."

"Aye. I like my time alone."

Callum nodded. "I suppose when ye share a wagon wi' a family there might be a need for it. Do ye have sisters and brothers?"

Roslyn's dark curls bounced as she spoke. "I do. I have two sisters, one a year younger than myself and another a wee bairn, and one brother."

Roslyn couldn't help but glow with pride as she spoke of them. "Mama and papa would've had more, but the Lord chose differently."

"Then it's as it should be."

"Aye."

He pointed to her hair. "I must say, I thought ye were a young lad at fairst." His eyes twinkled.

"At fairst?" She feigned an injured look, and then she giggled as she swept her hand in front of her and bowed low. "Robin of Locksley, at your service."

"Ah, I see. Ye could be him." He laughed. "Ye play the pairt very well."

Her brown eyes deepened in color. "Though my mama wouldn'tagree. She had a face like a bulldog chewin' a wasp when I chopped my hair on account of oor play, but I felt it had tae be duin. I would've liked tae make Robin proud."

He smiled. "I'm quite positive he would have applauded your efforts. And for your mama's sake, it'll grow, though I rather like the look of it 'round your pretty face."

Roslyn eyes widened. Her dark lashes fluttered downward and then back up again.

Callum looked out over the valley. He gave her a curious look. "What's it like traveling from place tae place? Are you content tae live on the path day in and out?"

Her voice was quiet as she answered. "I've known naught else so I'm not certain, but I love my family."

"They treat ye well?"

Roslyn brightened. "They do. Mama and papa are very kind tae all of us, and we're a close family. Though…"

Callum's look was thoughtful, but he didn't say anything.

Her voice grew wistful. "I do sometimes wonder what it would be like tae live in a home. I canna imagine anything aside from the traveling life."

Callum spoke quietly. "I'm quite certain it would be very difficult tae break ties from such a close-knit family."

"Aye, papa and mama are already seeking tae secure my future so that I'll have a place wi' them." She sighed. "Mama says I must marry a traveling man." Her cheeks reddened as she said it.

"And you're prepared tae do this?"

Roslyn gave a reluctant nod. "Aye." Then a frown crossed her brow, and she paced back and forth in front of him. "Mama and papa would expect it."

She stopped in her tracks. "Though I kind of wonder as I've been told my mind is in the clouds, and my feet are off the path. I rather think a stable man might make a better match. I've as much as told my mama and papa my thoughts, but it's as if they daena wish tae hear it."

Callum's hazel eyes were solemn. He spoke quietly. "So they give ye no choice in the matter."

"Oo, no! I'll have a choice, but mama and papa are quite certain about what's right. I love them dearly, and I wouldn't wish tae cause them pain."

Her cheeks suddenly grew warm. She put her hands to her face. "I've randered on so. I did not mean tae."

She backed away from him.

"Miss?"

"I shouldn't have spoken as boldly as I did. I apologize."

"No." Callum shook his head. "Ye must not feel bad for giving an honest answer."

Roslyn sighed and set to pacing again. "But a proper lass would never rander on about her private affairs the way I did. My Mama would be disappointed in me."

Her skirt rustled against the uneven ground as she turned abruptly. She took hold of the edge of it and lifted the corner. "I've so much as told ye some of my deepest thoughts when we're outright strangers, and it wasn't mannerly of me."

Callum smiled. "If ye please, I find it quite rare tae meet a lass as straight oot the gate as ye are." His eyes sparkled. "I admire your honest words."

She climbed onto a rock and stepped from there onto another one. She turned and looked conflicted. "Mama would believe you tae be quite bold. You must not speak as commonly as ye do."

She got down off the rock and went to him.

"Truly?" He laughed. "When you appeared tae me as Locksley? What would she say tae that?"

She gave him a shocked look. "Please! You must not tell her this, or papa!" The color in her cheeks heightened further. "They'd not allow me out again."

"They wouldn't?" He leaned closer and smiled. "Then you're saicret is safe wi' me as I'd rather wish tae meet up wi' ye again. Alhough they should know about the way ye jested wi' an aff the fair streenger."

"But ye won't tell them."

"No, I will not."

She eyed him curiously. "Ye do speak your mind, sir, without restraint."

"It seems wi' you I do. Though afore today, I've not been called into question. It's not ordinarily my way tae be so bold."

"It Is not?"

"No."

Roslyn gave him a puzzled look as she tugged at a curl at the nape of her neck. "Did ye tell the truth when ye said ye thought me pretty?"

He smiled. "I did." The expression in his eyes softened.

His horse suddenly danced and whinnied. "Whoa, Kurrie. The lass has no wish tae sidestep your hooves again."

The nervous animal quieted and quickly lowered its head.

Roslyn reached out and stroked its neck. "You have a way wi' her. I see it."

He spoke quietly. "Aye, we wark well together. A steady hand settles this traveler."

"Traveler?" She stared at him. "Why do ye say this?"

Callum let go of the leather rein.

The horse immediately lifted her head and snorted. Her gait was lively as she trotted to a flowery path and meandered down it.

"Look see." He whistled, and the animal immediately turned and trotted back to him. He took the reins.

"She listens tae ye."

He nodded. "Aye, she's safe wi' me, and she knows it."

Roslyn watched him curiously, and then she looked around. "Do ye have a home nearby?"

"I do, quite close. I've a flock of black-faced sheep and some land, and I'm rebuilding an old homestead."

Roslyn turned as a small warbler on a branch dropped to the ground next to her and pecked at twigs and dried leaves.

She put her hands behind her back and clasped them and sighed.

Callum took a place beside her. "Have ye given it thought tae what it would be like livin' differently than ye do?"

She turned. At first, she didn't answer. "I've thought a lot about this. Being raised the way I have is quite different than growing up in a home as a wee bairn. Sometimes I wonder if I might have thrived under the security of a stable place tae live."

"Though you've had a good life."

"I have, but it might have been good tae have had a bit of guidance at times. I'm a wee bit like your Kurrie wi' my mind in the clouds and my feet off the path as I was when ye fairst met me." She smiled. "Maybe I'd have been more prudent in my actions."

"Though we wouldn'thave crossed paths if ye had been."

A blush formed on her cheeks as she looked at him.

He steadied his horse again when it lifted its head. "Ye do lead a very interesting way of life. Livin' the way ye do is much different."

"Aye. Mama and papa barter wi' the townfolk while the youngsters play and run around. My sister and I tend tae the wee ones, and do what else is needed, though my mind quite often turns tae the land and places I travel through. And tae my books."

"I see ye care very much for your parents."

"Tis true. My family's close tae me. We wark hard, but at the end of a traveling day, we dance around the fire and sing. Faither will often tell us a bonnie tale."

The expression in her eyes softened as she turned in the direction she'd come from. "They'll listen tae my poems, too, and pretend tae be entertained by them."

Callum spoke quietly. "I'd like tae hear a poem of yours. Would ye recite one, Roslyn?"

She gave him an uncertain look. Her cheeks pinkened. "Surely ye have better things tae do than tae listen tae my ill-aft dafferie."

He took his hat from his head and held it against him. His eyes twinkled. "I'm thinking I'd rather like it."

"I daena know. I quite sure my mama wouldn't approve that I have shared such things." She looked away.

"Please, I've something in my saddle bag. I'll give it tae ye in exchange for a poem."

Her brows drew inward. "For one."

"Aye." He smiled. "And I think you'll be pleased wi' what I have. God must have willed that I brought it."

"I see you're quite persuasive." She put her hands behind her back and paced. Then she stopped. "I suppose I could, but only on account of my curiousity being roused. I'd be interested tae see what ye have in your saddlebag."

Callum smiled again.

She looked toward the rolling mountains separated by narrow, flat valleys in the distance. She put her hands to her side, and she stood there deep in thought.

She spoke quietly.

"In the grace of a moment
aneath dusty, violet mountains
that vanish in the whispy mist
the traveler, she chanced upon
one wi' a steady hand, a blissin'
leaving traces of splendor
in her heart."

He studied her quietly not saying anything.

"The words, they come in colors and sounds in my mind, not my own. They are the Lord's arrangements. I'm quite certain of it."

She breathed in the soft scents around them. "Tis a smaw one. I hoped not too silly."

His look was solemn. "I do not know how ye were able tae invent a piece so lovely in such a short notice. Tis a God-given gift, Roslyn."

She looked relieved. "I'm glad you approved of it."

"Very much so." He smiled. "Now, I've something for you." He went to Currie and opened a leather pouch. He reached inside and pulled out a hard-bound book.

Roslyn's eyes widened, and she gasped with delight. "Hech ay!"

He brought it to her and placed it in her hand.

"No! I daena deserve this." She smoothed her fingers over the cover. "Robert Burns! It's more than I can bear."

"My mother gave it tae me, but I know that God meant it for you." He looked tenderly at her. "I'm glad ye felt spendor today. That grace of a moment I believe might have involved a gray horse. Could it be?"

She put her hand to her mouth, and her cheeks pinkened. "I…told ye these things come tae my mind. I daena decide what comes out of my mouth. I apologize if it seemed bold."

"On the contrary." He shook his head. "I found your words comforting. You are able tae express honest truths."

Roslyn breathed a sigh. "Then I'm glad of it as oor time together has lifted my spirits this morn."

"It's a good thing you were not injured and that I gained a companion on account of your runaway thoughts."

She smiled then reached out and patted Kurrie again. "It's been a pleasure meeting ye, Mr. Crawford, in spite of the way it came about."

"Aye, it's been a bonnie time." He took her hand and held it in his as he watched her reaction.

She withdrew it as crease lines formed over her brow. "I daena think I should tarry longer. My mama and papa will expect me back soon."

"Despite that you were on your way tae town?" He smiled. There was a sparkle in his eye. "I'll walk wi' you if you'd like."

"No! You mustn't. My papa wouldn't approve. He'd not be happy wi' me this morn."

"We'd be back afore the sun is overhead?"

"You daena know my papa. He doesn't think much of…town folk." Her cheeks suddenly flamed again. "Though you're a very worthy man, and I know it. I daena mean…my parents…they…"

Callum smiled. "I understand. They daena want me tae swee ye from your traveling ways."

"We're a very close family."

He gave her an expectant look. "It's been a pleasure, lass. God surely had a hand in the way oor paths crossed. Maybe it's His will that we meet again."

"But mama and papa wouldn't approve…" Roslyn eyes widened.

"I've no desire tae injure you, or them, in any way." His voice was sincere. "I'll speak tae them."

Roslyn shook her head. "No, ye mustn't. They'd be unhappy."

"That we exchanged kind words and took pleasure in good company."

"I see no harm in oor friendship, but they'd surely see things differently."

"I'd prefer your parent's blissin, though it does not seem possible."

"They'd not consent."

"Then Roslyn, it seems we're in a quandary."

She stood there quiet and thoughtful a moment as she looked up at him.

She spoke softly. "I might walk down this trail afore nightfall and maybe come upon your horse by chance again so that we might talk. I suppose it would be no fault of oor own."

Callum eyes lightened. "I daena think it would, Roslyn."

She backed away as he mounted his horse.

He smiled. "I'll go now, but I hope tae see ye again."

She nodded. "Maybe." Something in her chest leapt quietly as she watched him ride off.

She put her hand to her chest stilling her beating heart. If she did meet him again, it would be a short visit.

Surely there'd be no harm duin wi' a bit of talk and a brief friendship. Her Papa and mama need never know about Callum as naught would iver come of it.

\*\*\*\*\*

# Chapter 3

The following morning, Ian stalked grim-faced past two men and stopped at the last shop on the street. He tapped his fingers against his side impatiently.

The owner looked up. "Do ye need something?"

"I'm looking for my prize black staig, the one wi' white marks on it. It was gone from my stable this morn." Ian shifted his stance as he raked his hand through his hair. His eyes narrowed, and he looked down the street. "There's a horse thief afoot who will be paying for it, and it'll be a harsh restitution they'll be facing when I catch them."

The merchant put out his hands. "I haven't seen it, Ian. Sorry, but I canna help you. Sales took place afore the early morn though. Ye know how it is around here at this time."

"I do know it." Ian tapped his fingers on his side. "But, I canna allow such swickery. I mean tae find out who it was who took it."

A voice came from behind. "Ye said a black staig?"

Ian turned.

A man behind him held the reins of a seasoned mare. His pudgy cheeks widened as he spoke. "With white marks? Were they on its chest?"

Ian nodded. "Aye. Ye think ye might have seen it?"

"I...I do." The man stuttered in his excitement.

"Ye must tell me. Who had it?"

The man nodded. "I believe it were that muddy, wee tinker's daughter. I saw her early this morning, holdin' it like it was her own. She took a cattle drover aside, a lowlander, tae speak wi' him."

Ian gave the man an odd look. "That wee lassie? Are ye certain of it?"

"I am." The man's voice got higher as he spoke. "I'd misgivings concerning the matter but not enough tae voice 'em. I thought she was selling it for her faither, but it seems not. She went away on foot in the direction of Comrie."

"Comrie?"

"Aye."

"Thank ye, sir."

The man rambled on while Ian turned and strode back to his horse. He didn't stay to listen or elaborate on the matter.

His jaw clenched as he patted the side of his animal and got on. He adjusted the reins in his hand. Heiress, my eye. He should have listened to Grizel. It seemed that the young lass *was* a clarty thief and a traveler.

He let out a breath as he shook his head. It was a good thing that cattle man had overhaird her conversation wi' the drover. Otherwise he might never have found out the truth.

And now he'd find out where she went and see that she'd pay for what she'd duin and not get away wi' pilking his property. The wee speeritie swick wouldn'tset foot in Comrie afore he found her.

It was lucky for her they'd put an end tae hanging horse thieves on Kind Gallows not long ago. Though there'd be no Highlanders touching their bonnets as they passed the hanging tree wi' their blissin's and damnations, though he'd see tae it that justice was duin and that she'd pay for her lawless act.

He looked back at the two men with a grim expression and then rode off out of town as he left the rolling lowland landscape behind at the edge of the sweeping hills of the highland.

*****

Ismay stole along the edge of the path between tall hedges that lined the way to Comrie, the small weaver's hamlet, west of Crieff, that was her home.

Most of what she'd passed over was Drummond clan acreage. Aberuchill Castle was west of the town, one of the clan's many properties in the area. It stood low in the valley amongst tall trees in the distance wi' its stark white stone and many windows and chimney stacks.

The grand mountains rose up in the distance. She drew in a breath as she stopped to admire them. A rugged, steep-sided river ran through the low valley just south of her, and a small loch had pooled at the end of it. She could barely make out a couple large trout treading water in it, side by side, near the banks while a common moorhen dipped its pronged feet in at the river's edge.

The weather was cool even with the sun shining through the misty reaches of fog that lay in patches over the valley.

She breathed in the fresh, brisk air and sighed. Och, the beauty of the highlands. Its boundless rivers and lochs and majestic terrain left her breathless wi' its magnificence.

And Comrie, her town, a place where three rivers met, sat quietly between the Grampian mountains and open moorlands to the north and lesser mountains to the south.

She sighed. Scotland was a bonnie place tae have been born despite being a hard taskmaster. Rich and poor alike, who lived in the land, were a sturdy lot enduring the hard, long winters and clumpy mounds of rocky soil.

Comrie, the affluent village in the southern highlands of Scotland, lay a couple miles from where Ismay had spent most of her days as a child. Her home and land had been given tae her faither by a relative of a famous clan leader himself through a series of unusual circumstances. If truth be told, more than one duel had been fought over the rights tae it. Yet, time had healed wounds, and peace had ensued for now. Ismay was the owner at the present and planned tae do iverything she could tae keep it that way.

She suddenly put her hand to her throat and groaned. But she shouldn't have stolen the horse for the cost of the taxes. Ach!

She looked back in the direction of Crieff about five miles to the east. She'd been walking since early morn and had made braw time. It seemed her troubles were behind her as she'd seen no one along the path.

The cattle drover who had bought the black staig would have been long gone afore anybody had seen him. She'd met up wi' that unceevil tax man and had given him the money, which he'd taken wi' relish, and quickly hitched a ride out of town. The black deed had been duin. She'd stolen in haste, and now it grieved her heart tae think of it.

Her cheeks suddenly grew hot. What iver possessed her tae take such strong measures and sink so low? She'd been rash and impulsive. How could she have duin what she did?

She cringed at the thought of the horse's owner finding his animal missing. When he did, would he go south tae search for the horse? And if he found it, would the cattle drover be blamed for her wickit act? Or would he expose her for the thief she was?

What a collieshangle she'd made. How would she live wi' herself efter taking such a dark turn?

She sat on a flat rock on the side of the road and looked at the rolling hills in front of her. Their slopes were grass-covered dotted with flocks of black-faced sheep bleating quietly to each other. Along the edges grew the breckan, wild ferns which fanned out against the rock strewn hillside.

She kicked a pebble across the path and jumped when a brown hare hopped skittishly into the underbrush. Och! She was jimpy. She needed tae compose herself. There was no danger now and most likely would be none.  She'd left Crieff behind and her wickit deeds as well.

Her eyes drew upward at the sight of a large shadow moving overhead.  It passed a grouping of Hawthorne trees across a field.

A golden eagle had spread its wings wide and drifted downwith on the wind past snow white clouds.  It was as if he were keeping a careful watch over his marked range.

Ismay shivered.  He'd most likely seen ivery one of her wrangous actions from his lofty vantage point.

She'd outwardly sinned by pilking another's prize possession.  She'd sauld the animal for her own gain.  What she'd duin was ill-deedie and braisant.  Her faither would be affronted by her devilish breach.  Would it be possible for her tae be forgiven for such a lawless act?

She swallowed drily as she got up and walked down the path her thoughts a jumble.  She wished she'd not succumbed tae the daurk course she'd taken.  It might have been better tae have been cast out of her house and tae have taken up residence on the streets than tae carry the horrible guilt around that plagued her now.

She sighed.

Maybe she should go back tae Crieff and turn herself in?  What had she thought she might accomplish by what she'd duin?  Tae become a thief and a liar.  She payed the taxes to her home, once again, but she'd sauld her soul tae the deil tae do it.

Goin' back and telling what she'd duin could set it all straight.  It would surely be the better path.  And she'd be right wi' God again.

Maybe it was what she should do.

She jumped at the sound of horse's hooves behind her.  Her nerves were frazzled since she'd returned.

"Ah, the wee heiress, is it not?" A harsh voice sounded behind her. "I wouldn't have believed a person wi' such a title would've found it necessary tae resort tae horse thievery."

\*\*\*\*\*

Ismay turned and looked up.

She groaned when she saw who sat atop a tall, brown mare which high-stepped nervously in the road. "Oh, no! The wutch's husband." Her heart skipped a beat as she stared fearfully at him.

The man's dark eyes narrowed. He gripped the prancing horse's reins tighter. "You recall oor meeting on the street? It appears you've been busy since then. Now where's the animal you stole?"

Ismay's cheeks flushed with pink. "Please, sir. You daena understand! I was confused. My mind was tapsalteerie! I was without a penny or a purse. Afore this, I've been unacquainted wi' scandal. I meant tae make it right."

"Haud yer wheesht! He got off the horse and went to her. He took hold of her arm and dragged her with him.

Ismay dug her feet into the earth and tried to pull away. "But, he's long gone wi' it. I sauld it tae a cattle man."

"Aye, right. You're the wee hen that never layed away." He didn't let go.

"I never said I did not do it, and I planned tae pay ye back." Her eyes were large.

He stopped and stared at her. His jaw was set in place. "Aye, ye will pay for what you've duin."

Then he looked at her skirt. He dug in her pockets and in the coin purse she'd slung over her shoulder.

Ismay gasped. "Sir!"

He pulled out a crumpled handkerchief and threw it on the ground. He gave her a look of disgust. "Where are my coins?"

Ismay stooped to get her handkerchief and wrung it in her hands.

He took her by the shoulders. "Come, lass. Tell me. Ye owe me the price of it."

"I told ye, I daena have it." She wiped a tear that slid down her cheek. "I'll pay it back. I promise." Her hands shook. "I meant tae get the money back tae ye, I did."

"But I want it now."

"I gave it tae the tax man. Otherwise, I'd lose my heirship, my faither's home." She wrapped a piece of hair around her finger nervously and looked up at him. "And I bought a wee bit of broth, too."

"The money wasn't yours tae use for what you wanted! You stole it!"

"But I'll wark for it!" She gulped. "I pledge it on my honor. Please, sir!"

He rolled his eyes and gave a harsh laugh. "You speak of honor, efter what ye did? Ye took the coins and were on your way out of town!"

"I know ye daena believe it, but I'm not so wickit and tairible as ye think. I meant tae pay ye back." Ismay stood straighter and pushed her hair over her shoulders. "My faither always said I was able and full of speeritie. I may look a wee smaw, but I can labor harder than any highlander."

He shook his head. "You shouldn't have sauld my horse. I canna have a horse thief warking for me."

"But, I canna get it back, and I daena have the money. I'd give it tae you, if I could and will. Your home is not far from here, though I daena know your name."

He groaned and gave her another dark look. "Ye did not see MacAllen emblazened on the side of my stable when you were sneakin your way in?"

"It was dark, sir."

"Ye understand I've the right tae send ye tae jyle where you might lairn from your mistake. A couple of solid walls and a lock might do ye good."

Ismay gulped. She put her hand on his arm. "Mr. MacAllen, please, sir. I'll not steal again. I'll wark for it and pay ye back."

Tears suddenly dropped down her face and mixed with the mud on her cheeks. "I saw a woman once dressed in sackcloth, and her feet were bared on that cold stone floor. They mocked her there tairibly having her sit on the stool of repentence for others in the town tae watch. She was made tae confess afore the whole county, and she was dead afore she left the place."

Ismay's eyes looked like pools of blue as she turned to him. "I am sorry for what I did. Will ye please allow me tae labor for the price of the horse? I'll pay ye back in full. I promise." She wiped the tears which dropped down her cheeks and gave him a pitiful stare.

Ian looked upward at the sky and groaned. "Hech ay! You're doin' my heid in!"

"Please, sir. I'll wark hard, but daena send me to the jyle. I tell ye, I would die there."

He let out an annoyed breath and shook his head. Then he sighed. "Dry your eyes, lass! I'll not send ye tae the jyle as I know what other ill-kindit suffering goes on there. But ye will wark it off, and you'll pay for all of it." He took hold of her arm clenching it tightly.

Ismay winced but didn't say anything. She looked up at him with tears still in her eyes.

He groaned again and loosened his grasp shoving her away from him. "Oo ay! I'm an ouf tae even consider this bletheration!"

"You'll get back what ye lost. I promise ye. And if I daena do as I say, you can take me tae the jyle. I give ye my word."

The man stared at her as if in disbelief. "If ye lie tae me iver, or if ye cause anymore trouble, you *will* go there."

"Please, sir, I won't be a burden tae you." She held her breath as she waited for his answer.

"I'll get my money's worth, and you'll do more than enough tae pay for the horse and make up for the dark deed ye took it upon yourself tae do."

She looked up again, and her mouth opened in surprise. "Oo ay! I will! I'll make it up tae ye. I will. You'll see!"

Ian's brow furrowed over his eyes. He seemed as if he wasn't sure what to say.

Then suddenly his horse gave a nervous snort, and he looked at his animal. "Whoa, Lillias. What is…"

The horse suddenly threw back its ears and sniffed the air.

Both Ismay and Ian stared at the animal as it gave another nervous snort. It whinnied and ran a distance away.

Ismay took hold of Ian's arm. She gulped.

"Lillias! Come!"

At that moment, there was a loud sound similar to an explosion, and the ground began to quake.

Ismay's eyes widened. She grabbed Ian around the waist, and they both fell to the ground.

"Och!" She buried her face in his cloak while tremors rocked the hillside and all around it. "No…" Her heart pounded, and her breath caught in her throat.

Ian's arms tightened around her shoulders. "Wheesht, lassie. It'll be past soon. There's naught tae fall on us."

The rumbling intensified, and a sudden rushing wind swept over them.

Ismay shuddered. Panic rose in her chest. She took a ragged breath. Since a youngster, and a time when she'd fallen into a crevice when the earth had been rocking and not been able tae get out, she'd been terrified of the quakes. Luckily, her faither had found her and had pulled her tae safety.

Oh me! How did Comrie have tae rest near a fault? Shaky town, as it had so been nicknamed, had been plagued by these tremors, and lately they'd been comin' on quite often.

Ismay held onto the man's waistcoat, and it seemed ages until the shaking slowed and disappeared altogether.

She gathered her wits about her and whispered to him. "I've an unnaitural fear. I..."

He pulled away with an agitated frown. "There'll be eftershocks." He stood and backed away from her.

She got up. Her cheeks reddened, and she straightened. "I know it."

She brushed herself off. "I apologize that I clung tae ye the way I did. I'm certain your wife wouldn'tbe pleased that I've been so forward, though I would've clung tae the darkest serpent of the loch if I'd been forced into it. These quakes rattle me so."

"It seems they do." He eyed her curiously as a small spark lit in his eye.

"Aye! More than ye know, and I'm sorry for it. I wouldn't have behaved as I did if not for the quakes."

He rolled his eyes again and made a gruff sound. "Well, ye needn't worry. Miss Hawthorne isn't my wife. Though I suppose she might not take kindly tae such things."

He got up and whistled for his horse as he looked toward the rolling hills in the distance. "It appears you're not so bold as I thought ye were. There were no trees or rocks nearby, nothing tae fear."

Ismay didn't answer.

Ian's horse galloped toward him and slowed. It stopped as it reached the spot where he stood. "Good, Lillias." He took the reins which dragged on the ground. "There's a braw mare." He petted the side of it's neck tenderly as the horse snorted and settled.

Ian turned to Ismay. "Come, lass, wi' me." He put out his hand. "We must wark this out between us."

"But, my house and clothing! The quake. I must see if all is as it should be."

He shook his head. "Not until you've paid me back in full. Ye owe me for the horse and have indentured yourself. My servant will find clothes for you, and you'll clean this clarty skirt."

"But…"

"Daena oppose my wishes, lass. You deserve the jyle, and I've allowed ye concessions for this. Horse thievery, a family's livelihood, isn't taken lightly here."

Ismay looked like she planned to speak again, but he shook his head. "It wouldn't be wise tae say more."

She held her tongue and sighed. At least the taxes had been paid, and the land wouldn't go tae another. Tom would see the the care of her house. She supposed she'd find a way tae get back there in time.

For now, she'd been lowered tae the peasantry status.

He lifted her onto the back of the horse and got on behind her. He dug his heels into the side of the animal, and they sped down the road in the direction of Crieff.


*****

# Chapter 4

"What?! You've taken that clarety tinker's daughter into your home?" Grizel's face turned red as she came bursting through the thick, wooden door. Her hand rested on the bronze latch.

Ismay swept the hardwood floor with a broom in front of a stone hearth. She didn't look up, but her movements quickened as she jabbed at the edges. She whispered under her breath. "Tinker's daughter? I'm an heiress, and not clarty."

Ian eyed the smaw orphant at the far end of the room.

Ismay moved efficiently without a break in her work. She'd begun her new position, assisting his cook and head housekeeper.

Over the span of a few days, she'd proved she was a warker. Chores had been finished handily, in neat order wi' vigor.

Afore her presence in his home, a hearty diet had been a rare thing tae find joy in. Now, the meals were greatly improved, and denner was a blissin, rather than a curse.

Though her previous actions had led him tae mistrust her, he'd come tae see her quite differently since she'd moved into his servant's quarters.

He studied the young woman as she moved about the room. Her tunic and leather shoes were clean but were a couple sizes too large.

Annag was the smallest of the servants, but Ismay still swam in the folds of the housekeeper's skirt and sark. If not for the plaid piece, tied about Ismay's waist, she would have had difficulty moving freely.

Washed and clean she appeared quite different. She was a bonnie lass wi' large, blue eyes and thick lashes. Her hair was the color of the black moors, tied behind her wi' a piece of leather, and her cheeks had a healthy glow about them. He wasn't surprised Grizel was full of fury about Ismay being there, as pretty as she was, yet there was no reason for her tae lose her head over the matter. He'd no plans tae set his sights on one of the servants.

"She owes me for the horse, Grizel. I'm taking my full payment for it. She'll wark it off in time."

Grizel lifted her chin and smoothed out her silken gown which was fastened at the neck with a silver brooch. She stared stoney eyes at Ismay. "You should be taking her tae the jyle instead, what she truly deserves."

Ian shook his head. "She'd rot away in the jyle. I might as well get what I'm owed."

"But you've no need of more workers. There's no sense in it."

"Grizel, the debt must be paid, and the lass will redeem herself. Say no more about it. My decision is made."

"Sometimes this code of honor ye hold so tightly tae warks tae your disadvantage. Ye must see this, Ian."

Ian's jaw tightened, and he clenched his fist. "I told ye that my decision is made, Grizel. I've wark of my own and no time tae rander on about this. You might go home and shew a bonnie skirt for the next ball, instead of attempting tae dissuade me from doing as I see fit."

Grizel couldn't hide her displeasure at his remark. "I've servants for shewing…and worthy ones at that." Her smile was curt, though she moved closer and took his hand in hers. "I'll have a gown for the event. I'm sure you'll be pleased wi' it when your carriage arrives, and I'll expect the fairst dance of the night."

She looked over at Ismay who was busy working. Her eyes darkened.

Ismay looked up briefly. She gave the woman an indifferent glance and started sweeping again.

Ian let go of Grizel's hand. He bowed. "It'll be my pleasure."

Grizel said no more, but she lifted her chin. She stepped outside the door and latched it behind her.

*****

# Chapter 5

The week had gone by quickly.

Roslyn's family pitched their tent for the night. Roslyn got up at the urging of her parents and twirled in her gold-striped skirt to music around the firelight.

Her mother's expression brightened, and her eyes twinkled merrily as Roslyn's sisters and brothers laughed and cheered.

Roslyn's papa played the fiddle while the wee ones clapped with a plucky, speeritie beat. He turned to Roslyn from where he stood. His eyes were tender. The full lit moon shone down on them as her arms moved in rhythm to the song and beat.

Though Roslyn smiled and danced, her thoughts drifted far from the campsite tae her own private musings.

She'd seen Callum again and another time, and then met wi' him regularily until she'd lost count of how many times they'd been together. Knowing her parents wouldn't stay in one place for long, she took walks in his company ivery evening before the sun went down.

An attachment had grown between her and him, and a commitment had blossomed in the wake of their friendship.

Roslyn turned from her family considering the possibility of someday leaving the tinker wagon and setting out in a different direction, one that would take her from them.

She loved her mama and papa, and it was never the reason for her discontent. They'd given her a braw life and had treated her well. There was little she'd lacked from their glad hearts and giving natures.

A home of her own, and space tae breathe had always weighed heavily on her mind, and now Callum was in the mix of these wayward thoughts.

She took a seat on a wooden box not far from the fire. She gazed at the flickering flames and drew in their warmth as she listened to the crackling sound. The charred smell of ash crinkled her nose.

Shona was the only one she'd confided in, concerning these matters, but in time, she knew she'd need tae also speak tae her parents.

She clasped both hands and rested them on her knees as a hollow feeling encompassed her.

Shona moved closer. "You're thinking of him again, aren't ye, Roslyn?"

Roslyn jumped out of her reverie when she felt her sister's gentle nudge on her shoulder. "Please, Shona! Daena say this so loudly. Mama and papa will hear." She put her hand to her mouth. "And daena scare me like that."

Shona gave Roslyn a solemn look. "Your goin' tae leave us, for him, aren't ye?"

Roslyn's brows knit together. She drew in a breath. "I daena know. I canna say." She put her hand on her sister's arm. "Please, daena tell mama and papa, Shona. It'll break their hearts. Callum will be in Perth. I'll look for him there, but there's no need tae cause them pain. I must fairst know without a doubt that his feelings for me are the same as mine are for him."

"Ye care deeply for him, don't ye? I see it in your eyes."

"I do. But, I must not think of that now. I must see him again."

She took a comb from a small box that sat on the back of the wagon and tugged it through her hair. Her curls had grown to her shoulders again. She sighed. "I know now why I cut off this frizzy taigle afore."

Shona giggled.

Roslyn smiled at her sister. "Do ye think he'll still have me wi' this snorly mess." She braided the pieces into two sections and tossed them behind her.

"You're enchanting, Roslyn, like a pretty woodland maid. Ye sing a merry tune. I'm certain he canna help but love ye."

Roslyn reached for her book and opened it. Poetry and romance. A gift from God.

*****

# Chapter 6

The head house servant went to Ian when he came into the room. Her blonde-gray hair was neatly clipped to her head, and her dark gray dress and white apron was stiffly starched. She handed him a newly pressed shirt.

He smiled. "It's a good thing I have ye, Annag. You see tae it that I'm well taken care of."

"Grizel wants tae see ye well-dressed, sir, as a gentleman must present himself in such a way."

His brow rose. He didn't say anything.

Annag wagged a finger at him. "You should pay more mind tae the lady, sir. You need a proper wife."

"Wheesht!" He put the shirt on a table next to him and scowled. "I've no wish tae be married. I've enough tae consider wi' this home and my wark." He took the shirt from off his back and handed it to Annag.

Ismay looked up and almost dropped her broom as she stared at him from across the room. Och! A bonnie man he was! She let out a gasp.

Ian glanced over at her and gave her a look of interest. He grinned when his eyes met hers.

Ismay put her hand over her mouth and turned away taking up her task again. Her heart raced inside her at her wayward thoughts. God might strike her dead for them.

Annag scowled at Ian. Her gray eyes darkened. "And daena be turning your head in the servant's direction. You'll only come tae ruin for it. There's no crossing onto that path, and ye know it."

Ian put on his newest shirt and his cloak. He didn't answer her. Grabbing the latch on the door, he opened it and went out.

*****

Ismay went to Annag. "I finished what ye asked of me. What else might I do?" She brushed off her skirt and leaned her broom against the wall.

Annag stared down her nose at Ismay. "And you daena be gettin ideas in your head about that one. A servant knows her place. You should turn away instead of gawkin' at him like that."

Ismay's cheeks turned red. She cleared her throat. "I know what I need tae do. I did not think he'd be dressing in the main room. It took me by surprise. I'll be watchful of these things in the future."

"Well, I'm glad ye have your head on straight." Annag's expression softened. "He does have odd habits and is a bonnie one tae look at. Noone can deny it."

Ismay nodded. "I'm here tae pay him back what I owe. I daena wish tae harbor thoughts of the maister in a way that others would blether on about. It'd braisant, and trouble for him and me."

"Then you are a braw lass. Tis true the gentrice class must be left tae their own." She pointed to the kitchen. "Now, go tae the cook and see tae her needs. There's always wark tae be duin."

Ismay left to find the cook in the kitchen and see what wark there was for her tae do.

*****

A month of debt had been paid for the horse. Summer neared an end.

Ismay looked up from working in the garden.

Ian's white-brick house stood tall and proud in the distance with overhanging vines laying trails against the side of the walls. Dark lanterns hung on hooks of posts set at various intervals, and small windows framed in black iron trim decorated the sides of them. Chimney stacks rose tall against the cloudy, gray sky behind it on top of the close knit, interconnected buildings forming a square inner courtyard and a gate for visitors to enter.

There was a cobblestone path that led to the main road, and to the right of it was the stables. Chickens nervously clucked as they pecked at the ground around the barn.

Ismay's cheeks reddened as she eyed the door of the stable. She recalled the night she'd spent there and her misgivings about what she'd done. A sick feeling welled up inside her.

It'd been wrong tae steal as she had. Though luck had been wi' her that she'd fallen into the hands of Ian MacAllen who'd spared her the cruelties of a just punishment. Sentences were most commonly severe for horsethievery.

She pulled ripe carrots and tatties from the ground. She brushed at the dirt from a large vegetable she held in her hand. Her fingers were dusty.

Her hair had fallen from its clasp. She pushed it aside as she accidently swiped the side of her cheek.

She reached for another carrot top and tugged on it when the heel of a woman's buckled shoe came down hard upon her hand smashing it into the dirt.

"Ouch!" Pain seared through her fingers.

Ismay heard a voice behind her. "You're where ye should be ye clarty thief."

Ismay pulled her hand out from underneath the shoe and held it to her chest. Angry tears stung her eyes. She looked up.

Grizel stood above her scowling.

Ismay frowned and quickly put the vegetables she'd taken from the ground into her apron. She got up. "I must bring these into the house. I've wark tae do."

"You daena deserve tae be here wi' these goodly people, a wickit thief without a coin tae your name."

Ismay tried to push her way past, but Grizel blocked her. "Please move, mem. They're waiting for me in the house, and I've denner tae prepare."

She tried to walk around the woman, but Grizel took another step in front of her. She held the apron full of vegetables close to her chest as her lips drew into a pout.

Grizel leaned over and whispered in Ismay's ear. "Let the maister be, or I'll see that you're let go, and if ye tell him this, you'll wish you hadn't."

"No, ye ill-faured wutch! I said tae move aside!" Ismay released her apron in all fury sending the dirty vegetables flying at Grizel who flew over backwards and onto the ground.

Grizel lifted the skirt of her silken dress and shrieked. "Now, look what you've duin!"

Another voice sounded sharply behind them. "Ismay!" Ian went to Grizel's side. His expression was grim. He spoke gruffly, and his brows formed a hard line. "What is this?"

He helped Grizel out of the dirt.

He gave Ismay a disconcerted look. "What have ye duin, lass. There's no excuse for such behavior. You must apologize at once!"

Ismay stared at her feet and didn't answer.

"Ye told me you'd cause no trouble in my home." He put his hand on her arm. "Ye gave me your word."

Ismay looked up. "But, sir?"

"It was a promise, and ye broke it."

Ismay gulped.

She wiped a tear from her face, then she turned to Grizel. "I apologize, mem. I did not mean tae be unceevil tae ye. My temper often gets the better of me." She bowed.

"Truly? This smaw joskin is the deil herself!" Grizel scowled at Ismay and then at Ian. "Ye shouldn't have taken her in."

"Wheesht, Grizel. She's not the deil."

Ismay got down and collected the vegetables into her apron again. When she'd taken all of them off the ground, she stood up.

Ian looked at Ismay's hand. He frowned. "What's this?" He took hold of it and studied it.

Ismay pulled away from him and shoved her hand behind her. She nervously backed away. "I...caught it in the door, sir. Tis nothing."

Ian's eyes narrowed.

Ismay lifted her skirt with her uninjured hand and stepped aside. "I'm sorry, sir, but I must go. Gladys will be looking for me."

She curtsied and turned to take the vegetables to the scullery.

She didn't look back as she went inside the home.

*****

Annag came into the kitchen. She looked concerned. "You've duin naught tae cause trouble, have you?"

Ismay looked up from where she sliced a potato at a wooden table in the middle of the small room next to Gladys. She shook her head. "I've not. What's happened?"

"I daena know. The maister, he wants tae see ye."

"Where?"

"In the study." Annag moved to the pots and pans. She took a large spurtle and stirred the mixture. "Go, I'll see tae this until you're back."

Ismay nodded. "All right. I'm sure it's nothing."

She thought of Grizel and what had been said. She hoped the ill-deedie wutch hadn't convinced the maister tae send her away. "I'll return shortly tae finish the wark."

She took off her apron and turned to Gladys. "I'll be back soon tae help."

Gladys nodded. "I'm sure you'll not be long."

Annag's brows gathered above her eyes. "You should definitely go, but it's a bit odd that he'd call for ye like this. Ye mind yourself wi' that one. Remember your place."

Ismay tipped her head and curtsied. "Aye, mem. I'll not forget it."

Annag watched Ismay with a stern look as she left the kitchen.

*****

Ismay entered the dim lit study full of rows of books and a desk with a wooden thriftie on it. Leatherbound ledgers were stacked in the corner. Painted papers covered the walls, and thick curtains draped in curves over long, thin windows.

She crossed a patterned carpet marveling at its rich hues as she approached the straight-backed chair where Ian MacAllen sat facing the fireplace.

The silence of the room drew her attention to the hot coals snapping in the hearth and the mantel clock nervously clicking in the light of the fire.

A tremor ran through her. She shouldn't hae thrown the tatties and carrots at Grizel. Why hadn't she controlled her temper? "Sir, you wished tae see me."

He turned and touched the seat across from him. "Sit. Here, Ismay."

Ismay didn't move. She smoothed out her skirt with her hands. "No, I prefer tae stand. It wouldn't be proper."

"Come, lass. There's no one in the room but us. There's no need for decorum."

She sighed. "But my scullery clothes are a clarty mess. I dare not sit on your fine plenishins." She moved nearer the fire and stood facing him, but didn't sit down.

He got up and went to her.

Ismay's blue eyes widened as he moved closer.

"You wark hard, and little muck is expected." He used the edge of his sleeve to wipe a smudge off her cheek. "Though it is a distraction tae me on that bonnie face of yours."

Ismay's heart skipped a beat at his touch. She didn't know what to say. What would Annag think? She said a quick prayer.

She spoke quietly, hoping in the dark he couldn't see her heated cheeks. "Why have you called me, sir?"

His voice was a soft command as he looked down at her hands. "I want tae see the one ye caught in the door."

She made a sound then shook her head. "No, sir." She put her hands behind her back. "It was nothing. It's not your concern."

He seemed a bit put out by her answer. "No?" He took a step closer.

"But…" Ismay lifted her chin.

"Please, Ismay."

Ismay hesitantly held her hand out to him. She let out a wounded sound when he took it in his.

He loosed his hold and lifted it to the light. "It wasn't caught in the door, was it?"

She didn't say anything.

"Ye must tell me what happened, lass."

"I told ye. I…"

"She stepped on it, didn't she? Miss Hawthorne."

Ismay looked away. "You told me tae apologize. You were angry, sir, and wouldn't have believed me."

"Is it broken?"

"It hurts, but I believe it's only bruised. It may not have been intentional. I canna say."

He sighed. "I should have listened, lass. I'm sorry for it."

Ismay stared at him in surprise. "But you've just cause tae distrust me, sir. I've wronged ye, and you've been kind tae me."

"Not as kind as I should've been, in this case, it seems." He spoke quietly as he studied her.

Then his voice lowered. "Miss Hawthorne doesn't understand oor agreement which I'm determined tae carry out. I believe wrongs must be payed for in full. I'll speak tae her so this behavior will not repeat itself."

"Please, sir. I'd rather not draw attention tae myself. I'll do my best tae avoid crossing her path from now on."

"But she canna treat my workers in this way whether it was intentional or not."

"Please, I'd rather ye did not."

"But, how? She should know it."

Ismay nodded. "I've no wish tae cause ye more trouble, nor for myself. I'd rather we let the matter go."

A muscle in his lower jaw twitched, but he nodded and stood back from her. "For now I'll keep it between us. But you must make it known tae me, if it happens again."

"I will, sir." She sighed.

"And you must tell Annag tae make a splint for your hand. I want tae see that it heals properly."

"I will."

The door swung open, and Annag entered. She looked around the room until she spotted Ismay. There was a hint of suspicion in her eyes as she stared at both her and Ian. "Pardon, sir. But, Ismay's needed in the scullery."

Ian turned. "At this very moment? The matter canna be taken care of another time?"

Annag went to Ismay and took her by the arm. "Gladys canna get the spices right. She canna remember which ones she used last time." She looked back at Ian. "Do ye mind, sir? Ismay's place is wi' us."

He turned to the fire and put his hands behind his back. He looked somewhat perturbed. "We're duin here, but efter this I'll make the decision as tae when I send my servants back or not. You're not without abilities in the scullery."

Annag gave him a curt nod. "I'll remember this next time. Come, Ismay." She put out her hand.

Ismay gave a quick curtsy to Ian. "Sir."

He tipped his head to her as she turned to go. He watched as both women exited the room.

*****

"Ismay, you must lairn tae separate yourself from the gentrice. Tell the maister that your help is needed elsewhere. No good can come of your being alone wi' him for such a period of time."

They walked down the stone passageways in a hurried pace.

Ismay sighed. "I'm not in the position tae speak so plainly, though I did nothing tae bring myself shame, and I daena have plans tae. Oor maister's a good man. He asked questions which I answered. There's no cause for your concern."

Annag shook her head. "I believe ye, lass. But I hope, for your sake and for his, this continues tae be true."

\*\*\*\*\*

# Chapter 7

Roslyn took nimble steps on the road. The day was coming to a close, and she'd spent longer than she should have in the grove by the loch where she'd told Callum to meet her. She'd been in the same place iveryday since her parents had taken up temporary residence again just outside the town of Crieff, but she hadn't seen a spot of him.

The woods were quiet. There was no sound but the light breeze that swayed the treetops since she'd stopped on the path. Not even a Tinker's wagon nor the lowing cow of a herder was anywhere in sight. Only a light wind swaying the treetops and the scurry of animals in the underbrush was heard.

She quickened her pace as she walked back toward the village thinking about her family and the wagon she called home.

Her parents had raised her and her siblings lovingly wi' time and attention given tae the children's needs. Their tinker ways afforded them close family ties yet allowances for individuality between them.

She valued the freedom a traveler's life presented. They moved when they wanted and went where they wished. Adventure lay ahead of them, and they were a tight-knit full of spirit family.

Much of Roslyn's way of life allowed her idealistic heart tae roam free from constraint and permitted her speeritie imagination tae run rampant wi' possibilities of poetry and musings. More often than not, she'd been lost in dreams and passions as the wagon wheels had turned around beside her.

Yet moments alone were few, and stability never seemed tae be within her sights. Iverything moved and bustled along. She'd only a smaw amount of solitude and a wee bit of space tae call her own.

How would it feel tae live in a home of her own? What would it be tae settle and no longer be on the move?

She kicked at a pebble in the road as she clasped her hands behind her. Her parents' plans, in regard tae her life, weighed heavily on her. She wasn't sure which way tae turn.

Her voice was soft, and she sung the words in a sweet melody.

"In the grove awaitin' word,
a sound, my love, a horse's hoof.
Faint I hear it, a whisper in the breeze.
The Lord he sees,
and brings my love tae me."

"Roslyn?" A voice sounded behind her.

She looked up. Callum was on his horse coming toward her.

"Callum! I knew I'd see ye soon!" She waited as he came to her.

"I'm glad tae finally see ye again!" He smiled as he reached down and tugged on one of her braids. "Where's my Robin of Locksley? Who's this lovely lass, and where did that sweet voice come from?"

She pushed her braids behind her shoulder. "From a maid in the wood." She smiled as she stood on the path.

"And a very lovely one." He got down and took a place beside her. There was a tender look in his eyes. "I kind of think I've seen ye on this trail afore."

Her cheeks glowed a rosy red. "Callum! I'm so glad ye came." She smiled, and she hugged him tight. I missed ye so."

"I've thought of ye often, Roslyn. I've missed you."

58

She shook her head. "And I you. I'd not forgotten the pleasant days spent in your company."

Then she suddenly backed out of his embrace while scanning the path.

Callum gave her a quizzical look. "What is it? What's wrong, my love?" He reached out to take her hand, though she withdrew it.

She sighed. "I'm thinking of my mama and papa. I knew I had tae see ye again tae know for certain how ye felt. I wanted tae tell them, but couldn't bring myself tae it."

"I've a mind tae marry ye, Roslyn, very soon." His voice was strong with emotion. He took the hat from his head and held it tightly. "It's true. I only need your answer."

"Callum!" She gave him a shocked look. She put her hand over her mouth.

"Let's go away, Roslyn, on the morn's morn. Marry me then, lass!"

"Callum, no! Though I do wish tae, ye must be patient and wait so that my family will care for ye the way I do. You're a good man, and they must see it."

His hazel eyes softened in the light. "Then it is true that ye do love me, Roslyn." He looked relieved.

"I do." She spoke quietly. "I only hope that they'll feel the same."

"You'll tell them then soon?" He leaned to kiss her, but she backed away.

She tossed her braids behind her and wagged a finger at him. "Ye know I must remain pure for marriage."

He immediately became contrite, though there was a gentle sparkle in his eye. "I apologize. I missed ye, Roslyn."

"I'll tell them soon."

She looked around again. "But for now, please walk wi' me tae the edge of town. Then we'll pairt as my father's wagon is in Crieff."

He nodded. "I'll be glad tae go this far wi' you."

She went to his side, and they took the path that led to Crieff. "Come, and I'll tell ye how I've been."

*****

# Chapter 8

Sunday came quickly. Ismay looked down the road from inside the carriage.

The gentrice and servants alike rode to a meadow at a loch where a picnic had been planned.

When Ismay's carriage stopped, she got out with Annag and Gladys.

She watched as a second carriage rolled to a stop, and the door of it opened.

Ian stepped out and moved to the side as Grizel stood at the top of the steps, and he offered his hand to her.

Grizel glanced at Ismay as she held onto Ian's arm. Her lips drew into a pout. "You treat me well, love." Her voice was like a cat's purr.

She eyed the steep slope of the hill and leaned closer to him. "It appears we've a wee bit of a climb."

He nodded without comment.

Annag whispered to Ismay and tugged on her arm. "Come, we're meeting over the hillock." Her look was stern. "And keep your eyes tae yourself."

Ismay started up the grassy incline behind a hired chaise loaded with supplies pulled by a short-legged brown, furry horse. John, the horse's owner, coaxed the small animal to pull the load.

Ismay wobbled in her ill-fitting shoes as she stepped behind the cart. She stopped occasionally to steady herself. Her over large skirt caught underneath her more than once. She tugged at the thick folds of fabric to keep from tripping. It'd take some time tae climb the hill in such a state!

Grizel laughed from behind. "The clarty servant is quite the bummlin, tripping over her own feet." She put her hand to her mouth and held it there as she watched. Her eyes danced as she spoke.

Ismay's cheeks burned. As her hands gripped her skirt, she tugged the edge of it higher. Her small feet slide in the overly large shoes which made it nearly impossible to walk. If she'd had her own clothing, she'd have had no problem reaching the rise at the top.

"John, stop." Ian spoke to the man in the cart.

The wheels slowed, and they came to a halt.

Ian lifted Ismay onto the back of the small wagon. He spoke quietly for her to hear. "You'll have a skirt and shoes of your own in time, love. Pay no mind tae the injurious talk."

Ismay's eyes widened, but she didn't say anything.

Ian motioned for John to carry on and then turned away.

Ismay held the edge of the cart as it jostled in a back and forth motion away from the others.

Annag and Gladys both sputtered to themselves. Their brows rose above their eyes, but Ismay didn't acknowledge them. She looked away.

She'd no control over Ian and his actions. She'd do what she saw fit in the circumstances as he'd been kind, and it was all there was to it.

She looked at the fields in the distance and breathed in the scents of the heather-filled glen which covered the side of the hill that led to the loch.

The sun had come out. It was a beautiful day. A song stirred in her heart as she waited in anticipation for the festivities to begin.

*****

Grizel cocked her head to the side, and her eyes narrowed as she stared at Ismay.

She drew in a breath of cool, autumn air.

The servant was trouble. Ismay's ploys by appealing tae Ian's considerate nature by playing the poor, dowie victim were pure swickerie.

The young lass was no innocent and quite adept in the art of turning many a gent's head her way wi' those dark blue eyes and that helpless act. There'd surely need tae be something duin about the young woman's ill-trickit behavior. It wouldn't do for it tae continue.

When Ian turned back to Grizel, she smiled and clutched his arm as she moved closer to him.

She cooed to him in a sweet voice. "I'm so very glad we came. I'm thinking it'll be a braw day." She flipped a strand of magenta hair behind her ear.

"As long as it doesn't rain." Ian stared at the sky. "But, I suppose it wouldn't cause much harm the way these things come and go around here."

"I hope it doesn't. I spent too much money on this gown tae see it soaked in a blaud." Grizel's nose twitched. "But then, I see ye brought a cloak. I'll be asking for it if it comes tae that."

He nodded, all the while glancing back at the cart.

\*\*\*\*\*

Ismay tucked her skirt into her plaid belt.

"Come, Ismay! Play wi' us!" Some of the children at the picnic waved to her.

Ismay put out her hands and pretended to dodge them when they came near. She laughed and giggled as she allowed them to catch her. She fell with them as they landed in a heap together.

"Ismay!" A servant boy of Ian's, smiled widely as he put out his hand to help her up.

"So, I've Cael on my side now!" Ismay patted his arm. "I'm glad for that!"

Another small child called out. "Here! Catch me!"

Ismay grinned at the young lass as she ran past. When the little one fell, Ismay got down beside her. The child laughed as Ismay tickled her.

Ismay got up and went to a blanket to sit down. She straightened her kirtle. "There ye go." Her cheeks were rosy as she took some time to catch her breath. "Oo aye! I must rest."

She turned to where Ian sat.

He leaned against a tree watching her. His eyes were intent with interest.

Hech ay! She put her hand to her chest. She couldn't deny the quickening in her heart when she saw him. He was a bonnie looking man.

His expression suddenly became solemn, and he looked away. His attention shifted to the mountains jutting out over the horizon in the distance.

Grizel was on a blanket spread out on the ground busily talking to two of her friends.

Ismay sighed. In the course of time, she'd inadvertently found herself increasingly attracted to Ian. Aside from his braw looks, and well-formed physique, he was also considerate and mindful of others. She'd seen the way he'd treated his workers. He'd been especially charitable in allowing her tae work off her debt tae him when she shouldn't have been worthy of his kindness efter having stolen from him.

These things aside, she'd no business setting her sights on the maister of home. It mattered not whether she owned property and was an heiress as she'd so proudly stated. Her faither had been a mere home owner, wi' a few cattle, of lesser means, and she was a servant. She wasn't Ian's equal. Grizel's status was clearly above her own.

Though Grizel was wickit in disposition, she was also very beautiful wi' her dark, reddish brown hair and large, almond eyes. Her heart-shaped face was almost without flaw, and she was noticibly practiced in the art of charm and appeal. Her movements were smooth and refined, and it was obvious how Ian found her agreeable.

Ismay turned when the other-worldly sound of the pipes played. The wailing cry of their melody melted her heart as she watched three kilted Scots march over a hill in blended harmony. A surprise!

Each of the men wore dark green jackets adorned with silver buttons and scarlet red plaids. Their sporan molachs, large goatskin pouches, hung from their sides while knitted highlander's bonnets, Tam o' Shanters, tilted against their brow.

The gripping howl of the wooden pipes lifted Ismay's spirits. The powerful melody ran right through her Scottish blood. Tae live fast and die tae that sound ringing in Ismay's ears would be an honor!

She stood when others danced. Servants hopped and skipped and tapped their toes while raising their arms to the rhythm. They beat in a merry melay. Laughter and song broke out in the midst of lively patterns of dance.

Though she wanted tae join in, it was nigh tae impossible tae do it gracefully wi' her overlarge shoes and skirt.

She moved back and forth to the beat as her thick, dark hair swung over her shoulder in gentle waves.

She turned to the sound of Grizel's voice. Grizel tugged Ian's arm as the others in the group pushed him to his feet. "Come!" She teased him playfully.

He reluctantly moved closer to her and smiled at the folk around him as he danced.

Both Grizel and he were skilled at the folk dance. Grizel bent her head to the side with a coquettish look. Her skirt swirled round in patterned waves, and she twirled to the sound of the pipes.

She turned and caught Ismay's eye and flicked strands of deep coppery hair over her shoulder laughing as she looked back at Ian.

Ismay's mood dampened, despite the lovely sound. She suddenly had no wish tae stay and watch the others.

She lifted her skirt and took a path that led to the edge of the loch below the hill where there was a large, rocky ledge to sit on. She took off her shoes and dipped her feet in the water as she listened to the bagpipes.

Looking out over the water she drew in a breath of fresh air. It was quiet and serene at the place she'd chosen, sheltered from the others above the hill.

She straightened the folds of her skirt and wrapped her plaid scarf around her waist tighter. She smiled at the cool, briny smell of the place and the soft squish of sand under her feet.

The water wove silvery patterns of light over the surface. It rippled gently against the rock-crusted shoreline as a light wind pushed the waves across the shimmering pool.

She raised and lowered her legs as she eyed the waves that splashed playfully in front of her.

She turned when she heard footsteps behind her and pulled her bare feet out of the water and under her skirt.

Ian came down the path and stood looking at her. "Ismay, I saw ye left the dance?"

She twisted a length of her hair in her hands. She gave him a worried look. "It's not proper for us tae be alone. What are ye doing here?"

He shrugged. "Grizel's occupied wi' more than one Scot vying for his turn tae dance wi' her, and the others have consumed enough Scottish whiskey tae take no notice of oor whereabouts. Whether it's proper or not is of no concern tae me."

"But..."

"I would've thought you'd favor a Scottish jig, Ismay." He squatted down next to her. "You did not wish tae dance?"

Her cheeks pinkened. She looked back over the loch. "I almost always shed a tear at the sound of the pipes. I love the music and the fun." She averted her eyes from him.

"But you're here. Why?"

"Wheesht, sir! You can hardly expect me tae dance wi' these shoes and clothes. I couldn't walk the hill without stumbling. I surely woulda made a spectacle of myself wi' this attire."

He eyed her skirt and shoes with a look of chagrin. "I hadn't thought of it. I'm sorry, lass. I should've taken this matter into my own hands sooner."

Then he smiled and put out his hand. "But, you daena need your shoes, and there's no one tae see ye but me if ye take a turn. Come and dance wi' me, lass. We've music and time for it."

The sound of the pipes spilled over the top of the hill in a melodic, rhythmic beat.

Ismay looked up at him as her eyes widened. "But none of them would approve of it, barefoot and dancing wi' the maister. It wouldn't be proper or wise of us."

"I told ye, lass, they're engaged in their own undertakings, and you're not tae blame for your lack of proper clothing." He took her hand in his and stood. He pulled her beside him. His eyes shone. "And as for your feet, the sands will be soft on them. Please dance wi' me, Ismay. I've no design tae malign ye in any way."

Ismay's heart beat loudly in her chest. She eyed the top of the hill and then him and took a step closer. She did love the dance! The beat of the music struck her deep inside.

She lifted her skirt and tucked it into her belt then took his hand. "I did want tae, sir. I'm a Scottish lass through and through. The pipes they make me want tae dance."

Ian pulled her to him and put his hand around her waist guiding her steps to the lively beat.

She twirled and hopped in quick rhythm as a smile worked its way across her face. She moved gracefully despite the sand and laughed at the excitement of the pipes bold sound.

"Hech ay, love!" Ian smiled. "Ye do know how tae jig, and ye do it well!" He turned her hand in his as she twirled on the wide, flat rock on the shoreline.

"You're a good partner tae have." She laughed.

Ismay quickened her step, hopping lightly from toe to toe and then swinging round and round on his arm in playful movements. She curtsied and then took his arm again twirling beside him. A smile widened on her face as her eyes sparked with delight.

They danced until the pipes ended, and there was a brief interlude of silence.

Ismay looked up at him, her face flushed. She smiled. "It's been a pleasure, sir. I thank you."

"I'm glad of it, lass." He smiled back and took her by the hand. "It'll be time tae go shortly, and they'll be looking for us. Come, we'll make oor way tae the others."

Ismay shook her head. "Oh, no, sir. I couldn't. You must climb the hillock fairst, and I'll follow efter."

He hesitated, and then he gave her a look of understanding. "I suppose, though I expect ye not tae be far behind."

He gave her a light-hearted grin, yet there was a questioning look in his eye. "You're not schamin tae skirt away from me again, are you? Go back tae your home?"

Her blue eyes widened. "Sir! I mean tae pay ye back what I owe. I've no plans tae leave until then."

"I hope." He touched her cheek and then dropped his hand to his side. He gave her a sidelong glance. "My meals would suffer for it, but I'd miss ye more."

"I'll not go. I won't be long behind." Her expression softened.

He hesitated a moment. Then he turned to walk up the hill, leaving her to make her ascent behind him.

She took her shoes in her hand and waited until he reached the top. Then she took the trail back to the others.

When she stepped over the edge of the rise, she walked down the path and stopped to watch the workers clapping to the lively beat. Four couples danced a jig in step to the music.

Ian had rejoined Grizel and watched the dance.

Grizel turned in Ismay's direction. She stared darkly at Ismay with a look of mistrust in her eyes while tapping her fingers against her side as if contemplating some ill-deedie scheme.

Ismay sighed. She gave the woman a proper smile and waved.

Grizel's green eyes narrowed as she drew her cape tightly around her. Her mouth pursed into a thin line. Her expression was indifferent as she turned and walked away.

*****

# Chapter 9

Roslyn's father paced back and forth in front of the fire. "Ye canna mean it, dearie. He's not a traveler."

"But papa, I love him." Roslyn put her hands on her father's arm.

Her mother shook her head. "Roslyn, dearie! You've not known the lad long enough tae say such a thing. Your papa and I canna agree tae such a thing."

"But, mama, you must meet him fairst, please."

"Roslyn, dearie! What can ye be thinking? You'll marry a tinker's son, a traveler. It'll make no difference whether we're acquainted wi' your friend or not. You'll not be content wi' a town man."

Roslyn's cheeks reddened. Her eyes glistened with tears. "But, how do ye know this when I plan tae marry Callum and want a life wi' him." Her voice was a whisper. "I've not told ye knowing what you and papa would say, but not for lack of love of him."

"Roslyn! Have ye no sense!" Her mother turned pale. "Go tae the wagon, and come out when you're able tae see reason!"

"But, mama! You daena understand."

"Roslyn, now!"

Roslyn climbed into the wagon. She sat on the floor and wiped away the tears that rolled down her cheeks. She lay down on a soft, wool pallet and turned over on her side drawing her patchwork quilted blanket over her.

She'd been abruptly dismissed. Her mama and papa had been unwilling tae hear any of what she'd told them.

She'd confessed tae having had met frequently wi' Callum and of her attachment tae him through his and her long walks and discussions together, but her mother and faither had only stared straight ahead.

Neither seemed tae understand the extent of her commitment tae Callum. She was sure she'd never have eyes for another. They coudna keep her from him. It wasn't possible.

\*\*\*\*\*

# Chapter 10

Ismay stood in front of a looking glass and turned. She smiled widely. Though the lavender skirt and white buttoned top were simple in design, and the brown leather shoes were practical, the effect with her dark hair and blue eyes was stunning. She spun round one more time and then tied a purple ribbon in her hair.

Annag watched from the corner of the room. Her expression was stoic. "He shoudna have bought ye such finery. Wi' the wark ye do, it isn't practical." She let out a snort.

Ismay sighed. "I daena believe he meant harm in it. I can kiver it wi' my apron."

"Ye should." Annag gave her a cross look. "Wi' the cooking and cleaning tae do, there's no time for such dafferie."

Ismay spoke quietly. "I suppose, but it's evening, and the chores are duin." She turned to leave. A walk about the grounds would do her good. She wanted tae thank Ian for the gift. She'd supposed she'd find him in the stables.

"Keep your head about ye, lass, and daena be causing trouble for the maister."

"You must not fret so. I've no plans for anything but a quick walk."

She reached for the door handle and went out.

*****

The light in the stable grew dim. Ismay hadn't seen Ian down the long lines of horses as she walked to the end.

She spoke quietly to the animals in the stall. "You're a braw one wi' such soft fur. A fine blissin ye are." She reached over and stroked the side of the pony's neck and smiled.

She turned when she heard a sound.

"Aw, my wee horse thief has come tae charm my animals again. I hope ye plan on staying this time." Ian watched her walk toward him. There was a questioning look in his expression.

"I thought I might find ye here."

"And may I ask why ye wished tae see me?" He seemed interested.

Ismay stood back and turned in the light of the square-cut window. "I wanted tae thank you for the clothing." She pointed to her skirt and curtsied. "And for you tae know how much I appreciated them."

*****

Ian couldn't take his eyes from Ismay as she swung around gracefully, eyes sparkling. She was a picture of loveliness wi' her long waves of dark hair and sweet smile. The lavender skirt he'd given her and purple ribbon were the perfect compliment to her bright blue eyes.

He leaned against the stable next to him and eyed her with a look of intent. "You're a bonnie lass, Ismay. It woudna matter what you wore. I'm glad ye like it."

*****

Ismay drew in a breath at the way he looked at her. Her heart quickened in her chest, and a blush set upon her cheeks.

She took a step back. "I do like the clothing, sir, and wanted ye tae know it."

He set down a bucket of oats on the dusty floor of the stall and stood against bars that fenced one of the horses in. He didn't say anything as he eyed her curiously.

She wasn't sure what else to say. She spoke quietly. "Well, I do thank you. I'm glad I found ye here." She stirred the dusty floor with her foot.

He smiled as he watched her.

She put her hands in the pockets of her apron. "But, now that I've said what I came for, I think it best I take my walk on the grounds afore evening is here."

He spoke quietly. "Wi' the sun goin' down, I doubt you'll have time for it."

"Sir?"

"I think it might be a wee bit late for a walk. It's almost daurk."

She eyed the shadows that had lengthened inside since she'd come. It *was* later than she'd originally thought.

She relented with a nod. "I hadn't noticed, but I suppose you're right. I would have liked a chance tae stretch my legs, though I daursay I should head back tae the house instead. Annag will be wondering where I've gone off tae."

"She's most likely retired tae her room, along wi' the other servants."

"Aye, so I must be off also." Her heart seemed to be skipping beats as he hadn't taken his eyes from her. Surely it would be a good time tae go. "So..."

"Ye wish tae skirt away so soon?" He looked at her fidgeting hands. "Ye seem a knitchie of nerves tonight, Ismay."

She took hold of her skirt playing with the folds of it. "It's late, and iveryone has turned in for the night. I fear we shoulda be alone. I daena believe it's proper." Her eyes turned a deeper blue.

Ian went to her side, and his voice softened as he took her hands in his. "Daena go. Stay here." He drew her closer to him. Leaning down, he whispered in her ear. "I've feelings for ye, lass."

74

Ismay drew in a breath. "Sir."

"Annag and the others wouldn't know if ye stayed back."

She stepped away, straightening her skirt and her hair. "No, sir, but God would know. I couldn't."

"Ismay…"

She spoke quietly. "I'm your servant. I'm in no position tae speak my mind tae you." Her cheeks heated. "I'm a mere house maid."

He gave her an impatient look. "I've not censured ye afore, have I?"

"You've not, but…"

He took a step closer, but she put out her hand. "No, sir, please."

Ian's brow furrowed. "I think of you often, and I've seen ye, Ismay, the way ye look at me." He raked his hand through his hair, then took hold of the stable door when a horse let out a whinny. "I know ye think the way I do."

Ismay swallowed and backed away. "Tis why I shouldn't have come. And ye shouldn't ask such a thing. I've taken vows afore my Lord and Savior tae remain pure for the man I intend tae marry. Tis what I expect. Ye should respect this, sir."

"But, I canna marry you, love, the way things are." His brow shot upward. "And ye know this. It wouldn't fare well for either of us. It's the truth of it."

Ismay looked at the dusty floor beneath her feet. "I told ye I shouldn't have come. I did not mean tae cause ye trouble."

Ian followed her as she went to the door.

She opened it to leave.

"Ismay, please."

Ismay let out a sound. "Miss Hawthorne." She backed away a sick feeling welling inside her as Grizel stepped into the doorway with a haughty look on her face.

"What's this?" Grizel gave both Ismay and Ian a halting look.

Ismay's cheeks burned, and she turned away. Och! What timing this ill-deedie wutch had!

Ian stepped forward. "Grizel, it's not what ye think."

Fire flamed out of Grizel's eyes, and her voice burned with anger. "The tairt came looking for ye, didn't she? Waiting until dark. I told ye she'd be trouble." She started toward Ismay.

Ian stepped between both women. He put his hand to stop Grizel. "She was here tae thank me for a new set of clothes, nothing more. You mustn't jump tae conclusions." He turned slightly when one of the horse whinnied.

"She came in the stable looking for you. I know it." Grizel's eyes narrowed. "It isn't her place tae follow ye the way she does! Ye should be careful allowing your servants the freedom ye do. As maister of the home you should see tae it that they behave properly."

The tone of his voice changed. "Enough, Grizel! My conduct in my own home is my own business, and I'll not have ye casting false accusations at any of my staff. There was nothing unorderly about Ismay's behavior." His mouth set in a grim line.

Grizel frowned. "But you should take a proper stance regarding your servants. It's only right that ye be this way. What I tell ye is for your benefit, Ian."

Ismay shoulders straightened. Her cheeks flamed in color. "I've duin nothing tae discredit myself, or Mr. MacAllen, and I'll have no such charges laid against me." She took a step closer to Grizel.

"Ismay." Ian took a place beside her and put his hand on her arm. "Say no more. I'll address Miss Hawethorne properly."

Ismay shook her head. "Och! Baurmie! I came tae thank ye, but there'll be no more of this."

Ismay re-tied a ribbon that had come loose around her chin and turned to face them both. "Ye might sort out your own troubles as I've chores tae do, a wee bit of time, and no occasion for your trifling concerns."

She curtsied and tipped her head to them both. "Good day, madame. Sir." Then she took quick steps back toward the house.

\*\*\*\*\*

Ian escorted Grizel back to the house. Luckily his business wi' her had been short, and she'd not caused him too much trouble over his dealings wi' Ismay.

He stood on the back porch under the fullness of the moon in the darkness.

The cricket's trill warnings permeated the air around him. He took hold of the porch rail as he recalled his words tae Ismay earlier.

Until now, he'd no time tae process what he'd said, nor make sense of it, other than tae regret his words and actions almost immediately.

He sighed with the realization that he'd allowed a bonnie face and pretty manners to persuade him so easily to denounce his own sense of propriety and values. What had he been thinking?

He groaned as he recalled the look on Ismay's face when he'd propositioned her the way he had. Whatever possessed him tae ask her the things he did?

He'd most likely given her the impression that it was in his nature tae request such liberties from women, yet he'd never duin such a thing afore.

He tapped his fingers along the wooden rail that surrounded the porch and paced back and forth in front of it.

Her living in his home presented a predicament for him tae be sure. He'd no right tae even regard a warker in his home as one he'd wish tae pursue. Yet, wi' Ismay, he'd found it difficult not tae. His attraction tae her was more than he'd iver possessed for a woman.

Wheesht! How could he continue this way? She'd so much as insisted on marriage as the only rightful and proper course of action tae take, and he couldn't blame her for demanding such treatment. Any prudent woman would be justified in doing so.

He stopped pacing and raked his hand through his hair.

But, surely this type of union between them couldn't take place. The trials she'd bear from others would surely outweigh the benefits of a marriage tae him. She'd not be recognized by "polite highborn" society as his equal, or accepted by others, in the way a wife of his should be. It'd be tae her disadvantage for him tae even consider such a thing. He could never allow a woman as her tae suffer for the sake of his selfish desires.

But what did he truly know about Ismay since she'd come tae live in his home? He needed tae consider this also.

Tae be sure, she'd demonstrated that she was a diligent warker, thorough in her duties around the home. She'd been competent wi' most any task she'd been handed and had convinced him that she'd the patience and efficiency tae deal wi' others ably. Surely, his staff hadn't suffered since she'd come.

Though she'd not been long in his employ, only months, and she'd not fairly proven herself tae him. Could he believe the lass when he'd been prevailed tae hire her as a result of her own misdeeds? Had she been honest wi' him since? He surely had misgivings.

She'd told him about heirships and dying family members efter having stolen his horse. She'd been muddy and alone in the country when he'd found her without a coin tae her name.

How might he know whether she'd been telling him the truth then or filling him full of tales? Were his coins in the tax man's hands or had they been used for another wrangeous activity? What other things could she be hiding?

He turned to go back inside the house.

None of his questions could be answered in a fortnight. There'd be no proven anything until he'd time tae sort things out. Trust wasn't something one gained easily, especially when it hadn't been there tae begin wi'.

*****

# Chapter 11

Grizel held her manicured nails to her face and stared at them. She looked up when a young lad, about ten-years-old, came into the room. "I asked for ye straight away, Cael."

Cael took off his hat and twisted it in his hand. He raked his fingers through his sun-streaked hair and stared at her with wide, blue eyes. "I had tae stay tae finish maister Ian's wark. I'm sorry, mem."

"I told ye, you'd be paid well. You do understand how your suffering family is tae benefit from this?"

"How much, mem, if I do it for ye?"

"You'll know it when you've completed the task."

Cael cast a wary glance at her. He tipped his head to the side. "I do not know. It doesn't seem right tae me."

"Ye should be more concerned wi' what I tell the maister. Would ye want your good name tairnished? I could swee him against ye easily enough." Her lips tightened as she stared darkly at him. "And, if ye lose your position wi' him, how do ye propose tae support your family then? I'll not give ye a shullin more."

"But..."

Grizel's face darkened. She pinched his arm hard. "I told ye, I'll not give ye another coin, and he'll turn ye out when I'm through wi' you. You mustn't fail in this." She let go of him and stared icily.

Cael backed away and rubbed his arm. He lowered his head. "I'll do as ye say. I canna afford tae lose my place wi' Mr. MacAllen. What is it ye want, mem?"

Grizel smiled and motioned to him with her finger. "I'll not ask much, but I do have a task for you. Come nearer, lad, and I'll tell ye what it is."

*****

Ismay extinguished the beeswax candles and lanterns in the brick-floored kitchen and then in the adjacent rooms. She placed a grate over the fireplace opening. The logs had burned to ashes.

She tiptoed past a couple of rooms in the servant's quarters and then went into her own bedroom at the end of the hall as she carried one last candle. She'd promised Annag that she'd put out the lanterns and fires afore she went tae bed in place of the young lad who was needed elsewhere.

She put on her nightclothes and then got into the hurlie bed and lay back against the bedding.

It took some time before her eyelids closed, and she felt herself drifting off to sleep. It had been a long day, and she'd warked hard.

*****

"Ismay!"

Someone shook her shoulder. She pulled on the covers and attempted to wrap them around her. "It's late." She groggily opened her eyes. "Ian? Sir? Why are you here?"

His voice was harsh. "The place is lowed up! Come!" He quickly lifted her to her feet with the blanket intact.

Ismay's nose wrinkled. A bitter smell of ash and heat coiled around her. Her eyes widened. "Oo!" The room was engulfed in white hot flames.

Ian raced through the doorway dragging her along beside him as they made their way into the yard.

Once outside, Annag ran to them. "Thank the good Lord! The maister got ye out!"

Ian left Ismay in the care of Annag and turned to help the others with the fire.

Buckets passed between men from the well and were thrown onto the building. A scream pierced the air as fire shot upward and lit a tree. Hot ash slipped downward onto the soft earth.

Ismay caught her breath and then joined the others in their attempts to put out the fire.

"How did this come about?" She shook the arm of another worker.

He stared at her blankly and didn't say anything in response.

Ismay swallowed drily as she passed the next bucket.

Through the night, the fire burned while villagers slung buckets of water at the home.

Though exhausted, Ismay worked late into the night to help the others put an end tae the fire.

She cringed at the thought of having taken on the task of closing down the grate. Had she errored the night afore? Had she duin anything tae cause the mishanter that had come about?

After recalling the actions she'd taken that night, she was sure she'd secured the fire and put it out. She couldn't remember having duin anything that might have compromised the home. She'd positioned the grate firmly in place and checked tae see that the coals were burnt down.

But would anyone believe it? Would they think she'd been careless? There'd be no way tae prove herself.

She gulped back tears as her eyes met others who woodenly stared at her without answering when she spoke to them.

No one seemed tae hear her explanation of what happened.

*****

"There's haurdly anything left. The house is gone. At least the stable did not burn like the rest of it." Ian raked his hand through his mussed hair. His eyes were dark. "Where's the lad? Wasn't he supposed tae put the grate over the hearth?"

Ismay shook her head. Her face paled. "It wasn't his task last night, sir. He was needed elsewhare."

Ian stared at the brick home which was charred and still burning from inside. "But, I daena understand. Cael always closes down the hearth. Who did this?" He looked around.

"It was me, sir. Annag asked me tae do it, and I made sure the grate was closed. I'm certain of it."

Ismay went to him. Her voice broke. "I daena understand how this happened."

He didn't say anything as he stared at her blankly.

His look was one of disbelief as he eyed the house again with a defeated expression. Then he got up and walked in the direction of the stable. He didn't look back as he unlatched the door went inside.

*****

Grizel turned to Cael. She grabbed him by the collar. "It wasn't supposed tae burn out of control, ye ouf!"

Cael flinched. "I tried tae stop it, but the flames were too much for me."

She shook him. "You were supposed tae put it out. Ismay was supposed tae be the one tae suffer. But this! Ian's lost iverything! There's nothing left tae his name but his horses."

The boy covered his face. "I'm sorry, mem. I did not mean for it tae take hold the way it did." His lower lip quivered. "Though ye had your wish. The young miss was blamed for it."

"Daena speak of it again, Cael. No one should know the truth of it." Her eyes darkened. "But, ye must know that if they do, you'll pay dearly for it. It could be very bad for you and your family."

The young boy shook his head. "They'll not know it, mem. I'll not see my family harmed."

"They willna if ye know what's good for you." Grizel reached out and patted the top of his head, ruffling his hair.

She opened the door and stared down her nose at him. "Now, go your way lad, and have no more tae do wi' this. Away wi' ye!"

The boy nodded. He quickly turned and walked off, his boots clicking slowly down the hall.

*****

Ismay couldn't sleep. Morning came early for her. She got up from the bedroll on the floor of the small room packed with servants. She swallowed drily. "I'll be back. There are things I need tae tell the maister."

Annag frowned. "Ye think ye can make restitution for this? What else can ye do?" Annag looked out the window.

"There's my heirship and a bit of land. I might offer it tae him."

Annag sat upright. "In Comrie? Ye truly have a place there?"

"Aye, though he might not believe it."

"He's quite changeable and in a fowl mood, and you'll get nowhere wi' him."

"Maybe, but he's lost iverything. He should listen tae what I have tae say." She got up and gingerly stepped over others who were scattered on the floor sleeping. "I might be able tae convince him."

Annag shrugged. "There needs tae be something duin. I suppose it's worth a try."

Ismay went outside and took the path that led to the stable.

When she got there, she grabbed hold of the latch to the door and opened it. She went to where she knew Ian would be and stood beside him waiting for him to acknowledge her.

Ian was on a wooden crate.

He looked up and stared blankly at her. There was a hollow expression on his face.

She swallowed drily. Her voice was soft. "Sir?"

He didn't answer.

She took a breath and clasped her hands together to keep them from shaking. "I've my heirship. It's a braw piece of land and a home."

Only the sound of a couple neighing horses answered her. The acrid burnt smell around them made her twitch her nose.

She scuffed her shoe against the hard floor as she clasped her hands behind her back. "I'd give over the property for restitution. It isn't as grand as yours, but it's a worthy plot. I can offer naught else, but I'll take ye there."

She sighed, clasping her hands tighter. "I daena know what else tae do." Her voice was quiet.

"The wee heiress." He chuckled bitterly. Then he looked up. "Ye rander on about this, Ismay, when ye have naught tae your name. Can ye not be truthful wi' me now?"

"Sir…" She moved closer to him. Her cheeks reddened as she straightened to her full height and looked him in the eye. "I've told ye nothing but the truth, and ye still will not believe me."

"Why would ye think I'd believe ye, when you've not been not trustworthy from the beginning? Ye stole my horse and sauld, claiming ye were an heiress when ye wore the marks of a tinker's daughter." His look was one of incredulity. "And now you've burned down my house and deny ye did it."

"I daena think I did." Her expression was contrite. "But, I've a home, and I'm not a tinker! My faither and mother died, I tell ye!" Tears filled her eyes, and she wiped them away. "I'm alone and an orphant, as ye said yourself, but they did not leave me without a shullen."

She knelt beside him and took his hands in hers. "Please, take me there, and I'll show you. I'll give ye what I own. I promise I will."

He gave her another incredulous look. "Wheesht! Lass! Ye keep goin' on about this, and I've haird enough. I want no more of it. I canna believe anything you say tae me. You've no heirship or property tae offer me. Ye want tae go tae the highlands and skirt off and away since there's nothing left for ye here."

"No, sir, I tell you, I've a home there. You're mistaken. Come wi' me, please. I promise, if ye do, I'll not speak of it again. You've nothing tae lose." She gave his hands a gentle squeeze and then let go taking him by the arm. "Please."

He rolled his eyes and groaned. "Away ye go! I did not know ye were so headstrong."

Her brows knit together. "You might think me stubborn, but you're too proud tae see the truth. Why can't you believe what I tell ye?" She got up and paced across the floor. She stopped to tap her foot on the floor and stare at him.

"When you've duin nothing tae deserve it?" He frowned. "I trust only a wee bit of what ye say."

"I told ye, I own property and a home. It's not a lie!" Her eyes were wide with credence.

He raked his hand through his hair and rolled his eyes upward. He stood and went to her taking hold of her arm. "All right then. Ye want tae show me and have your way? Then ye will."

Her mouth opened slightly, and she stared at him.

"We'll go there, but you'll not be given the opportunity tae run off, ye hear? The matter will be settled once and for all, and then I daena want tae hear of it again. We're only taking one horse."

"Tis a bit of a distance. Ye might consider two."

"You'll ride wi' me, or we'll not go. One will suffice."

Her brows slanted downward, and she shook herself free of his hold. "If you insist, we'll take one."

"I do." His jaw tightened as he spoke again. "And when this is over and duin, I daena want tae hear about any of it again."

She sighed. Her expression was solemn. "Come, you'll change your mind when ye see my land and home. I can do something for you."

"Let me saddle a horse, and we'll go. Tell the servants we'll return later in the day, and then meet me at the gate so that we can settle this matter and be duin wi' it."

*****

# Chapter 12

The horse climbed a steep hillock, and when it reached the top, it threw back its head and whinnied.

"Comrie's past that treeline down the road." Ismay pointed to the top of the rise. "See the hill. From there, it's only a short distance from my home."

Ian's brow rose. He tightened his grip around Ismay. "So ye did not plan on leaving me behind in that gorge we just came through."

"Deil's Cauldron? I told ye I was taking ye tae my home, sir." She stared at him and rolled her eyes. "So ye believe this tae be trickery?"

"Maybe." He half-smiled. "Sending me into that boiling cauldron and treacherous river wi' the water elf might have been the answer tae the fix your in."

"Efter what ye said tae me at the stable, it might not have been so bad an idea. Dealing wi' that water elf might have been what ye deserved."

He turned away as he looked to the rise of the hillock.

They continued their ascent without saying more.

When they neared the flat ground at the top, a man on a horse approached them. He lifted his hand in salute. "Hullo! What hae we here? Ismay?"

"Robert!" Ismay waved back.

"It is you, lass! Where have ye been?" A ruggedly handsome older man with a red plaid and blue jacket rode to where they stood. His eyes shone as he gazed appreciatively at her.

Ian gave the man a cautious look. "And this is?"

"The man who's most likely cared for my property while I've been away. My neighbor. His wife is my friend."

"Wife?"

"Aye, they live quite close tae my home. Maybe now you'll believe me."

She turned back to Robert. "Ye must tell Barbara hullo for me and that I'll be back again. Let's ride together, and I'll tell ye why I've been away. Much has happened."

\*\*\*\*\*

While they made their way over the grassy hillside, Ismay gave Robert a truthful account of why she'd not been back in the Highlands.

Her cheeks blazed red as she spoke. "I've duin wrong, but have been attempting tae pay my debt. I regretted it dearly."

Robert spoke gently to her. "You were distraught, lass. You'd lost so much in so short of time. You lacked your sense of what was right."

"Aye, but this did not make what I did right."

"Tis true. It's good your making amends."

When they cleared the rise, Ian got down. He lifted Ismay to the ground. He scrutinized the traditional highland blackhouse in front of them and the coarse and poorly drained land spread out around the property. He said nothing.

Ismay turned to her friend who had also gotten down from his horse. She went to Ian's side. "This is Ian MacAllen whom I've been warking tae pay what I owe."

She looked at Ian. "Robert Shaw was my faither and mother's dear friend. He and his wife have supported me in difficult times."

Both men shook hands.

Ismay tugged on Robert's shirt sleeve. "Please tell him, Robert, that this is my heirship. He doesn't believe me, but it's true that I'm an heiress, isn't it?" She stood straighter and lifted her chin. She turned in the direction of the home.

Robert nodded. "Aye, it is, and ye are what ye say. Tis your home and land. Your good mother and faither entrusted it tae you. Iverything is as it was other than the drovers and your cattle. Without your faither, I suppose the drovers figured there'd be no repercussions in making off wi' your stock."

Ismay looked at the gated pen next to the stable. "I hope their black pudding will stick in their throat for what they've duin, or their precious whiskey runs dry. Though I suppose it should matter little tae me as I'll be handing my birthright over today."

She took Ian's hand. "My estate isn't as grand as yours, but I can make restitution tae you for what's happened. Below the glen, there's a bonnie servant quarters, large enough for a staff the size of yours and a stable. The stable's not so large, but enough tae house half your horses. You could build more of them."

Ian spoke quietly. "You told the truth, lass."

"Aye, it is my property, and I'm prepared tae sign my house over tae ye so that I might make amends for what I've duin."

"Relinquish this and the servant quarters?" Ian looked doubtful.

"Aye, you've lost your home. I owe ye this and for the horse. I'll wark for the remainder of the debt." Ismay spoke quietly. "Though I hope tae remain here as a servant efterward as I daena wish tae leave my home."

Ian nodded. "You'll certainly be welcome to remain efter the debt is paid."

"Thank you."

He didn't take his eyes from her. "I fear I was wrong tae doubt ye, lass. You've been tellin' the truth. I'm sorry I did not see it."

Ismay sighed with relief, but her look was solemn. "I'm sorry for what happened. I thought the fire was out and covered."

"What's duin is duin. We canna go back tae it."

Robert took hold of the reins of his horse. He turned to the hill in the distance. "Ye wish tae stay for a meal? Barbara will want tae see you, Ismay."

"I wish we could, but we must get back tae Ian's home. The servants are waiting for us." She smiled. "There'll be time for it when we return. Please tell her hullo."

"I will. She'll be glad tae see your bonnie face again." Robert tipped his head to the both of them, mounted, and then rode away.

Ismay turned back to Ian. "I suppose we should return and notify the servants of this new plan. We'll want tae get back afore nightfall."

"Aye, we've wark tae do." Ian tugged on the reins of his horse and pulled it closer. He lifted Ismay onto it and got on, behind her, giving the animal a tap with his heels.

"Come, Lillias. That's a braw mare." He turned the animal in the direction of Crieff. The horse took them along a ridge and then down to the main road.

Ismay let out a relieved sigh as the realization struck her that Ian had a tae move tae her place, her home. She missed Comrie, and her friends, and couldn't wait to be living here again.

She smiled at the thought that it wouldn't be long before they'd be settled here for an indefinite amount of time.

*****

Ian and the members of his household had packed what things they could salvage. They moved from Crieff to Ismay's highland home in Comrie in a very short time.

They arrived tired, and a bit disconcerted, but glad for the shelter and a place to stay.

Fortunately for them, there was food and clothing in the new home. Ismay's possessions were there and her faither's also. Some of the house uniforms still hung in the closets. Though the cattle were gone, it seemed the drovers weren't interested in household items or anything else on the homestead.

Ismay derived pleasure in the fact she'd be back in her own home again. She couldn't wait tae be able tae visit her friends. Ailsa would have wondered where she'd gone off tae.

*****

After Ismay and the others had time to settle and establish their routines, they rested on the first Sunday.

Ismay set out early in the morning as she walked along the road to town. The air was fresh and clean, and the day was bright. The sky was unusually blue this day, and the high hills in the distance were a rich, smoky green.

Ismay stopped briefly to pick some pink gillyflowers which dotted the edge of the path. She walked alongside a thick, stone wall that separated the road from the fields and three terraced gardens beyond. In the distance, a herd of red deer grazed in a remote glen. She marveled at the number of them and how they seemed so peacefully unaware.

She smoothed out the folds of her blue linen skirt and drew her green plaid cape closer around her shoulders. For the Sunday services at the kirk, she'd abandoned the simple style of a serving maid and chose clothing from her former wardrobe instead. She'd even tied a bright yellow ribbon in a bow on the top of her head in the style of the unmarried women.

When she reached the main street that wove through the town of Comrie, she eyed the quaint, traditional highland cottages built of dry-stone and clay with low-thatched roofs on both sides of the road. Though she did own one worthy pair of leather shoes, the weather was fair enough to walk about freely without them. The stone path beneath her barefeet was flat and smooth, not too difficult to maneuver.

The white kirk stood tall and welcoming at the end of the street in the heart of the village. It's prominent tower and spire appeared as if it watched over the town like a kind guardian.

Her eyes were drawn to the striking, stained-glass windows which rose upward on all sides of the building, and the colorful artistry in the designs which shone brightly as glimpses of sunlight streamed into them.

She stepped to the side of the road when the rattle of a sleek horse and cart startled her from behind. The wooden wheels of the vehicle bounced over the road and caught a stream of pebbles in them which rolled into her path. She stepped over them gingerly.

Square and round-cut stone buildings lined the street. Ivy trailed their walls like plaids over a shoulder, and tall chimney stacks stretched upward in neat rows against the blue cloudless sky.

She passed headstones scattered at the one end of the kirk amidst a small grouping of trees as she listened to the rumbling, bubbling sound of rushing rapids of the river Earn along the back side of the street.

Ismay breathed in the fresh scents of the air from the wide stream. Despite the lovely picturesque village and charming buildings, she'd grown to know so well, she hesitantly approached the kirk doors. Other parishioners were going inside.

A new parish minister stood on the path as he greeted the people who came up the walk.

She turned in the man's direction, and a chord of guilt suddenly struck her heart. She was tae step foot into God's place and look upon the meesionar! Could she do this wi' a right conscience efter what she'd duin?

Her sins suddenly weighed on her as she recalled the stable and the horse she'd taken. She'd stolen another's possession and sauld it! And here today, she'd sit in the very pew that she'd sat in as innocent bairn!

She took a deep breath and turned when someone whispered her name from behind. "Ismay!"

"Ailsa!" Ismay ran and pulled her friend aside. "It's been so very long! We're together again!" She gave Ailsa the handful of the pink gillyflowers that she'd collected.

Ailsa, a waif-like lass with white-blonde tendrils of thick hair and large, luminous hazel eyes reached out and took the bouquet. Leaning over, she drew in the sweet scent as she smelled them. Her eyes welled with tears which she immediately wiped away. She pushed pieces of hair from her face and smiled from beneath the thickness of it.

Ailsa's parents directed half-hearted smiles at Ismay, and Ailsa's mother was brusk. "Ailsa, we're goin' in tae take oor place. Ye must not linger."

Ismay sighed as she adjusted the scarf that hung over her shoulders. Surely news hadn't been randered about town concernin' her recent troubles? She'd no time for such ill-deedie blether. Ailsa's mother wouldn'ttake kindly tae such information.

Ailsa excused herself from her parents who went to the kirk door.

Ailsa's mother took the parrish minister's hand and shook it as an ingratiating smile widened across her face.

The meesionar tipped his head. "Mrs. Finn, tis always good tae see your bonnie face. I must say that the scones ye baked the other day were a gustie treat."

Ailsa's mother tipped her head. Her eyes shone. "I thank you. I'm glad ye liked them."

He smiled back then turned to Ailsa's father. "Mr. Finn." He shook Mr. Finn's hand.

Mr. Finn tipped his head and took his wife's arm. They turned and went into the kirk together.

Ismay walked down the path beside Ailsa. They stopped before they got to the doorway.

Ailsa hugged Ismay again. "Where have ye been, dearie?" Her voice was hushed. The paleness in her cheeks made her dark hazel eyes take on an almost eretheral glow.

"Tis a very long story, which you'll hear about soon enough, but for now I'm home again."

Ismay shifted her stance so she was looking away from the parrish minister. "Ye look bonnie, Ailsa."

Ailsa took her arm and smiled. "I'm glad tae see you, friend." She pushed her hair back from her face again and peered out from behind it. "I missed you, Ismay."

Ismay sighed with relief. "I missed you also." She reached out and adjusted a violet-colored ribbon in her friend's hair. "Ye still wear this."

"And my cloak tae match." Ailsa fingered the outer fabric of the green and violet plaid hooded garment. "Your mother was kind tae give it tae me."

Ismay sighed. "She cared for ye very much, Ailsa."

"It kept me warm many a day."

Ismay smiled. "I'm glad." Then she sighed as she looked at the doorway of the church. "I see that we've a new meesionar."

Ailsa moved her foot back and forth while toying with a pebble on the path and nodded. "Aye, and a worthy one. His words set the heart tae stirring."

The parrish minister, a young, broad-shouldered man with clear, blue eyes and a wide smile, shook hands with people going into the kirk. He greeted each of the guests heartily.

Ismay swallowed. She eyed the man warily. "I hope not too much. I canna bear much more conviction."

Ailsa's eye widened. "He's caring and kind. Whatever you've duin canna be so bad. I know ye well, dearie."

"Efter ye laern what's happened, ye might not be so sure of it."

"It certainly canna be as bad as ye say. You'll fancy tae tell me why you've been away so long when we have more time tae talk."

"Efter the meetin'." Ismay reached for the meesionar's hand and shook it politely. She quickly moved away.

She turned to Ailsa. "Shall we?"

Ailsa took Ismay's arm, and they went into the building together.

They sat in the pew next to Ailsa's parents. Neither spoke as they looked around the church. Lilting music of a German flute echoed through the great hall.

Ismay's eyes were drawn to the long, stained-glass windows which were rounded and peaked at the top as sunlight streamed into the warm room. Heartfelt music filled the hall, and prayers were softly uttered by church members while verses of the Bible were read.

Ismay's hands twisted in her lap when the minister got up to the pulpit speak.

He lifted spectacles across the bridge of his nose and pointed to the Scriptures. "God will speak tae your very heart if ye spend time in his Word. Ye must not deny yourself the joy of it."

Ismay looked at her hands and sighed. She'd not opened a Bible in what seemed weeks.

"Oor God loves us very much, so daena turn from Him." The meesionar's voice softened. "And we must allow Him tae guide us in His will."

He turned in Ismay's direction.

Her heart sank. Ismay drew in a breath. Lately she'd duin nothing tae deserve the Lord's love.

It suddenly seemed as if the meesionar was looking directly at her, like his clear blue eyes could see into her very soul. Did he know her saicret? Had there been rander about her in town? Her stomach lurched. Had something been said!

"God's folk mustn't swee from his path. Listen tae that still, soft voice and abide in it."

He looked at her again. "If your sins are weighing you down, then go tae Him. Give an honest account."

Ismay put her hand to her chest. Her heart sunk, and she felt sick inside.

It was a holy commandment not tae steal, but she'd duin it. Och! Would this sin and others take her tae Hell?

Her thoughts stirred within her. Would she be able tae come each Sunday and hear what this meesionar had tae say when she felt as she did?

She counted on her fingers the good deeds she'd duin since she'd come tae Comrie. She'd made meals, cared for the sick and was kind tae the other servants. She'd given the possessions in her home tae the people living there.

Would this be enough? Surely it would?

A sickening emptiness filled her as she wondered what Hell would be like if she were tae end up there? Was her faith strong enough tae keep her from that place?

Ailsa patted her arm.

The tender gesture and words of love and grace spoken aloud at the pulpit calmed her, yet she couldn't help wondering about what had been said. She wasn't worthy like Ailsa and the meesionar. They were surely goin' tae heaven someday, but her? She shivered.

As the parrish minister spoke, Ismay looked across the aisle of the church to the full rows of pews.

Cael, the young lad, who was a servant in Ian's home, sat a couple pews in front of her with his family. He'd given her a couple quick looks back but didn't return her smile. He seemed almost afraid to look at her. She thought he might have been shy.

Ismay scanned the faces of other people in the kirk. It had been some time since she'd been back in town, and there was something comforting seeing those her family had been close tae.

She looked from one person to another and suddenly drew in a breath. Mr. MacAllen?

Ian sat in a pew near the front of the kirk. He was intent on the meesionar's words.

A sick feeling ran through her as she studied him. What was he doing here? It was her kirk? He hadn't gone tae the town of Crieff for worship instead?

She nervously tugged at the folds of her skirt. It wasn't bad enough that the meesionar kept staring at her strangely. Now she'd need tae contend wi' Ian MacAllen in the same kirk as her.

He seemed tae know she was behind him, because not long after she laid eyes on him, he turned and looked directly at her.

His eyes suddenly lightened, and an amused expression spread over his face when their eyes met.

Her cheeks heated, and she quickly looked away. Surely, she'd never be able tae come tae the kirk again, wi' him sitting in the pews reminding her of her misdeeds. What was he doing? What would others think if they knew what she'd duin?

She played with the leather bracelet on her wrist and wriggled uncomfortably on the hard, wooden bench while she looked back at the meesionar.

Indeed! He wasn't without reproach himself. He'd also would have tae answer tae God efter what he'd asked of her in the stable.

She lifted her chin and stared straight ahead. It mattered not what he or others thought. She was most likely on her way tae the loch of fire anyway. The meesionar did not mince words.

She shrugged. She might speak wi' Ailsa efter the meeting for reassurance. Her friend woudn't judge her and would know what advice she needed tae here.

It was difficult tae concentrate on the meesionar's words efter seeing Ian. When the man spoke of the cross and payment for sin, she'd not felt particularily comfortable.

She tapped her fingers against the edge of her skirt and sighed. There'd be the end of it soon.

When the service finally was finished, Ismay practically dragged Ailsa out of the kirk and onto the path. "Come, there's much tae tell ye. I'm not sure where tae start."

"Ismay?" Ailsa leaned nearer. "What is it? You seem troubled. Is it so tairible?"

"Aye, very much so."

"Come, I'll have none of this. We'll go tae my home, and you'll tell me what's happened."

Ismay sighed. "You'll not quite believe it, but will know soon enough."

As they walked down the path, a low, quiet voice sounded behind them. "A good day tae ye, Miss Innes."

Ismay turned cautiously and watched as Ian walked down the path toward them.

He had a spark in his eyes. "Tis a bonnie day tae see ye in the holy house this morn's morn."

Her cheeks colored. "Sir? Ye did not think that I'd attend the kirk on Sunday?"

"I wasn't sure. I daena see too many horsethieves sitting in the pews." Ian studied her with interest as a smile stole across his face. "I hope ye confessed."

Ailsa gave him an odd look but didn't say anything.

Ismay cheeks blazed pink. "Ye know I'm paying ye back restitution. But I daena know why you showed your face there efter what ye asked of me?"

He moved closer, and he smiled again. "I suppose I need a good dose of the meesionar's words as much as you do."

Ismay tapped her foot against the stone walk. She placed her hands on her hips and looked up at him. She spoke quietly. "Efter treating me like a common limmer the way ye did, I think ye would. I just wonder what the meesionar would think of it."

"Ismay!" Ailsa tugged on her friend's arm. "We're outside the kirk doors! What are ye thinking?" Her voice was just above a whisper. Her face was pale.

Ismay didn't move. "He shouldn't be speaking so braisantly either."

Ian's brown eyes suddenly lightened again. He laughed. "Now, lass, there's no reason tae wark yourself up tae high doh. I'm only teasing ye." He looked behind them. "See, there are others comin' out, and we're standing in the way."

Ismay moved aside. She gave him a dark look.

Ian smiled again. "I daursay your friend is right tae say that it's not the proper time tae be reminding each other of oor sins just outside the kirk doors. Instead, ye might make introductions as I know few people in the town."

He glanced at Ailsa who still had hold of Ismay's arm. "Are ye kin?"

Ismay took a breath. She scrunched up her brow. "Ailsa's been my closest confidant since afore I could remember. Miss Finn. I'll be stopping by her place on the way back."

She turned to Ailsa. "Mr. MacAllen's the new owner of my home. He's a tae allow me tae wark there."

Ailsa stared at her with wide eyes. "Ismay! This is true?"

"Aye, we've an agreement." Ian spoke quietly.

Ismay smoothed out the folds of her skirt and nodded. "I clean and mostly cook."

"Och!" Ailsa drew back.

Ismay took Ailsa's hand. "I've much tae tell ye so we'll walk the path together. We'll visit a spell."

Ian didn't say anything, but eyed them both curiously.

Ailsa nodded. "Aye, we've much tae say. I've not seen ye for some time."

Ailsa turned and curtsied to Ian. Her dark hazel eyes looked large on her face. Her voice was barely audible. "I'm glad tae have met ye, Mr. MacAllen. I hope tae see ye again."

Ian tipped his head to her. Then he put his hand on Ismay's arm. "When do ye plan tae return?"

"I haven't seen my friend for quite some time, sir."

His eyes rested on the carriage across the street. "There are clouds overhead. You might get caught in a blaud. You could ride back wi' me."

"Tis gray this day, but the sun is out, and I've my cloak." Her blue eyes were like pools as she turned to him. "I like a brisk walk and haven't seen my friend in ages."

Ian glanced between the two of them, then he reluctantly shook his head. "I suppose I canna keep ye from Miss Finn's company, so I'll inform Gladys you'll be back tae help wi' the meal later."

"I'll not be long, sir."

He didn't answer, but tipped his head to Ailsa. "Miss Finn, it was a pleasure meeting you. I hope your visit wi' Miss Innes goes well. Good day."

"Good day tae ye, sir."

Ismay and Ailsa watched as he turned and walked down the path. Then he got in the carriage and rode off.

*****

Ismay went with Ailsa into her parent's quiet, candle-lit home.

Ailsa's faither stoked the fire while her mother wiped her hands on a dishcloth in the kitchen. Neither looked up but kept on working.

Ismay eyed them curiously. They tolerated her presence, yet she never felt particularily welcome in their home as Ailsa's mother seemed to prefer a more solitary existence.

The room was dimlit. Iverything was neat and orderly.

Ismay took her plaid shawl from her shoulders and laid it across her arm. She didn't speak. She didn't want to be the first to break the silence.

"Come." Ailsa tugged on Ismay's arm and led her into a sparsely furnished bedroom in the back. She closed the door, and they took a seat on a heather mattress which was covered with a clean but well-worn, embroidered quilt. "You must tell me what happened when ye disappeared. How did Mr. MacAllen came tae own your property? Hech ay! It's your heirship, Ismay."

Ismay took Ailsa's hand. "I might have given more thought tae it afore I did some things that put me in such a poor light wi' oor heavenly Faither. Now I must bear the shame that comes wi' it."

"But how does this concern Mr. MacAllen?" Ailsa moved closer. "Did ye take his horse?"

102

"Aye, it's true." Ismay turned away. "Oor cattle died, and I couldn't make the money for the taxes. I took it and then I sauld it when the opportunity arose. Ian MacAllen might have sent me tae jyle, or worse, but instead he allowed me tae wark for what I owe."

"Ismay! Ye should have come tae me fairst afore you chose tae do such a thing. I would have helped you."

Ismay nodded. "I suppose I should've. I daena believe I was thinking straight at the time."

"Efter the service ye said some things." Ailsa's voice was a whisper. She blushed. "Has Mr. MacAllen treated ye wrongly?"

Ismay sighed. "He gave me reason tae believe once that he desired a more intimate exchange between us, yet there was no offer of marriage."

"Ismay! What did ye say tae him?"

"Of course I told him I wouldn't have it." Ismay's cheeks reddened. "You do know that I'd not allow such a thing. He's said no more about it."

"Tis what ye should've told him, Ismay."

"Aye, I'll have none of that."

Ailsa smiled.

Ismay suddenly turned to the sound of a broom against the stone floor in the main room swishing back and forth. She gave her friend a concerned look. "Are ye happy, Ailsa? Are they treating ye well enough?"

Ailsa's eyes widened. "They see tae my needs."

"Providing and warkin and goin' tae the kirk on the Sabbath are worthy enough, but you're their wee ane. You deserve more than a place tae stay."

"It's the way of oor home, Ismay, and ye know it. Do ye believe it can be any different?" Ailsa looked at the door. "What can I do, but wark hard tae prove myself each day and show my love for them?"

Ismay frowned. "Yet I've seen them wi' others, goin' out of their way tae be kind, doing their good deeds. They should do the same for you, Ailsa."

Tears welled in Ailsa's eyes. She spoke softly. "The truth is I daena believe they want tae see the good in me. Though I'm not sure I want their flattery either."

"Ailsa, you're hurting."

Ailsa stared at her fidgeting hands in her lap. She put her hand to her mouth, her dark hazel eyes large against her pale skin. She was like an elvin creature peering out from the shadows. "Ismay, I've haird something."

"What is it? Tell me, dearie."

Ailsa looked at the door. She leaned close to Ismay. Her voice quivered. "Yesterday I lairned of my own mother cursing the day I was born, having nothing tae do wi' me as a wee bairn. It seems even then she'd no love for me."

She spoke in a whisper. "A nursemaid took over the task of caring for me when my own mother wouldn't."

"Ailsa!" Ismay tapped her fingers against the fold of her skirt. "How could this be?"

"I daena know. How does one understand such things, mine own folk turning out a helpless babe?" She wiped the tears on her cheeks away and pushed the thickness of her hair over her shoulder.

She sighed. "I told them it was wrangous, and now they say that I'm tae blame for speaking my mind and making a collieshangle of things. I'm about tae lose my mind!"

"Their talkin' nonsense! A bonnie lass ye are, honest, and good, asking for so very little."

"I'm not so good. Am I not tae honor the ones who gave me birth, the ones the Lord put in my paith?"

"Ye speak the truth and nothing more. You're not tae blame for the direction they've chosen." Ismay put her hand on Ailsa's arm. "You're the Lord's creation, dearie. A precious gift ye are and loved by the Faither who made you. Daena despair. You're beautiful tae Him. Your flaws He doesna see." Her voice broke. "They've wronged ye, Ailsa. I know God's wrath will someday rein down upon their heads for this."

"Ismay!"

"No, the meesionar said this very thing. They've sinned against ye most tairibly, and the Lord will make it right in the end."

Ailsa straightened. Her eyes were large. "I know that oor God is just and true. I only hope they're brought tae repentance afore they're made tae face what they have duin."

"And this is why I daena understand them. Ye put me tae shame, dearie." Ismay smoothed back Ailsa's hair.

Ismay tugged on a gold chain hidden in the neckline of her dress. She brought forth a sapphire pendant. "Faither gave it tae me. Look. Do ye see the inscription?"

"Daughter of the King." Ailsa studied the back of the pendant and pointed to some small letters p-l-p-d etched into the bottom of the gold backing. "Do ye know what those mean?"

"No, my faither did not tell me the day he died." Ismay ran her fingers along the letters. "I only understood a little bit of what he said."

"No doubt he was in a badly state."

Ismay nodded. "He was very sick, and I daursay you're right."

"He loved ye, Ismay. I'm sorry ye lost so much." Ailsa spoke quietly.

"He wanted me tae have this piece, and I've worn it around my neck iver since. He told me God in heaven was my Faither."

She sighed. "I want tae believe that the Lord will take me wi' Him someday. Though sometimes wonder whether

He'll have me when I've duin the wrong I have. I know I daena deserve His grace."

"Who hasna duin wrong?" Ailsa took Ismay's hand. The look in her eyes softened. "You should talk tae Him."

"Now?"

"Aye, He loves ye, Ismay. Speak tae Him."

Ismay shivered. "But I'm not good like you, Ailsa. I've always been high-strung and spiritee. I've a temper and sometimes it gets the better of me."

"You daena believe oor Almighty God is able tae forgive you?" Ailsa smiled. "Did He not bring the murderer on the cross wi' Him tae heaven the very day He died?"

Ismay drew back. "Aye, He did."

"Sometimes I canna quite believe the love He has for us, but it's true. I know it."

"For me too?"

"If ye pray for it." Ailsa nodded. Her eyes shone. "Oor God wants us all as His."

Ismay sighed. She suddenly moved to the floor and got on her knees beside the bed. "I've no mother or faither, on this Earth, no one tae guide me or instruct me in the way tae go."

"Then ye need Him as much as I do."

"I suppose." Ismay swallowed. "It seems what I should do."

She bowed her head and closed her eyes. She spoke quietly. "Forgive me, Lord, and take my sin. I believe ye. Guide me on the paths I should go."

It was humbling tae be lowered onto the floor beseeching God the way she did. Though it seemed right, and she didn't mind it in the least. She'd chosen to listen to Him and believe that He would show her the way.

Suddenly something lifted inside her heart. The heaviness that fell on her shoulders weighting her down was no longer there. It was as if she could breathe easier, and that all the worries she'd previously held close inside her had faded quite soundly away.

It was true that He could do great things for His people if they trusted Him. God could change hearts.

She lifted her head and breathed a sigh. "I do think He haird me, Ailsa. I believe He's taken my sin."

Ailsa nodded. "I know it's true, dearie. Oor God is so very good."

Ismay got up and sat back down on the bed. She wiped tears from her eyes. "I should've duin this afore. I know I'll meet my faither and mother someday. I'm sure of it."

"Ismay! I'm glad."

Then Ailsa eyed the closed door. Beyond it was the clattering of dishes in a tub of water and shortly after a set of heels clicked against the hardwood floor across the room.

She pushed her thick, blonde hair from her eyes. Her smiled faded as she looked down. "She's unkind, Ismay. Faither is the same. I canna please them."

Ismay tugged on Ailsa's skirt. "But ye please God just as ye are."

"I trust Him greatly. I know He's been wi' me since I was a wee ane."

"He loves strongly. He doesna condemn. I'm sure you've stolen His heart, Ailsa." Ismay touched an open Bible on her friend's bed. "We'll read and pray, and God will bring us tae a spacious place. He'll see tae both oor needs."

"Aye, Ismay." Ailsa wiped tears from her eyes. She leaned against the bedpost. Her look was solemn. "Oor God is verra good."

"He's given me peace."

Ailsa nodded. "Aye, I know it too, and a heavenly home I can put my hope in."

Ismay squeezed Ailsa's hand. "I'm glad tae be back in Comrie. I missed ye."

"I've missed ye too." Ailsa stood and smoothed out her skirt. "You must visit often."

Ismay got up as she retied the ribbon in her hair. "I'm sorry for your struggles. I'll pray for you and think of ye often, and I'll come calling again."

Ailsa nodded. "God be thanked!"

She looked toward the door and fidgeted with her hands. "I suppose they'll expect me tae set the table shortly. We'll be eating a meal soon."

"Aye, there's wark awaitin' us both." Ismay smiled.

Ailsa's eyes turned a deeper shade. "You're a braw lass, Ismay. I was downcast without ye, but am glad your back again."

"Someday things will be made right, Ailsa. God will provide a way for you."

Ailsa nodded. They went through the main room and hugged.

As Ismay closed the door behind her, she heard Ailsa's mother immediately issue an order in a curt voice to Ailsa. Ailsa answered quietly. "Aye, mother. I'll do it straight away."

Ismay prayed as she walked down the path and opened the gate. "Lord, may ye bring peace tae my friend while ye lay evil tae rest. May the beauty of Ailsa's character be allowed tae shine in the light of Your great love. May Ye protect her wi' Your blessed strength."

Then Ismay shook off any of her apprehension and unease trusting that God would meet all Ailsa's needs.

She looked back one last time then took a short cut through a field in the direction of her home.

*****

Ismay wasn't surprised by Ailsa's revelation.

Though the townspeople had no knowledge of what went on in Ailsa's home, it had been no saicret tae Ismay that Ailsa had been rejected by her mother from the time she was a wee bairn. It was difficult tae believe a young lass as caring and kind could be treated as she'd been.

Ismay recalled her first encounter wi' Ailsa, when their friendship had fairst begun.

She'd been walking the forest looking for mushrooms and had heard a soft voice from behind a tree.

When she'd peeked around the base of the trunk, she'd seen Ailsa. The young woman had been skittish, a blonde-haired lass wi' large eyes. She'd stared at Ismay in surprise.

Ismay recalled jumping at least a horse-length when she first saw Ailsa as she'd considered her tae be some sort of wickit faerie on the path wi' her dark green eyes and wild, untamed hair the color of sunlight. She'd thought Ailsa might have been a meesterious changling who had come tae lure her deeper into the forest.

Ailsa had immediately apologized and assured Ismay she was neither in which they'd made fast introductions and quickly formed a friendship.

Since that day, they'd been the closest of confidants, and there was little Ismay didn't know regarding Ailsa and her family.

To this day, they'd comforted and prayed for each other ivery day. Nothing had changed, even in the event that Ismay had been away for a time. God was good tae have brought them together.

Ismay suddenly looked up when she noticed a movement at the edge of the field. She put aside thoughts of her friend for a time.

A small chestnut colored Highland Pony stood directly under an alder tree in the distance. It lumbered along while grazing near a trickling stream.

"He has no bridle, and his reins are falling free."

Ismay watched as he quietly munched on the tall, weedy grass beside him. He seemingly had lost his way.

"I should take him tae his owner. Someone's most certainly looking for him."

She moved toward the pony and spoke softly to him. "Hullo, wee one. Are ye lost?" She took small steps in the pony's direction quietly talking to him.

After a few minutes of moving closer, waiting and watching, and speaking tenderly to the small horse, she'd finally managed to move near enough to take the reins in her hand.

"A Highland Pony ye are and a braw one at that." She smoothed her hand over the side of the animal's neck in a firm stroke as she cooed to it.

"Come." She tugged on the reins and guided the pony across the field.

The animal's wide feet and broad knees moved sure-footedly over the bumpy terrain.

Ismay smiled. "We'll see what the maister has tae say about you. He can take ye tae the nearby farms and see where ye came from."

She took the pony to a tree that had fallen over. Part of it had formed a cracked stump.

She stepped onto the stump of the fallen tree and pulled the pony to her. She quickly got on the pony's back and patted its sides. "There, there."

She nudged the pony with her knees and gave it a firm heel with her bare feet. "Away!"

It moved across the field.

Ismay smiled. The wee pony was a bonnie one. Someone surely missed the little beauty wi' the cream-colored mane and strong, swift legs.

She rode for a time when she suddenly noticed Ian MacAllen who was on his own horse.

He came across the field toward her edging beside her and taking the pony's reins as he pulled the animal aside. "Whoa!" His voice was low and firm. He eased both horses to slow their pace until they stopped.

He gave the small pony an odd stare as he waited for Ismay to speak.

Her cheeks pinkened. "He was in the field without an owner. I planned tae bring him back tae the house. I did not take him."

"Ye found him?"

"Aye, I did." She frowned as she studied his face. "But you believe I stole it, don't you?"

He tugged on the reins and drew the pony to him. "I don't know."

Ismay got down. "Truly?" Her eyes narrowed. "When I'd taken your horse I'd lost my faither. I had no one. They wouldn't take me on the cattle run." She looked away. "I was wrong, but at the time I felt I had no other choice."

"Ismay, this is not your pony."

"I know that." She stepped back putting her hands on her hips. "He was in the meadow without a rider." She turned walking in the direction of her home. "I did not take it."

He got down and took her by the arm. "But you were on it." He swung her back around.

"Bringing it back I was." Her blue eyes darkened. "I gave you my home, all of it. Ye have iverything. Do ye not understand the kind of person I am."

He let out an exasperated breath. "I do not."

"I was taking him back, though it seems you've made up your mind."

They both turned when a rider on a sleek, black horse appeared in a distance headed their way.

Ismay leaned forward squinting as the animal trotted toward them.

When the man was close enough that they could see him, he called out. "Ismay! You're home! Where have ye been?"

Ismay pulled her arm aside and wiped her tears with her shawl. She gave Ian a cross look.

Her voice softened. "Tom Drummond! Hallo!"

Tom eyed the small animal next to them. His face registered surprise. "My horse threw me this morn's morn and ran off. I've been looking for him."

Ismay reached up and pet the side of it. "If I'd known it was yours, I would have ridden it tae ye."

He smiled. "Tis not the fairst time you've extended a neighborly hand. You're a fine lass, ye are, Ismay."

She stood straighter and gave Ian a sidelong glance. "I am glad you know my worth, Tom. Though I canna say the same for others."

Tom brushed a piece of sandy hair from his eyes and got down from his animal. He went to her.

His expression suddenly changed when he got close enough to see her face. "Are ye well, Ismay? Are those tears?"

He cast a suspicious glance at Ian who stood next to her. "Hech ay! What's got my bonnie lass so cast down?"

Ismay had no wish to explain what had come to pass between her and Ian. She dabbed at her eyes with her scarf. "The pollen's strong this time of year. I'm glad you found your horse."

She went to the pony and took the reins as she spoke softly it. She tugged on the leather straps and took it to him. "Here, I'm glad you came when ye did. Now ye can have him."

He tied the pony to the saddle of his horse then lifted his hand to her cheek. "Ah, Ismay, I've missed my wee lass. I'm sorry for your loss. Your parents were honest folk, and I'm sad ye lost them."

She gave him a wistful look. "I thank ye both for your help. I miss them very much."

Ian hadn't spoken but moved close to Ismay.

Tom eyed him curiously. "I've not seen you in these pairts. How is it you've come tae know my Ismay?"

Ian looked the other man in the eye. His voice was cool. "I own her property, and she's under my employ. We were on oor way back."

"Ismay? Is it true?"

Ismay nodded. "Aye, Tom, it is. This is Ian MacAllen." She tipped her head in his direction. "Ian, Tom Drummond."

Both men acknowledged each other with a nod but said little. There was an awkward silence.

"I'm wagering we'll be seeing each other around." Tom finally spoke.

"Indeed, it seems we will." Ian's voice was gruff.

Ismay turned to Ian. "I hope your acquaintance wi' each other will be beneficial as you are neighbors."

Then she looked back over the hill in the distance. "I suppose they'll need me in the scullery. I ought tae get back afore Gladys comes looking for me."

"Ye do wark for him then?"

"Aye." She looked at Ian.

"Annag asked for ye too. We wondered where you'd gone tae."

"I'm sorry." She put her hand on his arm. "I'd have been home sooner tae help her if not for the pony."

"Come, I'll take ye back." He turned to Tom. "I'm glad ye have your horse. You must visit sometime."

Tom took hold of the front of his hat and tipped it forward while eying them both with interest. His clear, blue-gray eyes shone. "I thank ye both for the help you've given. I'll come tae your home shortly. I'm very happy tae see ye again, Ismay."

Ismay curtsied to him and smiled. "And I you, Tom."

They watched as Tom mounted his horse and rode off with his pony trailing behind.

Ismay turned to Ian. "I'll walk back. The meadow is a short distance."

"Ismay." Ian pulled her back around. "I believe I owe ye another apology. I should not have rushed tae the conclusions I did."

Ismay's cheeks reddened. "I'd not taken it, but I suppose ye had reason tae doubt my word, sir. Though I hope tae win back your trust in time. I did take your horse but daena plan on anything of the sort again. I hope someday you'll see this is true."

"I've wronged ye, lass." He bent down and picked a flower from the edge of the field and held it out to her. "Here, I must make amends."

"No please keep it." She shook her head. "I canna take that."

"But…"

"I'm sorry." She crossed herself. "I daena mean tae seem ungrateful, but it's like a Banshee, sir, one of those wee wickit fairies dressed in white. I daena pick white flowers. I'm afeart of them."

"A Banshee? Do ye see long, fair hair or silver comb extending from the petals?"

His eyes sparkled as he looked at her. "Do you not believe God could save ye from such a thing? Come now, Ismay." He laughed and winked. "Your talkin' mince. Tis a silly superstition."

She put up her hand and frowned. "A Banshee isn't anything tae trifle wi' in the event that those childhood stories might ring any bit of truth in them. I won't have it."

He laughed again as he tossed it to the ground. "Oor God has power over all things, even those tales from auld. You should believe it."

"Well, I do, but I would think oor Lord would want us tae stay away from such deeviltry."

He leaned down and picked a different blossom with pink petals on it and held it out to her. "Will this suit you?"

She took it from him. She lifted it to her nose and breathed in its sweet scent as she looked at him. "I suppose, but have no wish tae die on account of seeing the other one."

Her lips drew into a pout as she slipped it into her pocket. "Though we mustn't stand here the day. Annag will wonder what has happened tae us, and we've little time tae waste."

He smiled. "Come, we'll ride back together. I'll see tae your safety. There's no reason for you tae walk."

He didn't wait for her answer as he lifted her onto his horse and got up behind her.

Ismay felt his arm curve around her waist as they rode back in the direction of the home. Hech ay! She turned in her seat and looked at him. "There's no reason for us tae ride together, sir. I can get down and see myself home."

He gave her a curious look. "You daena appreciate my gesture, Ismay?"

Her cheeks reddened. "I do. It's only I daena wish tae be an imposition tae ye when I'm capable of walking."

He gave her an easy smile.

"Please, sir. I prefer it."

"It's no imposition on my pairt. Annag's most likely warked up tae high doh by now and will want ye back soon. Please say no more about it."

Ismay sighed. She looked out over the rocky hillside as they took one last climb to her faither's place and down the path.

There'd be wark when she got back tae the home.

Annag awaited her. She supposed it best tae focus on the chores that would need tae be duin.

\*\*\*\*\*

# Chapter 13

Ailsa finished scrubbing the floor. She urged her mother to look at it. "See, there's not a speck of dirt anywhere. It's clean."

Her mother squatted down and touched the wooden slats beneath her.

She eyed Ailsa suspiciously, then her eyes grew slightly darker as she brushed a fleck of dust from her hand. A thin frown flitted across her face.

"Ailsa, do ye see this? Look."

Ailsa swallowed drily. Her voice was barely audible. "I warked very hard. Truly mother, I did."

"When ye left dust? Look at the panels. You said you're duin but there's still dirt. What are ye thinking?"

"But…mother. It is clean. I see nothing tae the contrary."

"Wheesht! Ye know nothing. Are ye worthless?" Her mother took the bucket and poured the soapy water onto the floor. She grabbed the brush and scrubbed the corner of the floor. Her hand moved vigorously back and forth. "I thought you'd have lairned what I expect from you, though I should have known what I would find. If ye had, there would be no reason for this ridiculous discourse. But because of this, you'll need tae do it again until it's clean!"

She tossed the wire brush into Ailsa's lap and scowled. "Come, daena dally anymore. Keep your scrubbing until it shines. Lairn tae do as your asked."

Ailsa's eyes filled with tears. "But…"

"Wheesht!" She gave Ailsa a shove. "Daena cry and blether on. Do your wark. Quit sitting here and sobbing like an ill-deedie joskin!"

Ailsa quickly pushed the brush back and forth as tears dropped from her eyes. She didn't dare reach up to wipe them from her face. Crying only led tae more misery. She watched her tears mix onto the wet floor.

"Come now. You'll never sleep tonight if ye refuse tae put anything into your wark."

"Yes, mother. I'll do what I can." Ailsa secretly wept as she worked.

Her mother got up and stood above Ailsa with her hands on her hips. "And wipe the sullen countenance off your face. I want tae see none of that. No more talking."

Ailsa's arm ached. She gulped back more tears as her mother's words stabbed her heart. She scrubbed harder burying the pain inside her. Being too truthful wi' her emotions always led tae more consequences.

When Ailsa's mother finally left the next room to work on her embroidery, Ailsa breathed a sigh. At least there'd be respite from her mother's constant berating words and harsh criticisms, and soon she'd slip off tae the bedroom without further provocation and find rest.

While she finished she thought of what Ismay had said.

What was it she'd spoken of? That they were both daughters of the King and significant tae God and that He wouldn't condemn His people?

She drew in a breath. Could she truly believe such a thing? Was it possible? She wasn't sure.

Maybe if she were beautiful like Ismay, she might be able tae believe it, but she was an awfy pie-faced lassie, pale and shy wi' frizzy hair. She was unworthy without merit. She'd not the talent of dancing, or song, or speaking well, and her reputation had been tarnished by the very mother she'd tried so hard tae gain respect from.

She'd not a kind word from either of her parents and had seen their condemning looks. She'd haird what they'd said about her. When she failed in ivery way tae please them, those who were suppose tae love her without fail, she wondered how she might she please the Holiest One of All?

Though she'd fully put her trust the Lord, sometimes she couldn't quite see herself as worthy of such a title. She never quite understood the Lord and how He warked, why he'd chosen her, and this perplexed her beyond her ability tae understand.

She wiped her hands on her skirt and dipped her brush back into the bucket.

What could He possibly have been thinking tae have allowed her, as ordinary as she was, entrance into His Divine Kingdom?

She who was unloved, without merit or favor in her own home, granted a place of honor at His table? And He'd come tae save her?

When she'd pleaded wi' Him tae be hers, His presence and comfort had been continuous. His mercy had shown no bounds. He'd offered her His guidance through His Holy Word and saw her through ivery difficulty she'd faced. It was what the meesionar had spoken of.

But how did such things happen? How could they be true? And could she believe them to be?

She pushed the scrub brush against the flooring and eyed the slats of wood shining beneath her fingertips.

Another tear slipped from her eye, but this time she managed a smile as she recalled God's great love, so unfathomable, so pure, so difficult to understand.

During her darkest times she'd reached out tae Him wi' more vigor, and it was then that her prayers and the time spent wi' Him seemed all the more meaningful. When life seemed harsher, always His light kindled brightest within her.

She supposed she'd no control over what He did and little understanding of His profound ways, but what she did know was that she loved Him and that He loved her when no one else in her home had.

She quietly crept out of the kitchen with the scrub brush and bucket in her hand. She emptied the water behind the house and put the brush into the bucket. She set them both on the porch to dry. Then she snuck back inside carefully closing the door to pull it shut and made her way to her room.

She breathed a sigh once she was safely in bed under the covers. She pulled her blankets to her chin, tucking them carefully around her. "Lord," she whispered, "Protect me and keep me from all that's wrong in the world. Thank Ye, Lord, for your great love. I owe Ye much, and I thank Ye much."

She turned to her side allowing the night to take her to places far from herself. Her imagination stirred as she drifted off to sleep.

\*\*\*\*\*

# Chapter 14

Roslyn's mother extended a sigh. "You're a wanderer, Roslyn. Do ye understand the sacrifice you're making when your deciding to make such a choice? You'll regret leaving us for the sake of your fleeting thoughts. You'll want tae travel wi' us in time, but then it'll be too late."

"No, mama. Nothing will change what I feel when I marry Callum." She drew her knees up to her chest and hugged them to her. She pushed her braids behind her.

Her father crossed his arms. "You're a dreamer, dearie. When your muses take ye tae a standstill, you'll wish ye were dancing in the firelight and breathing the wayfaring air reciting your poems and singing. You'll be like a restless pony in no time, and you'll fancy you were wed tae a man wi' the same spirit as one of us."

"But I've accepted Callum's proposal, and we're determined tae settle down together. He's buildin' a home."

Her mother put her hand on Roslyn's arm. "We've no doubt ye care for this man and have your heart set on him, but we want tae know whether he can truly make ye happy."

"He will, mama! I know it! I love him!"

"Roslyn, we see that you're determined tae marry him." Her mother drew her aside. "But there's a plan ye must consider fairst. You must honor oor wishes afore ye take the marriage vows."

Her faither nodded. "There's no reason tae be hasty. Ye must think this through."

"Papa?" Roslyn moved closer to him.

"We'll grant oor consent. We will." Her faither sighed. "But only efter you've proven tae us that this is what ye truly want. Ye must be happy, Roslyn."

Roslyn went to her father and took his hands in her own. "Och, papa! I'll do it! I'll prove it tae ye!" Her dark eyes shone.

She stared at the wheels of their wagon and whispered out quiet words of a poem.

"A movin' over tired
ole dirt and mud,
leavin' it behind.
For scents of heather
still and fresh as the day,
where earth stands still like
heaven aneath me."

She breathed in the scents around her and clasped her hands together.

Her papa shook his head wearily, though he couldn't contain a smile as his eyes rested on her. "You must prove tae us that ye can live this way."

"Please, pappa. Tell me what I must do tae gain your approval, and Callum and I will be wed." Roslyn practically danced around them.

Her mother reached up and pushed back a piece of her hair. "There's time, dearie. You're young. Daena be hasty."

"I daena understand."

"I have a friend just outside of Crieff. I want you tae meet her."

"A friend? Mama…" Roslyn's brows lifted upward. "What has this tae do with Callum?"

"Do you recall Lorna Bissett?"

"No."

Roslyn's mother pointed to the road. "She recently indured hardships. Her husband died, and then a month later, she injured her arm."

Roslyn gave her a puzzled look.

"So she's in need of assistance. She wants a companion to help her wi' her garden and chores for a time, until the splint can be removed."

"In Crieff? I'd live at her place, wi' her?" Roslyn's eyes grew wide. She tugged excitedly on her mother's arm.

Her papa spoke quietly and raked his hand through his hair. "You'd be off the trail for a time."

"You'll allow me tae stay?"

Her mother nodded. "Aye, we will. But ye must promise you'll not marry the lad, and she'll chaperone the times you're together."

"I'll see him?" Roslyn looked as if she were going to burst with excitement.

"In Lorna's presence mind ye." Her mother glanced at Roslyn's father. "We want ye tae lairn if living off the wagon is truly what ye want. Efter months of it, ye might ache for the traveling cart, and family, and wish ye hadn't have been so hasty tae accept the proposal of a land owner. Your papa and I want ye tae be sure of what ye want."

"Mama, papa! You're good tae me!" She hugged them both and laughed. "I must meet your friend at once and move in wi' her. Please, you must take me tae her straight away!"

Her mother and father smiled, yet their expressions were solemn.

Her mother nodded in the direction of the wagon. "Come, we'll get you a trunk. Tis time for you tae meet Lorna. She'll take the proper care of you."

"I trust your choice and canna wait tae meet her."

Roslyn's face suddenly saddened. "Though I'll miss ye both dearly, and my sister, and the wee ones too. I must take leave of all of you soon. It'll pain me tae go. Shona's my closest confidant."

Her father spoke softly. "We'll visit in the spring and see you then. By that time, you'll have made your decision."

"I'll wait until then. I promise. I'll get my things and go tae your friend's home.

\*\*\*\*\*

A knock sounded on the door. Ailsa turned to her mother. "It's Ismay come again tae call."

Her mother rolled her eyes. "Tell her you're ill and ye don't wish tae see her. There's wark tae be duin."

"Mother, it's the Lord's day. It wouldn't be proper."

"Wheesht! Ismay will hear you. Do ye have any sense in that head of yours?"

Ailsa's mother stared at the door sullenly when the knocker on the door sounded again. She let out a low breath. "Oh, all right. Go then have ye, but be back in time tae set the table."

Ailsa stood quickly and grabbed her shawl from an oak chair next to her. "Oh, thank ye, mother!"

Her mother eyes darkened, and her voice turned gruff. "Find your other shawl. That one looks ridiculous wi' your dress. You'll need a plaid tae match."

Ailsa's cheeks heated. "I'm sorry, mother. I'll take this one." She grabbed a second shawl that hung on a hook by the wall nearest her and put the other one on a nearby bench. She raced to the door and threw it open wide. "It is true! Tis my friend! I knew she would come."

Ismay peeked inside. "Hullo, Mrs. Finn. I came tae walk wi' Ailsa tae the river."

Ailsa's mother tipped her head. Her response was cool, and she smiled with a polite stiffness. "Bring Ailsa back in time tae help wi' supper. She shouldn't take much of oor day."

"We won't be long, mother." Ailsa turned away quickly.

After the door closed, Ailsa and Ismay latched arms and headed down the footpath together.

They laughed and giggled until they almost bumped into Ailsa's brother, Murdock, who came up the walk.

"Och! Murdock!" Ailsa's face paled, and she took a step back.

Murdock gave them a guarded look. "Shouldn't ye be in helping mother?" He pushed a shock of red hair out of his eyes.

Ailsa's voice quieted to a whisper. She took a small step back. "It's the Lord's day. She canna very well make me wark all efternoon?"

Murdock stared at them both. "Maybe so, but when ye run off as ye do, there's no telling what mischief ye might get into."

"I finished my chores, and mother said I could go."

A frown appeared over his brow. "I daena know why. She shouldn't trust the two of ye together."

Ismay stared at him. "I'll have ye know that your sister is a good friend tae me. She treats me kindly." Ismay crooked her arm in Ailsa's. "Come dearie, let's not waste oor time randering on with this one."

She turned and pulled Ailsa down the walk. She let out a breath after he went inside. "I'm sorry, Ailsa, but he puts on such airs. He shouldn't speak tae others the way he does. I canna help from saying what comes tae my mind when he berates ye so." She stared at the path. "In all conscience, I daena know how anyone can live wi' such an ill-fashioned, porridge stick. He's about as dry as a piece of toast, that brother of yours."

Ailsa covered her mouth and stifled a giggle. "Ismay, ye shouldn't say such things efter coming from the kirk! My mother and faither would disown you."

Ismay laughed aloud. "I suppose I shouldn't, but my own faither taught me tae speak my mind. Murdock's behavior is unbecoming, and it seems he could use someone tae boldly reveal the truth tae him. Otherwise he might never find happiness, for such things require a humble heart."

"Murdock's been told he's much like a saint. I wouldn't dare lower him. But it's odd tae hear ye say these things as I've not thought of him the way ye do." Her eyes widened as she turned to Ismay.

Ismay smiled mischieviously, but then she sobered. "Maybe he'll tend tae his own sin in time, rather the misdeeds of others, and understand oor Lord's profound ways."

She turned on the path. "But I suppose we must put this matter tae rest as I presently did not come here tae discuss that ill-deedie brother of yours. I wanted tae find out how you've been and whether you were in need of anything."

Ailsa drew her cloak tighter around her thin shape. She seemed to disappear within the folds of it. Her face paled as she spoke. "I'm well enough, but ye know how hard mother can be. I scrubbed the floor three times over yesterday and afore that I'd spent the morn's morn tearing seams out of a dress I'd made. The size of the stitches wasn't smaw enough tae please her. Tis difficult when she judges me so. She's not critical around others, but quite different when I find myself alone wi' her."

"Well, Ian MacAllen might hire ye in time. It'd be best for you tae skirt away from that home of yours and start afresh. They've treated you so woefully."

"Maybe in time I could lairn tae please them. I suppose I deserve the things I do when I make such a collieshangle of iverything. I'm not much at cooking and cleaning, and I am not sure how tae speak tae them. Murdoch seems tae know how tae make mother happy, and faither has his own wark tae do. You know how it is."

She took Ismay's hand as they neared the creek bed. Water gurgled and bubbled over rocks that stuck out of the middle of the stream.

They both sat next the the river's edge on a flat, rounded stone.

"Ailsa, ye make excuses for them. You're a commendable person and kind tae others. Ye daena deserve this treatment. If you'd leave them, ye might someday see your worth. Ye deserve tae be loved and see the beauty God has placed in you."

Ailsa smiled and spoke quietly. "I thank ye, Ismay, as ye truly understand, even when others daena. They canna see past the deceptions of my mother's gracious smile. I thank you for trusting my words."

"Your mother has a bonnie face, but a brimming smile does not always mean a kind heart. You've duin nothing tae deserve her scorn, and someday I'll see ye in a good place safe from harm. I promise."

Ailsa plucked a flower from beside her and raised it to her nose. She drew in a breath. "The forest and fields are my haven. There's much beauty around me here."

"It is lovely." Ismay looked around.

"I only wish I weren't so alone. Without you, Ismay, I've no good company. It can be lonely here."

"Maybe you'll meet a good man who'll keep ye from harm."

Ailsa's eyes widened, and she giggled. "I might not know good from bad if I saw it. I'd fear I wouldn't see the truth the way ye do and find myself worse off than I am. Then there would be no way out of it."

Then she sighed. "But I do wonder how might I keep food in my mouth and a roof over my head any other way. If I daena marry, they'll never allow me tae leave."

Ismay didn't say anything. She picked up a stone and threw it into the river.

Ailsa shuddered. "Mother's friends think me addled in the head on account of her tales. I see it in their eyes. How does one fight such blatant lies? She does her many charitable deeds and spreads her flattery all around, but then is so unkind in the home. I daena understand it and then wonder if I'm tae blame for it all. I begin tae question my own wits."

"No, Ailsa! Your candid words are not tae blame. To want for love is not a sin. God is good, Ailsa, and has a place for you in His heart. You're His daughter, and ye must never forget that."

Ismay pulled out the necklace her faither had given her. "Remember, you're the Lord's daughter, and He's loved the way ye are." She flipped it over for Ailsa to see.

Ailsa ran her hands over the letters, and a tear struck her cheek. "He's a very, very good Faither, isn't He?"

"Aye, that He is. My earthly faither's at rest, and yours may not have your best interests at heart, but oor heavenly Faither is all around us. He watches over us and makes all things right in His time."

"I am thankful ivery day for Him."

Ismay smiled. "As we should be, because of oor Kingly heirship. He's laid down His life for us, and we've a place, because we trust in Him."

"The thought of it brings me great joy."

Ismay nodded. "Aye, dearie. Ye must keep these words in your heart."

Then she looked at the sun which lowered in the sky. She got up and offered her hand to Ailsa. "I suppose we must be getting back. Your mother said tae not be late."

Ailsa took her hand. "Oor time has been quick, but it is true that I must go."

"Ailsa, I'll come again, when I can, or send for ye if I'm not able."

"Aye, soon. I'm very glad you're back."

"I'm glad for it, too. I've missed ye, friend."

"And I you."

They walked back down the path to the home.

Ismay left Ailsa behind praying that Ailsa's mother would be less harsh with her this evening. She headed back to her home knowing there'd be wark tae be duin there.

*****

The day was nearly over. Dinner was prepared.

Ismay carried a tray with venison steaks, turnips, and nettles into the cozy sitting room where a fire in the hearth burned brightly. Gathered round the snapping flames were a handful of guests. All eyes were on Tom Drummond who sat nearest the hearth.

Tom laughed. "Tellin' this legend ought tae keep the Fians from risin' again, and if ye daena hear it another time by the morn's morn, ye better recite it yourself tae keep the life-blood of the Celts moving."

The others in the room laughed.

Grizel's lips drew upward into a pout, and she put her hand on Ian's sleeve. "These dreich auld tales are senseless, sully things." She gave Tom a hard stare. "Why should we be forced tae bear one more of them?"

Ismay stopped short and whispered under her breath. "Surly? Any true Scot would want tae hear a tale by the hearth. Who could deny anyone the pleasure of it?"

When the others turned to stare, she blushed and spoke quietly. "You must pardon my impertinence. I've not the right tae say such things."

Grizel's mouth turned downward as her amber eyes darkened to coal. She put her hand on Ian's sleeve again. "Your scullery maid speaks her mind too freely. I daena believe it tae be prudent tae excuse such behavior."

Tom took a swig of drink from his mug and wiped the corners of his mouth. "Ismay shouldn't be warking in the scullery or have had tae give up her heirship the way she did. This is her land and home!"

"Hech ay!" Grizel pointed a finger. "The swick should've been in jyle, or hung, for pilking Ian's horse and causing his house tae burn."

Her brows slanted downward. "If it weren't for him, the clarty orphant would have nothing. I still canna understand why he's treated her as well as he has."

"Miss Hawthorne, wheesht! There's no need for your harsh words." Ian gave Grizel an admonishing look. "Ye musn't go on about it."

Ismay straightened. "I'm warking for the debt and making reperations. It's a fair trade." She set the tray on the table.

"I canna understand why a braw lass wi' a bonnie heart is being made tae wark off something she clearly had nothing tae do with." Tom scratched his head and took another drink. "Ismay wouldn't have had a hand in such things."

"No Tom. I've duin much wrong, and I'm sorry for it." Ismay lifted her hand to the dark hair which swung freely about her shoulders and pushed a strand of it behind her ear. "Only time and hard wark will pay the cost of it, but I plan tae uphold my pairt of the bargain."

She looked down as a blush rose in her cheek. "Now, Annag has need of me. I must go and finish my wark."

130

"None of this seems proper, nor does it set well wi' me." Tom's mouth set in a grim line. He shook his head and turned back to Ian.

Ian spoke quietly under his breath. "She's clearing her name, what she's proposed tae do. It's her choice tae make reparations."

Ismay gave a quick nod as she curtsied to the others. She didn't say more.

Tom scowled, and his brow dropped low, but he said no more as he watched Ismay cross the room.

All eyes turned away from Ismay as she slipped out of the room. She caught the last of their conversation and thought she'd heard the words 'cattle' and 'faither' as Grizel chimed in.

She dusted her hands off on her apron and sighed.

She'd hoped she'd seen the last of Grizel for some time, but as it turned out the woman had found her way tae Comrie quicker than a jack rabbit could hop. She wondered what the ill-deedie wutch and her faither had in mind tae do?

Though Grizel's faither hadn't joined them for the fireside tale that evening, earlier he'd disappeared with Ian into the study. They'd been there for the better part of the day when Tom had joined them for the evening meal.

Ismay thought she might ask Tom at the morn's morn what she wanted tae know. He'd surely be of service tae her as there was no disputing where his devotion lay. He'd tell her why they'd come, if he haird anything.

The week had been an ill-faured one. Ailsa was troubled and without the support she so desperately needed. Ian had wrongly accused her of stealing Tom's horse, and now Grizel had suddenly appeared at their home. The morn's morn could only be better.

Ismay took quick steps to the kitchen and smoothed the sides of her skirt as she closed the door behind her.

She moved to the open hearth and used an iron spade to scrape the freshly baked shortbread cakes from the metal pan sitting on legs above the coals. She placed them gently on a large serving platter that she held in her other hand.

"Do ye know why they came, Gladys?" She set the platter on the table and wiped her hands on her apron.

"Her faither has a mind tae invest in a smaw head of cattle. He's asked Ian tae keep them in the Highlands where they can graze, most likely a scheme of Grizel's cooked up tae spend time here."

Ismay rolled her eyes. "I'm not surprised that ill-trickit woman would find a way onto my land, and if the maister iver marries the auld wutch, he'll not find his time wi' her a blissin."

Gladys had turned to the hallway that led into the sitting room, and her eyes widened. She didn't respond.

Ismay quickly looked over her shoulder and lifted her hand to her mouth when she noticed Ian at the doorway.

He tipped his head to them both. "I came tae apologize for the way the others spoke tae ye, but I see it hasn't affected you as I thought it might have." He looked at Ismay. "Ye seem as speeritie as iver, lass."

"I'm sorry, sir. I shouldn't be speaking of such things. It wasn't my business tae blether about ye in this manner." She wrung her hands together as she glanced at Gladys.

Ian's tone was direct. "Ye slight Miss Hawthorne wi' your rander."

Ismay's face scrunched into a frown. She fixed the ties on her apron and spoke quietly. "I apologize, sir. You'll hear no more of it."

Ian nodded and looked around the room at the desserts. "I hope ye busy yourself wi' your wark instead. I must see tae my guests." He turned to go back into the hall. He left through the open doorway.

Ismay took quick steps after him.

"Ismay!" Gladys' warning was curt.

Ismay ignored the cook. She went into the hall and tugged on Ian's shirtsleeve. "I did not mean tae cause ye harm, sir, but it bothers me that you'd find yourself in trouble wi' that woman."

She looked up at him as he turned with a start.

He moved closer eying her curiously.

She took her hand from his sleeve and stepped back. "She isn't kind, and you must see this."

"And why would my business wi' Miss Hawthorne concern you?" He touched her cheek as his hand trailed over the wild, dark strands that fell onto her shoulder.

Ismay swallowed drily, and her blue eyes widened.

What a bonnie man he was wi' his excellent, dark features and fine, strong brow which perceptively drew inward. At first, she didn't know what to say.

She took a breath. She couldn't allow her feelings tae become entwined wi' what should be a proper response. "You're a good man and a deservin' one." Her voice was a whisper. "I only want for you tae be happy."

He took hold of her arm and gently pulled her closer. "Your interest in my affairs leads me tae believe you might care for me, love."

She heard the clank of a pan in the kitchen and moved away from him. "I must not as it stands. I only believe you should consider a different lady than Miss Hawthorne, a woman in high social standing who's your equal. I'd not find acceptance wi' those of your stature, and I'll not be the ruin of your life or my own."

"Your faither wasn't without merit, Ismay. It's clear you've been raised in polite society."

"In the Highlands as a cattle farmer. I daena believe this is equal tae you." She sighed. "Please, I must see tae the desserts. There's wark tae be duin."

Ismay's cheeks colored when Grizel stepped into the hall from the sitting room.

The other woman's brow arched highly, and she stared at Ismay. "I would think it proper that your servant stay in the scullery." She pointed to the other room. "It seems the hired help in this place canna keep themselves from their betters. Though wi' her preference for stories, I suppose she believes the elves will do her wark for her."

Ismay curtsied stiffly. "I've sweets tae see tae, sir. The shortbread cools which I'll bring to the sitting room. I hope it will meet wi' your approval."

Ian didn't answer her, but he tipped his head and watched as she left through the passage to the kitchen.

Ismay stopped on the other side of the door as Ian and Grizel made their way back to the hearth and into the other room. She pulled her hair behind her and tied it with a scarf she'd taken from her belt.

She sighed. Nothing improper had transpired between her and the maister, even though keeping it this way proved tae be difficult.

\*\*\*\*\*

# *Chapter 15*

The next day, Roslyn dreamily looked out the window of her new home as Callum walked up the path.

She smiled as he stopped to adjust his white shirt which had been loosely tucked into his navy plaid kilt.

He reached up to tilt a dark green rounded hat sideways on his head. When he saw her, he grinned.

She quickly grabbed her plaid wrap and threw it around her shoulders. She practically danced through the open door as she closed it behind her. "Callum!" She skipped toward him as her red skirt reeled around her.

Her soft, brown hair fell loose from its two, long thick braids, and she ran the rest of the way to him. She threw her arms around him. "My love!" She peppered his cheek with kisses while he laughed.

"My braw lass, my sweet traveler." He drew her back and smiled. "Nothing could keep me from ye."

Roslyn lifted her hand to his face. Her dark eyes had a warm, appreciative look in them.

The door suddenly slammed behind them, and there was a rustling of skirts.

A curt voice called out. "Roslyn Marie Day, where have ye gone tae?" A middle-aged woman with black hair tightly wound on the back of her head, and a splint on one arm, came marching out of the house and across the way. When she reached Roslyn, she took hold of her arm.

Roslyn smiled. Her cheeks were rosy. "Lorna, it's Callum. He's come tae call!"

Lorna wagged her finger at Roslyn. "The young man whose stolen your heart, is it?

"Aye." She giggled.

Callum tipped his head to Lorna.

"I promised your papa and mama I'd allow no improprieties tae take place between you and any young men comin' round the home." She shook her head. "I'll have ye know that there'll be none of this business anymore. I'll not stand for it."

Roslyn lifted her hand to her mouth and held back a giggle.

Lorna looked at Callum. "I plan tae teach this young woman tae be a lady of the proper sort so that she might be the wife of a gentleman. I expect more from you than this. If ye wish tae call on Roslyn, you'll need tae do it properly and address me fairst."

Callum cleared his throat. "How might I address you, mem?"

"By calling me, Madam Bissett." Her eyes raked over him critically. "And this is Miss Day, no longer a tinker."

Roslyn sighed. "May I go wi' Mr. Crawford? We'll stay within sight of the house." She smoothed out her woolen skirt and straightened her scarf around her shoulders. "Callum, I mean Mr. Crawford, is a very worthy friend. Mama and papa are aware of my feeling for him. We musn't turn away respectable company."

Lorna made a miffed sound. "You're here tae lairn townfolk ways and assist wi' the chores, but you may go, though ye must stay within sight of the home. I'll need you at the hearth within the hour."

"God be thanked!" Roslyn took hold of Callum's arm and leaned closer. "I've been waiting so very long for this!"

Callum released her hand from his arm and tipped his head to Lorna. He gave a broad wink at the older woman. "No injury will come tae Miss Day, Madam Bissett. I'll see tae it."

"And I'll see tae it too!" Lorna pushed a strand of hair behind her ear. "Now, I've gardening tae do."

Roslyn nodded.

When Lorna turned to her work, Roslyn stood on her tiptoes and quickly gave Callum a kiss on the cheek.

He set her away from him.

"You daena want me near you?" She giggled.

"Not when I'm told tae keep my distance." Callum raked his hand through his hair and looked back Lorna. "I believe I must prove myself a trustworthy man fairst, my good lass, as I'm not sure she sees this."

Roslyn gave him a curious stare then to the gate beyond. "I told ye I'd marry you. It won't be long afore we'll have a home."

He smiled again. "Aye, my traveler. And I'll tell ye about this very thing, oor house. Someday I'll take ye there."

She skipped ahead and turned around once dropping into a flower patch. She looked up at him. "Is there a place tae cook? Will we have a well wi' water and a hearth?"

He laughed. "Is this how ye'll always smell like the honeycomb?"

"Maybe."

She got up and took his arm again. "I imagine it's a bonnie home wi' a pretty sign on the door and a thick, brass knocker!" She sang a pretty tune.

Oor home wi'
purple heather 'round about
on jeweled loch
aneath fair skies this day.

Och, sing, my love
of spice-laden mountains
and black-faced sheep,
where rivers canna wash
oor love away.

He grinned at her and tugged gently on one of her braids. "Whatever ye want, Roslyn, I'll build it for ye. Be patient, and I'll tell ye what I've duin. God's been a blissin tae us in many ways."

Roslyn smiled widely. "He was very good tae put me in your path. I must hear it, and then I'll tell ye what I'll bring tae the home."

They walked alongside the garden hedgerow past clusters of wild thyme and fragrant flowers in the warmth of the day.

Rabbits played along the edge of the field in the distance amidst craggy rocks. Roslyn pointed to them while they passed.

Callum smiled. "They seem tae be here for us."

"Maybe so." Rosyln laughed. They stopped for a time and watched and then continued on their walk.

They both sat down on a large flat rock not far from the home and spoke of their plans and what they hoped to accomplish before Roslyn's parents would finally come back for her.

When the hour ran short, Callum dutifully took her hand and pulled her in the direction of the house which was still in sight of their path. "I suppose we ought tae go back now."

Roslyn sighed. "Oor time went by too quickly, but Lorna will expect us, and we shouldn't disappoint her."

Callum nodded and took her arm. "I daena believe we should."

They walked toward the home and to the doorstep where he took her hands in his. "I'm glad you've come tae stay."

"Oh, Callum!" She kissed his cheek. "I'll wait for your return. How good ye are tae me."

"I'll be back soon, my love." He smiled. He let go of her hand and stepped aside. "Sleep well, sweet traveler."

"And you as well." She reluctantly went inside, leaving him to walk down the path alone.

She sighed at the window as she watched him take the last turn in the road.

In time, Lorna would surely see Callum as the considerate man and a worthy provider Roslyn knew him tae be.

\*\*\*\*\*

The sun rose early the next morning. As Roslyn drew open the curtains, she felt a tug on her skirt. She turned around.

"Stop moving, lass. How am I tae take your measurements when ye won't quit wiggling? If I'm tae teach ye tae be a lady, I must see that ye have the things ye need."

"You've seen tae that already, Lorna. I must have a dozen linen and wool gowns and skirts and more than enough places tae wear them. My parents did not send me here tae change my ways, only my heart if needed."

Lorna readjusted the hemline of the skirt she'd altered. "They may not have, Roslyn, but I see an advantageous future afore you, and it seems ye already have your heart set on living in a house. I'll see that ye dress well while you're in my home."

"But, you've given me many gowns."

"I'm glad I kept what I did in that auld trunk. I knew I'd make use of them someday. I aim tae make a proper lady of ye tae attract a proper man."

Roslyn's brows knit together. "Callum."

"Mr. Crawford," Lorna frowned, "is fine enough, though I think you'd do well tae set your sights on Mr.

Featherstone instead. Did ye see the land he owns and his bonnie house? He's a wealthy laird who's noticed ye, Roslyn. Someday, ye might be mistress of a grand estate if ye set your sights high enough."

Roslyn sighed. "I've no interest in Mr. Featherstone, Lorna. Callum's a braw man. Did ye not see the look in Mr. Featherstone's eyes. He's skullky, and there's darkness 'round about him. He stares at me so strongly."

"Wheesht! You've got your head stuck in the clouds. That Callum has ye turned tae him, and you're not thinking straight."

She wagged a finger in the air. "You should listen, lassie. That gleam in your eye will only last so long when hard wark takes its place and there's nothing tae show for it. Mr. Featherstone's not so handsome tae look at, but he's well set and can provide for your future in a way you've never known."

"I'm a tinker's daughter and well accustomed to tough times. Callum's a worthy heart, a good man wi' laftie dreams, and he loves oor Lord and Savior. He cares for me deeply."

Lorna frowned. "Laftie dreams will haurdly pay the price tae live. You must think of these things, Roslyn."

Roslyn dropped her hands to her side when Lorna \ measured the length of her skirt. "Mr. Featherstone is coming tae denner tonight, isn't he?" Her cheeks reddened. "The reason for the newest gown."

Lorna didn't answer. She mumbled something about the hem and how it needed to be altered.

The room suddenly quieted enough to hear the snap of sparks in the hearth and the soft patter of rain on the roof.

Roslyn eyed the extra seat at the table and let out a sigh. Convincing Lorna of her love for Callum and his worth seemed an impossible task. It might have been easier for Callum tae have joined the wagon instead.

George Featherstone had a mansion, a set of fine clothes, and a stack of coins locked safely away, but he'd no bonnie smile or hearty laugh like Callum. His jaw was set like a prison door, and his soulless eyes lit only at the prospect of attaining more property. And so it seemed that she'd become his latest conquest.

*****

"Sit wi' us, Roslyn. Mr. Featherstone's here."

Roslyn held onto the edge of the window sill and looked out. She sighed.

"Denner's ready. You should eat."

Roslyn hesitantly walked to the table and sat down. "I'm not hungry, mem. I've much on my mind."

"But Mr. Featherstone brought ye news from town. You'll want tae hear it. Your parents sent ye a post."

"Here." Mr. Featherstone stared hard at Roslyn as he held the piece of folded parchment out to her. "They gave this tae me in Perth. I told them I'd be comin' by this way."

"Oh!" Roslyn brightened. "Please, I've not spoken tae them in so long."

He laid the note next to her and leaned back in his seat with a pleased smile.

Roslyn picked up the parchment and unfolded it. She read it silently to herself.

*Dearest Roslyn Marie,*

*We miss ye greatly and want ye tae know that we'll be passing through soon. We pray you've been thinking hard about the choices you're about tae make and that ye hasten tae recall the blissins in your upbringing as a traveler.*

*We've met many fine, brawly men at the tinker's campsites. They'd treat ye well if ye were iver tae consider them. Never forget oor family and oor ways and the times we've spent together.*

*The fires at oor camp burn bright under the stars at night. The song and dance is as it's been, a merry time, but less so without you here tae give oor spirits a greater lift.*

*Oor wee bairn's a size bigger and is walking on her own now. Shona delights greatly in her company but misses you dearly. She canna wait for when we visit and she sees you again.*

*Papa sends his love. He speaks of a time when you'll return tae us. You're in oor hearts wi' each passing hour.*

*Yestermorn, this wealthy gentleman came forward tae greet us as a friend of oor dear Lorna. He was very anxious tae ingratiate himself in a worthy and humble manner. We're glad for his goodly service in delivering oor note tae you. Lorna would consider this highborn man a worthy prize if ye choose tae live your life outside of the wagon. You must thank him for his attendance tae you.*

*Until we meet again, oor wee ane,*

*Mama and Papa*

Roslyn wiped a tear from her eye. She looked across the table. "I appreciate what ye did, sir. I've not spoken tae my papa and mama for some time." She held the letter close to her chest.

Mr. Featherstone smiled at Lorna and tipped his head. Then he dipped a spoon into his soup and lifted it to his mouth. He had the same pleased look on his face again.

Roslyn quickly turned to Lorna. There was a sudden sense of urgency in her voice. "Did Callum send word that he'd be paying us a visit?"

Lorna gave Roslyn a silencing look. "No, he hasn't sent word. His behavior has been rather unpredictable."

Mr. Featherstone brushed a spot of lint off his dinner jacket and tipped his head again. There was an unusual glow in his eyes.

"No one has haird from him?"

"None that I know of, lass." Lorna shook her head. "But, we've a guest this evening, and it'd be proper tae give him oor full attention. You mustn't fret over what ye canna change and put your trust in an unreliable man."

"But Lorna, Callum's not unreliable. There's a reason he's been waylaid. He'll come soon. I just know it." Roslyn put her hands in her lap. "Ye shouldn't speak of him the way ye do. Ye know I care for him very much."

Mr. Featherstone smiled again yet his eyes were stony. "If I might be so bold as tae speak my mind, Miss Day, I'd warn ye about setting your sights on a man not worthy of a woman of your beauty and grace. You could be a great lady someday, very well set, if you'd be willing tae consider other possibilities."

"Sir, I've given much thought tae the matter, and I'm quite certain your mistaken as I know my own mind. I believe it would be best tae keep your thoughts tae yourself."

"All the same, I've legitimate concern for you and want tae see tae your best interests." He lowered his spoon and looked down his nose at her. "It makes no sense for you tae retain a friendship wi' a young man who can offer you no title or position."

Roslyn's brow rose. "I'm a tinker's daughter, sir. I'm not of highborne status, nor have lofty ambitions. I'm happy wi' a little more than a roof over my head and a modest meal on the table."

"When there is a more comfortable prospect?" Mr. Featherstone let out a weary breath. "The choice is clear. A good woman would accept a worthy gentleman. If ye allow your feelings tae run away wi' you, you are settling for the lesser option. If this man cared for you, he'd be willing tae step aside so that you might increase your property and possessions."

Roslyn stared at him from across the table. "Mr. Featherstone, it isn't your place tae be concerned wi' my affairs. I've asked for no opinion, nor lecture, and I'd appreciate it if you said nothing more about it." She clenched her fingers tightly around the spoon in her hand.

A couple veins in Mr. Featherstone's neck thickened as he leaned forward. "Miss Day, your best interest is my concern because I care for ye very much. I'm a shrewd business man and have seen such matters take a sour turn. It would be good tae take my advice, and allow me tae assist you. It seems ye know little of these things."

"Sir! I daena relish the condescending tone in your voice. You've no right tae speak so boldly about my private affairs." She put her hand to her mouth and then back in her lap. "And I'll have no more of it."

"Roslyn!" Lorna shook her head. "'Tis not proper tae speak in such a passionate way afore highborn society. Clearly you've shown disrespect for your betters."

Roslyn looked at the ceiling and groaned. "Och! Will this denner never end?"

Mr. Featherstone cleared his throat. He dabbed a napkin on his forehead and swallowed. "I apologize if you thought me condescending, Miss Day. It wasn't my intent, but you must understand my disappointment as well. You should trust that my interests in your affairs are completely honorable."

"I trust you less than I trust Callum." She took a drink of water. "You speak of provisions, guinea notes, and money, but it matters little tae me."

"But Miss Day, how might I gain your trust when you provide me no opportunity? I presented good reason why you would be better off without that young man. My words are not without merit."

Roslyn got up from the table. She tapped her fingers against her skirt. "I can see that my words hold no merit wi' you, and I've lost interest in this conversation."

"Roslyn." Lorna looked bewildered. She got up and put a hand on the younger woman's shoulder.

"No, please." Roslyn shook her head. "I've no wish tae hear more."

Mr. Featherstone seemed at a loss for words. He muttered quietly to himself. "Another day. We'll speak of this when you've had time tae think about what I said."

Roslyn stared at him and Lorna. "I've no more tae say. If it pleases you, goodnight, Mr. Featherstone. Goodnight, Lorna."

Mr. Featherstone stood next to his chair. He nodded to her. "Miss Day, I'll see ye on better terms another time."

Roslyn turned on her heel. She said nothing in return and took quick steps to the end of the hall without looking back.

She quickly opened the door of her room and went inside. She'd no intentions of seeing Mr. Featherstone again. She hoped Lorna understood that she wanted nothing more to do with the man.

\*\*\*\*\*

# *Chapter 16*

"Get up and put on your clothes." Ailsa's mother's voice had a tinge of anger to it. "And daena be long. We're making a trip tae Crieff."

Ailsa opened her eyes and groggily looked around. She sighed as she hurriedly pulled the covers on her bed back. Patience wasn't one of her mother's virtues.

"But it's Sunday. We're not goin' tae the kirk?"

"We'll tell the meesionar we went tae services in Crieff. The tinker did not bring me the fabric I wanted. He'll be leaving town, and I canna miss him."

"So we'll go tae the kirk there?" Ailsa sat up in bed. Her brow furrowed as she swept her hair aside her face.

Her mother stared down her nose at her daughter. "We've no time for it, but no one will know." She frowned irritably. "And no one needs tae."

Ailsa wanted to tell her mother that they'd be lying to the meesionar if they said they went to the kirk in Crieff and did not, but she bit her lip instead and got out of bed. Nothing good ever came from having honest words wi' her mother. In fact, she'd pay dearly for speaking her mind so she chose tae remain silent.

She got dressed.

"Hurry now!" Her mother's eyes darkened. "And dress well. If you befriend the tinker's youngsters, he might not charge so much."

Ailsa did not appreciate being used as a means of bargaining for a better price, but again she dared not raise any objections. "Yes, mother." She spoke softly as she pulled a comb through her hair and threaded a ribbon across the top of it, tying it underneath.

She sighed as she went to the door to go out. She hoped the day wouldn't be too difficult.

\*\*\*\*\*

"Ailsa, I've two different fabrics tae consider for curtains in the home. What would ye think for the front room near the hearth?" She fingered a pale blue color.

Ailsa sighed. "That one looks good." She pointed to the fabric in her mother's hands. She didn't dare pick the plum swatch which lay on the table, yet she fancied it over the other when she pictured it draped over the rods matching the stonework of the fireplace.

"I don't know. Maybe the light green." Ailsa's mother lifted her chin slightly and smoothed her hands against the fabric. "I've been in the Drummond's grand estate settled in the valley and saw a great deal of green in it. I believe this was the color." She looked pleased.

"Yes, Mother." Ailsa sighed. She still fancied the plum but would never dare say it.

Her mother lifted the fabric. "Victoria Drummond thinks herself so high and mighty wi' all the money, but my smaw home matches hers in design and style."

She turned to Ailsa. Her brows drew into a frown. "I thought I told ye tae go and talk tae the little ones. And daena give such a dreich look. Do ye not know how tae smile?"

Ailsa turned quickly her hair covering her face. "I'll see tae them." She thankfully left her mother's side and went to talk to the children who stood watching. She'd smile for the youngsters, but not for her mother. Her heart and soul was her own. It was one place her mother could not touch.

\*\*\*\*\*

Ailsa's father scowled at her as she got into the wagon and took a seat. The frown over his thick brows drew inward as he waited for her to get settled and then snapped the reins and clucked to the horses.

He turned to Ailsa's mother. "She's not wearing her scarf or covering her neckline. The young men will think her a low-born hissy the way she's flinking herself around them."

"No, faither! I wouldn't!" Ailsa put her hand over her mouth and let out a sound. "Mother told me tae play wi' the children. I did not mean tae…"

"Ailsa!" Her mother turned in her seat and glared at her. "I never told ye tae flirt wi' those boys."

Ailsa gulped back tears. "But, I did not…"

"Haud yer wheesht!" Her father's voice trumped her own. "Ye dare argue wi' your mother or I, when we know very well what ye were doing?"

Ailsa's hair fell into her face, and she broke down in tears, as she shook her head back and forth.

She hadn't meant tae do anything but play wi' the children as she'd been told, but there wasn't a thing she could say in her defense. Neither her mother or faither believed anything she told them so it was futile tae say more.

Her father stopped the wagon. His voice was deep and cutting. "And you'll stop those ridiculous tears from running doun your face. If ye continue in it, we'll see that ye have something tae cry about."

Ailsa swallowed and wiped her eyes as her heart pounded at her faither's brusk words. She gulped back her choked sobs willing herself tae obey his command.

"I'll wear my scarf next time, faither. I'm sorry. I should have not duin what I did." She shivered, her cheeks drying in the wind. "I'll not do it again."

Her mother rolled her eyes and gave her father an exasperated look. Neither of them answered.

Ailsa sighed with relief at escaping her faither's heavy hand when the wagon wheels started turning again, and the cart rattled down the road.

She curled up in the corner of the wagon bed staring out over the rolling countryside.

She pushed back a tear making its way down her cheek. Her heart struck inside with a mixture of sorrow and anger. She'd not meant tae do anything ill-deedie. She hadn't even understood what she'd duin.

She shivered and clasped her hands bringing them up to her chest.

She sighed. How many times had it been this way, their finding fault wi' her at ivery turn? How many times had she forgiven them and cared for them in spite of their indifference? How could they not see her heart, or the love she had for them?

She'd not understood their resentment toward her nor their bitterness. Too many times there'd been accusations. Did not one's parents naturally have a great love for their child? Could they not see how hard she'd made attempts in gaining their approval?

She bowed her head. Lord, she prayed, I lay my sorrows at your feet. Grant tae me grace. Grant tae me joy. From this day forward, show me your peace. Show me your path.

\*\*\*\*\*

Ismay rapped on the door. No one answered.

Why hadn't Ailsa been at the kirk? Where might she have gone? The house was empty.

She walked around the back of the house to the garden. A lone chicken pecked the ground on the path. Other than the nervous, meandering bird the place seemed deserted.

She heard a shuffle behind her and noticed Ailsa's brother, Murdock, at the gate.

He opened it and stooped beneath the arch overhead and strolled down the path. "My sister's not here." He stared dully at Ismay while holding a broken reed in his hand, rolling it between his fingers. "She's wi' mother and faither."

"Where?" Ismay stepped back when he came closer. "I did not see them at the kirk."

He threw down the broken reed which rolled off the path. "Tae Crieff in the wagon about an hour ago. Mother needed some things."

"But Ailsa doesna miss services. She'd have wanted tae hear the meesionar and been pairt of the worship." She pulled her scarf tighter around her shoulders. The chill air made her shiver.

His eyes narrowed. "Ailsa? My ill-deedie sister?" He chuckled to himself.

"Not ill-deedie. Your sister's sweet and canna wait tae hear the meesionar talk about the Good Book." Ismay put her hand on her hip.

"Sometimes ye speak of that hizzie as if she's a saint, Ismay. She'd more likely be goin' tae the kirk tae look over those sword-dancers who've come tae town." He swallowed drily as if he'd stuffed his mouth full of haggis.

Ismay tapped her toe against a flat rock on the path. "You shouldn't talk so poorly of your sister. She's a braw lass, kindly and good."

His mouth drew into a grim line, and he looked down his nose at her. "Ailsa's been trouble from the time she was a wee bairn, crying and conniving. Braw lass? Wheesht!"

"Your head's full of deceptions, and ye fail tae see it. Ailsa's a devout young woman and has duin nothing tae deserve the ill-fashioned treatment she's been handed by you or your parents."

"My parents?" Murdock stared at her in disbelief. "Their goodness canna be matched. Ailsa's brought her own troubles doun on her." He tugged anxiously at the neckline of his shirt. "She's caused my family tae suffer more times than I can count and deserves tae be treated the way she is."

"Your mother might have the whole town believing tales about Ailsa, but she's wrong tae have blethered on about her daughter this way. It's not decent the way she has tarnished your sister's reputation when Ailsa's duin nothing but attempt tae escape her scorn."

Murdock lifted his chin and crossed his arms in front of him. "You're as daft as a tattie, Ismay. Your friendship wi' Ailsa seems tae keep ye from rightly seeing the truth. My mother has never had a reason tae injure Ailsa, and I've never haird a hatesome word from either of my parents." There was a cool tone to his voice.

"Ye raise yourself in your pride, and your mother and faither also." Ismay pushed on his chest with her fingers. "I've seen what ye do. Without Ailsa tae blame, you'd need tae look at own yourselves which is where the lot of ye should be pointing your fingers."

Murdock gazed at her with amazement. "Wheesht! Silliness! Ye rander on about these things, Ismay, when it's clear that the wutch has used her trickery on you. Ye point your fingers at me, when ye have three pointed back at yourself."

He took a step nearer and grabbed her arm. His voice bordered on hysteria. "Daena think, lass, that you can speak as ye have about oor family without repercussions. I'll not have anyone, including you, slanderin' my good mother and faither.

I'll see tae it that folks in town despise ye greatly if you attempt tae lower my parents in anyone's eyes."

Ismay wriggled out of his grasp. Her icy blue eyes narrowed. "You can do nothing, Murdock Finn. Your threats daena frighten me. I'll come back when Ailsa's home again, but I want nothing more tae do wi' you."

He grabbed her arm again and held it tight.

"Let go! I told ye I'm leaving, Murdock!"

His fingers dug into her skin. "You'll not speak of this. I'll not have it, Ismay."

"Stop! I told ye!" She attempted to break free, but found herself unable to escape from his hold.

Suddenly the sound of horse hooves beating against the road caused Murdock to loosen his grasp and back away.

They both looked toward the gate.

Murdock muttered under his breath. "Heidy winch blethering on. Ye better keep it tae yourself."

Her eyes narrowed. "As if I had a mind tae talk about you, ye Eejit."

Ian MacAllen got down off the horse. He stood at the end of the fenced in entrance to the yard eying Ismay's flushed face. He locked gazes with Murdock and then turned back to her. "Ismay? Are ye all right, lass?"

Ismay breathed a sigh of relief and nodded.

She quickly ran to the gate and opened it. "Ian!" Her face was flushed as she wiped tears from her eyes.

Murdock snorted and dusted off his sleeve. "Pensie missy." He spat and walked up the steps of the home and onto the porch where he turned back with his arms crossed in front of him.

Ian studied Ismay, and a frown drew over his brow. "What is this, lass? You are distressed."

She stopped short of him. "There's no need tae worry. It's only that Ailsa's gone tae Crieff, and I daena wish tae be at her home alone wi' her brother."

"Did he hurt you?"

"No, we had words but they are not worth our time." She closed the gate behind her and latched it.

"Come, I'll take ye back tae the house."

Ismay hesitated but then looked at Murdock who leaned against the house watching them. "I thank ye. I'd rather not walk today."

"Here." He got on the horse and lifted her behind him.

She reluctantly clasped her hands around his waist and nodded. "I appreciate ye comin' when ye did."

He dug his heel gently into the horse's side. His voice lowered. "Ismay, efter this you must meet Ailsa at the kirk. It would set my mind at ease."

"I suppose it would be best, though I truly am not afeart of Ailsa's brother. He randers on about his sister and family but nothing more. He's not the sort tae carry out a threat on account of tarnishing his good name."

"Ah, I see."

Ismay nodded.

The rhythm of the horse's pounding hooves steadied the rhythm of Ismay's heart. She breathed in the scents of the purple heather as they passed a flowing river and moss-covered rocks that dotted the barren, rocky shore. A steep rise led to the water below.

Ian took a course along the edge of the stream until they neared Ismay's father's land. Light sprinkles of rain fell around them in the crisp, cool air. The sky turned a cloudy gray, and the air dampened.

When they reached the gated entrance, he lifted Ismay off. "Go, get warm, and I'll see tae the horse. You're shivering. Stand near the hearth."

The cold ground water seeped through her shoes, and she lifted her skirt to keep it from dragging in the mud which pooled on the path.

"I suppose Scotland wouldn't be itself without a spot o' rain, would it?" She smiled.

"No, it wouldn't." He tipped his head to her.

Ismay stepped away from the horse. "Thank ye again. I'm glad ye showed up when ye did." She curtsied and turned to unlatch the gate as she allowed them both to go through.

Nothing more was said as she ran back to the house through the rain which beat down forming quick streams that trickled off into the pasture.

*****

Ismay coughed lightly as she lifted a loaf of bread out of the hearth. She laid it on the wooden countertop and stood upright, then she rested the back of her hand on her forehead.

"Your cheeks are flushed." Gladys stared at her. "Your shaking, Ismay. Are ye warm?" She put a hand to Ismay's arm and frowned.

Ismay tied her apron around her waist. "I should've taken off my wet boots. I thought they'd dry quicker by the hearth." She coughed.

They both turned when Ian came into the kitchen. "Are ye ill, lass. You should have dressed properly."

"The rain was a wee bit cold, but I'll be fine. I have a mind tae keep myself in now and dry myself by the hearth."

"I believe she has a fever, sir. She's shivering. Glady's voice was firm. "And her cheeks are red."

"Have ye been this way long?" Ian studied her as he spoke quietly.

Ismay coughed again. "I might have caught a chill, but I'll be well soon enough. Glady's tattie soup and a warm pair of socks will most likely put me tae rights again."

Ian went to her and touched her forehead. "Och love, you're burning up, and your clothes are damp."

He turned to Gladys. "Where's Maisie? Ismay belongs in bed. She needs a change of clothes and help getting into them."

"Maisie's in one of the back rooms." Gladys handed Ismay a cloak. "Here, dearie, go back tae the servant's house, and wait there. Mr. MacAllen will send someone efter you."

Ian took Ismay's hand and put her cloak on a wall peg. "I'll not send her out in that rain again when there are rooms here. There's no need for it."

Ismay put her hand to her side to steady her shaking. She looked at Gladys. "You've nothing more for me tae do here?"

"Denner's almost ready. You rest, Ismay. I'll send ye some soup when it's finished."

Ismay nodded.

"Here, come with me." Ian motioned to the door. "I'll find one of the maids tae help ye."

She followed Ian through an arched doorway and into the hall.

He let go of her hand and touched her flushed cheek again. "Here, go in the fairst room. It's unoccupied." He opened the door and led her to the end of the bed.

She sat down. "I'll be fine, sir, if ye send for Maisie."

He began to untie her shoes.

Ismay reached to unlace the boot, but he brushed her hand aside. "Nay, I'll do it."

He worked adeptly to remove both the boots and Ismay's socks. He handed her a pair of warm, woolen ones he'd taken from the wardrobe. "Here, put these on."

He added quietly. "I'll find Maisie while ye get these wet clothes off. She'll help ye wi' the rest."

Ismay waited for him to leave and shivered as she unbuttoned her dress and slipped out of it leaving only her undergarments. She crawled beneath the covers and waited for the house maid to come with a change of clothes and warm stones to put beneath the bed.

*****

Maisie opened the door to the room. She brought Ismay a set of dry nightclothes and helped her into them. She pulled back the covers.

"Ye must lie down, lass. I'll bring ye some warm soup and stones tae warm your bed so that you'll soon be well and duin wi' the fever."

"Thank ye, Maisie." Ismay nodded sleepily. "I am tired, but there's no need for you tae stay while I sleep."

"Mr. MacAllen told me I wasn't tae leave ye long, mem." Maisie curtsied at the door and tipped her head. "I'll be back soon tae watch over you. I'm sure you'll feel much better once you've had some rest." She turned and exited through the arched opening of the room and closed the door.

*****

"She's shakin', sir. I daena know what else tae do. She's burnin' up and won't quit the cough."

Ian held a cold compress to Ismay's head. He pushed back the hair from her forehead and studied her. His brows drew into a frown. "I thought they sent for the doctor hours ago. Where is he?"

Maisie brought a porclain bowl with broth in it to the bedside stand and set it there. "I thought he'd be here, sir,

156

though there's not a whole lot he can do at this point. Sometimes these things must run their course."

Ian didn't answer, but reached for a spoon and dipped it into the soup. "Sit up, Ismay. You should eat so you'll be stronger."

Ismay squinted at him and wearily got up. She shivered and coughed as she took the bowl into her hands. "Please hand me the spoon."

Ian gave it to her and watched as she took small sips of hot broth.

Between coughs and shivering, she finished half of the contents and then set the bowl back on the stand. "I canna eat more." She wrapped a blanket around her and curled onto her side. "I feel quite duin in."

Ian bent over and felt her forehead. "Maisie, bring more cool compresses. These are warm."

Maisie nodded and left the room.

Ismay tossed and turned. She mumbled to herself. "I'm cold."

\*\*\*\*\*

Ian took a chair next to her bedside. How many hours could this sickness go on? It had been almost a day since he'd sent Cael for a doctor. When would the fever break?

He tapped his fingers against his side as the sun poked rays over the horizon. Another day, and she hadn't shown improvement. Maybe the illness would soon come tae an end soon as Maise had predicted. At least the room wouldn't be so cold with the morning rays spilling into the room.

How much longer would it be afore she was well again.

\*\*\*\*\*

Outside Lorna's home, the same sun rose higher into the sky.

Roslyn waved to Lorna from a distance as she walked down the road. "Good morning. I'm out for a walk this morn's morn. Would ye like tae come?"

"I'll finish here, but you go ahead." Lorna looked up from the garden row where she worked. "Ye might see Mr. Featherstone on the way. He told me he'd be stoppin' by tae visit."

Roslyn would have preferred seeing Callum, though he hadn't been tae see her for quite some time. Maybe she'd pass him on the road. She wondered why she hadn't seen him and where might he have gone tae?

A sick feeling welled up in her. She looked to the end of the trail thinking of her parents and their traveling home.

As she walked, she hummed a tune, one her mother had sung when she was a little girl.

Wee baloo,
my bonnie bairn,
 came tae me
one sunlit morn.

Over the hillock,
blissin galore,
came tae me,
my bonnie bairn.

Her mama had sung it tae her, but also tae a smaw bairne who had lived with their family for a time. For some odd reason the tune had filled her thoughts just now.

Though Roslyn's mama and papa had rarely spoken of the young child, neither Shona, nor she, had forgotten the wee lassie wi' the large, blue eyes and dark curls who had played wi' them as a youngster.

Roslyn wondered what had become of the little girl who would most certainly be a young woman now. She hoped someday she'd meet up wi' her again.

Roslyn turned to the click of horseshoes clomping down the road.

Mr. Featherstone's buggy came to a halt alongside her. His eyes roved over her as he spoke. "A new dress. Lorna's duin well wi' ye, Roslyn. Apart from those braids, no one would wager that ye came from the humble beginnings of a tinker's wagon."

Roslyn rolled her eyes. She looked at him wearily. "Good morning, Mr. Featherstone. If you're here tae see Lorna, she's at the house."

"I hoped tae see you." He put out his hand and motioned for her to stop walking. "Wait, I'll hitch the wagon tae a post ahead and walk wi' you."

Before Roslyn could answer, Mr. Featherstone set his horse in motion and rolled it to the hitching post. He quickly tied it and took to her side.

Roslyn tapped her fingers against the folds of her skirt as she walked. She took a deep breath before she spoke. "What's brought ye tae oor home, sir? Do you not have wark tae do?"

Mr. Featherstone reached up and smoothed back a slick piece of hair that had fallen onto his damp forehead. He chuckled to himself. "I daena believe that ye understand, Roslyn. My position and walth afford me great luxuries others aren't privy tae. I wark very little."

"I daena understand why you place such importance in your coins and grand home when the good Lord in heaven sees little value in them. There are many of us who find contentment in a wee bit of bread, and broth, or the sight of the sun shining across the meadow."

"You appear tae enjoy the fine clothes and fixings Lorna has provided you wi' since you moved in." Mr. Featherstone's look of triumph did not go unnoticed.

Roslyn fingered the newest gown, a pretty blue mixture of linen and wool that Lorna had given her. "Tis true I value what God has seen fit tae give me. His blissins are ten-fold." She smoothed out her skirt. "Yet these things never satisfy for long. They're temporary on this earth."

Mr. Featherstone took hold of Roslyn's arm and moved closer to her. His eyes glinted a murky gray. "But you would satisfy me, Roslyn, if you'd marry me." His arm went around her waist, and he chuckled. "There's nothing that would please me more, if you'd someday accept my sentiments as your own."

"Mr. Featherstone!" Roslyn pulled away. Her cheeks reddened as she stared at him with a look of shock. "I've formerly given my consent tae Callum and have no intention of goin' back on my word. I can promise ye nothing but friendship. Please, daena speak tae me this way again."

Mr. Featherstone's eyes suddenly smoldered black. His fist tightened. "You heidy, daft lass! I told ye tae end that ridiculous promise. Why won't ye listen tae sense and break away from that poverty-stricken joskin?"

"Wheesht, sir! I'll hear no more of this!"

Roslyn lifted her hand to strike his face, but it was intercepted by him.

"In time, I believe you'll come tae regret your ill-fashioned words and your unceevil behavior. It's unbecoming of a lady, Roslyn." He tightened his grip on her wrist and frowned. "Daena cross me. You'll fancy ye did not."

"Are ye threatening me, sir?"

He stared at her with dark eyes and breathed deeply. "You're a stubborn one, Roslyn Day." He let go of her arm. "But, it doesn't need tae be this way. I'm a respectable man. In time, I'm hoping you'll come tae see this."

Roslyn's chin lifted slightly. She spoke quietly. "I told Lorna my walk would be a short one. I must go back now."

"She's expecting me also."

"Efter oor conversation, I daena believe it would be wise for you tae stay."

Mr. Featherstone gave her a displeased look but nodded reluctantly. "I suppose it would be best tae pay my visit when you're in better spirits. I'd be obliged if you'd inform Lorna of my change of plans."

Roslyn tossed her head indignantly. "I'll make her aware of it."

"Until then, Roslyn."

"I bid you good day, sir."

She turned and walked back to the gate lifting the latch to go inside.

He got into his carriage and rode off in the direction he'd come from.

Roslyn went through the door and back into the home. Maybe later in the day she would see Callum. But for now, she'd help Lorna with the chores.

*****

Ian got up from the upholstered chair he'd been sitting on. He reached for the medicine the doctor had left with them hours before. "Her chills are gone." He let out a relieved sigh as she opened her eyes and looked at him.

She coughed. "I'm better and hungry. I daena believe I have a fever now." She fingered the lace at the bottom edge of her sleeves.

Ian got up from the chair. "I'll see that Maisie brings you another bowl of soup." He reached out and covered her with a blanket.

She eyed the empty chair next to her bedside curiously. "You stayed here?"

"Maisie left at midnight." He spoke matter of factly. "The others were asleep."

She nodded as she pushed her tangled hair over her shoulder. "You've been kind, and I'm very grateful. I've not been so sick afore."

"I was concerned, but am glad you're better. I'll send for Maisie."

"Thank ye, sir."

He gave her a brief nod and left the room.

*****

# Chapter 17

"They told me you were ill, lass." Tom reached out and took Ismay's hand. "I see ye are much better on account of Mr. MacAllen's care. It seems he cared for ye the way a lady deserves."

Ismay gave him an odd look. She pulled her hand away. "He treated me kindly, but I'm quite certain he would have duin the same for any of the servants."

Tom chuckled good-naturedly. "Aw, Ismay, I believe you underestimate the effect ye have on your good maister. Even I have backed away from the thought of stealing you from him."

"Tom Drummond!" Ismay's mouth drew open. "You shouldn't say such things. I'm a servant there! You should know I'd do nothing tae compromise the agreement I have wi' Mr. MacAllen."

"You wouldn't, but I believe Ian might see things differently."

"He told me once it was not possible for us. It's my intention tae wark hard and pay the debt I owe. I'm happy tae have been allowed tae remain here in my own home."

She took the pail of water she held in her hand and started back toward the house. "Mr. MacAllen will not have me, and I'll thank ye tae not think differently."

Tom called after her as she reached the doorway of the home. "You're a stubborn lass, Ismay Innes. You daena see what is plain beneath your nose."

"You may think this, Tom, but I'd rather not get caught up in fancies that will come tae nothing. Now I've wark tae do, and you should see tae yours." She gave him a determined look, curtsied, and went into the house.

*****

When the last meal for the day was done, Ismay took off her apron and hung it on a hook.

She went to her room in the servant's quarters and changed into an emerald-colored skirt with a white blouse. She grabbed a dark green and red plaid wrap for her shoulders and put it around her.

She'd a few hours to spend with her good friends, Barbara and Robert, who'd come to visit.

She went outside and took the path. She looked up when she heard wheels of a cart rattling from a distance.

"Hullo, Ismay!" Robert called from the wagon.

Barbara sat next to him with a weathered shawl wrapped around her plain and simple clothes.

The woman's skin wrinkled upward at the corner of her eyes as a smile revealed a missing tooth on the side row of her mouth. Her face lit. "My darlin' lass!" She spoke quietly to Ismay. Her voice was breathless, and her pale blue eyes sparkled. "It's so good tae see ye."

Ismay eyed her friend tenderly.

Though Barbara was quiet, and plain in appearance, she'd an inviting, secure presence that drew others tae her. The woman never lacked company and was hardly iver out of sight of wee ones for long. They flocked tae her like townfolk tae pipers.

"Tis been long, my friend." Ismay hopped into the wagon and took a place beside Barbara. "I missed ye, dearly. I hope you are farin' well enough."

"I've a few aches and pains, but ye know how it is wi' this sickness that the auld doc canna cure."

"It's back?" Ismay stared at Barbara solemnly.

"Aye, I thought for a while I'd escaped it, but I know God will care for me."

Ismay held the side of the wagon as it lurched forward when Robert clucked to his team.

She sighed. "Can I do anything? If there's anything ye need, ye must send for me. I can make meals and send them tae ye."

Barbara smiled and patted Ismay's knee. "There's no need. My own mother's at with me, and I am busy wi' the grandbabies. I've no time tae think about my troubles. There's a new great grand bairn now, a wee lad wi' the bonniest smile. I do love the little 'uns."

"Well, I know ye do, but ye must care for yourself and take the rest ye need."

"They spared me this morn, Ismay, and it's sunny and warm. Look what God's given us, time tae spend wi' each other."

Ismay lifted her face to the sun and closed her eyes. She smiled. "It's a lovely day. I do feel God's presence when I'm wi' ye, Barbara. He assuredly brought us together."

Robert slowed the wagon as they neared the town. "Whoa!" He called out gently to the horses as they neared the kirk.

Barbara took Ismay's arm. "Let's sit there while Robert's doing business in town. We'll pray together."

"Aye, for God's healing, Barbara, that you'll soon be well again. This is what we'll do."

"You may, though my family needs it more than I. The home they live in is smaw, and the little ones will need warm clothes this winter."

Ismay nodded with a warm look in her eyes. Her friend almost always directed her thoughts to others when she was clearly in need herself. If she could be so selfless.

They got off the wagon, and Robert waved as he headed down the street.

Barbara and Ismay went into the kirk and sat down in a pew in the back. With no one else inside, the room seemed much larger. The sounds echoed with their every move.

"How can I pray for ye, lass?" Barbara simply stated. "Ye lost your dear faither and mother."

When Ismay didn't say anything, Barbara spoke. "I'll pray that your heavenly faither makes His presence known tae ye."

"You're a good woman, Barbara." Ismay's eyes filled with tears. "And I'll pray for your health, and for Robert."

Barbara smiled.

Both women bowed their heads and silently prayed. Though prayers were not aloud, Ismay sensed God's presence and His listening heart in the midst of them. How good it was tae be back in Comrie wi' loving friends.

She looked up when they finished. "Barbara?"

"What is it, dearie?"

Ismay cleared her throat. "I've something tae ask ye. I need your advice."

Barbara didn't say anything but tilted her head. There was an interested look in her eyes.

"I am conflicted. I am not sure which way tae turn."

"I'll listen." Barbara smiled. "I might be able tae given ye some sound counsel."

Ismay's cheeks reddened, and her voice quieted. She looked around. "I'm not sure where tae start, but I've no one else tae talk to."

Barbara nodded. "Tell me what ye know."

"There is a man I believe is forming an attachment to me, but I am not sure it is wise for me to pursue the matter."

"And ye wish tae know if ye should." Barbara spoke quietly.

"You've always given me council. I should know what your thoughts are."

Barbara smiled. "I'm afeart I'm not so wise, but I'll hear ye out and tell ye plainly what I think."

"Barbara, I wouldn't come tae ye, if I did not believe you could help me." She sighed. "The man is above my station, not my equal."

"The maister? Ian MacAllen?"

Ismay's cheeks colored. "Hech ay! I've not told anyone."

Barbara's eyes twinkled. "Robert so much as said. Ian canna help but love ye, lass. I would have thought it myself."

"Wheesht!" Ismay looked around the empty church. "He's not said it tae me!"

"Though he did pay particular attention when you were very ill."

"As he would do wi' any of his staff."

"Maybe, lassie." Barbara shook her head. "But Robert told me that Ian was duin in over it, that he never left your side."

Ismay stared at Barbara with questions in her eyes. "I've no idea how he feels, but I know it wouldn'tbe a proper match between us. Society doesna accept these things well."

Barbara nodded. "I suppose he knows you'd be treated poorly by his equals and suffer for it. Such an arrangement wouldn'tbe well thought out."

"Aye, ye know the back draw of it." Ismay sighed. "Though I'm a wee bit distracted presently. He's been very kind, and I'm not always certain about what I should do."

Barbara turned slightly. She eyed the cross on the altar in the front of the kirk. Her voice was soft. "Always appeal tae the Lord fairst. Take His path." She smiled. "I'm prettie sure He'll know what He wants for you."

Ismay let out a light laugh. A look of relief swept over her, and she gave a slight nod. "Barbara, you've suffered so many hardships in your life and have fared so strongly through them all. Ye understand how important it is for the Lord tae guide my thoughts."

"He's given me great peace which has surpassed my own understanding when I've needed it. I've seen the deaths of my closest of kin too many times, and have had tae lay them in His hands. Tae trust Him is all anyone can do. And when we do, He does more than we can fathom. His love is deep and wide."

"So, I'll do as ye say and give it tae Him. God be thanked for His great love and care."

"Aye, God be thanked."

Barbara and Ismay got up from the pew where they sat and went to the door to go out.

"The sun is still shining. And look! Robert's comin' across the way. We timed that well enough."

Ismay nodded. "Aye, I'm afeart oor time has come tae an end." She climbed into the cart after Barbara who sat beside Robert.

"We'll have a good amount of time tae talk on the way back."

"We will," Ismay smiled, "and I'm glad of it."

They chattered on as Robert drove the cart in the direction of Ismay's home.

\*\*\*\*\*

Robert let Ismay down from the wagon when they neared her home.

Ismay stepped back and waved. "I'd forgotten how lovely oor times have been, Barbara. Thank you, Robert, for bringing us tae the kirk. Please call if ye need anything."

Barbara smiled and nodded. "We'll be seeing ye around, dearie. Love ye, lass."

Ismay nodded as she watched the wagon roll away.

\*\*\*\*\*

Comrie's rolling green hillsides and meadows of pretty bluebells against the backdrop of the distant mountains caused Ismay to stop a moment and draw in a breath as she strolled the paths and took in the sights around her.

When she climbed a hill and came to a flat and rocky bed that overlooked a narrow, deep gray-blue loch, she sat and breathed in the scents of lavender-colored heather that covered the grassy fields below her. The autumn breeze was cool, yet the rare sun streamed through the clouds. It was a perfect balance to the day's temps.

Ismay eyed some movement at the edge of the loch. She was surprised to see three deer race out from a wooded area at the bottom of the hill. It seemed an odd sight because they appeared confused.

Then they suddenly stopped and stood a moment sniffing the air. They seemed jittery as if they knew something in nature was out of order.

Ismay assumed her presence was what startled them until a shaking beneath her jolted Ismay out of her reverie. The rocks beneath her rattled as she realized that tremors shook the ground.

She laid flat and crawled to the top of the hill while the shaking intensified. A couple boulders rolled past her as a small crack split the face of a flat granite rock a distance from her. As the tremors slowed she reached the wide expanse of the grassy area at the top of the hillock.

The deer she'd seen before had bolted along the edge of the loch.

"Och, Lord!" She prayed as the shaking stopped.

She waited holding tightly to the ground. Her breath came in gulps as she looked around. Was it duin?

She got up and stared dully at the landscape around her. She wanted to sit back down but willed herself to walk back to the house. It was rare there was only one.

She contemplated the possibility of aftershocks. How might she fare alone in this place if there were? A chill went through her that made her shiver.

"Dear me!" She lifted her skirt and ran as tears fell onto her cheeks. Her heart pounded at the thought of what might have happened at home.

Were Ian and the others safe? Was the house standing? The quakes weren't small.

Luckily she wasn't far from the estate, and it was within her range of vision. The home was still intact, and people milled around it. Some of the servants held children and others animals.

"Ismay!" Ian came over the nearest hillock. He walked toward her. "Are ye injured, lass? Do ye need anything?"

She ran to him and allowed him to put his arms around her. "I wasn't hurt, though I thought the house might have collapsed and…" She was unsettled with her thoughts.

He shook his head. His voice was calm. "There's no damage. I saw no one hurt."

"This time, but…"

"Wheesht, Ismay. Iveryone's safe. Daena be anxious, love." He wiped the tears from her cheeks and wrapped his cloak around her.

She looked around the area, her eyes widening. "The deer ran off, and I couldn't get my foothold. The rock split."

"Och, lassie, keep the heid! You know the quakes are common. Come, I'll take ye tae Annag. The tremors are over, and there was no damage." He grasped her hand, and they walked toward the house.

Ismay looked up.

Though he appeared unshaken by the incident, his jaw was tight, and a muscle twitched at the side of it. He clearly wasn't as confident as he tried to appear.

He'd come quickly to her, and she'd taken note of the uneasiness in his eyes when he'd first seen her. He plainly was affected by her absence.

As they neared the home, Annag came around the bend.

The older woman eyed them curiously. "Are ye both safe from harm?"

Ismay promptly let go of Ian's hand and gave him his cloak. "We are." She sighed. "I've a mind tae stay close tae home for a while."

Annag nodded. "Sir, ye must see tae the stables and tend the horses. Come, Ismay. I'll find ye back safely."

Ian hesitated, then moved away from Ismay. He tipped his head to her. "Ye must go with Annag, lass. I'll not be far." He seemed reticent to leave but turned and walked off toward the stables.

Ismay watched. Oo aye! He'd come for her and showed such concern. She put her hand to her chest and held it there. Maybe Tom wasn't wrong. Maybe Ian did care for her.

Annag tugged on her arm. "If you knew the truth, you'd not be thinking of him the way ye presumably are. You should know what's happened afore ye say anything you regret."

"Truth? What have ye haird?" Ismay looked toward the stables. She sighed, tapping her toe against the path.

Annag looked at her with a scowl, though there was also a look of pity in her eyes. "That he's asked her tae marry him, Miss Hawthorne, that is, and that she's goin' tae be his wife."

"Married?" Ismay turned with a look of shock. "But he would've said. It's not true."

Annag frowned. "While you were out, it was made known tae the staff. He knew what had tae be duin and what's expected of him. He's a duty bound man."

"But, it's so sudden. Why? When he's never spoken of it afore?" Ismay's voice weakened to a whisper.

"Her faither's dying, and she'll lose her properties tae her cousin if she doesna marry afore he's dead and gone. If she and Mr. MacAllen combine properties, her future will be secured."

"But her faither wasn't a wee bit unweel when I saw him." Ismay looked back at the stables again. "Mr. MacAllen canna possibly believe that rander."

She choked on her words. "The ill-deedie wutch has swicked him she has."

"Whether she has, or not, their engagement's been made public." Annag opened the door and pulled Ismay inside the kitchen. "He might have an eye for ye, lass, but it'll go no further than that. This be the truth of it."

Ismay took her shawl from her shoulders and hung it on a hook. She put on her apron and took supplies from the shelves for making the supper meal.

She scrunched up her brow. "It matters not tae me what he does. I turned him away once already. He can have his grand lady." She mixed ingredients to make bread dough and laid it out to knead. "Now, there's wark tae be duin, and I've no desire tae discuss the matter further."

Annag chopped vegetables for soup with a paring knife. "It's what's best, Ismay. He's doing what should be duin."

Ismay didn't answer. She broke the dough into pieces and formed it into loaves.

When a pained emptiness pervaded her heart, she briskly pushed the feeling aside. She couldn't think of it.

172

She'd let go of too many of her own kin as of late and too many of her possessions. It was impossible tae think of letting go of him too.

Ismay put the loaves neatly into the greased pans and placed them inside the oven shutting the door. She wiped her hands on her apron and turned back to clean the table behind her.

She needed to keep her mind on her work. She couldn't think about the things she had no control over.

Ian decision was made, and she could do nothing about it. She'd not change his mind now.

She only wished he'd given more thought tae the grave mistake he was making.

*****

Grizel paced back and forth in the drawing room of her home. She stopped to slip five gold coins into Cael's hand. "Are ye sure of it?"

Cael nodded sheepishly. "I daena believe the maister would appreciate oor discourse. Ismay's duin nothing tae deserve such treatment."

"Ye say he had his cloak about her? And she embraced him?" Grizel's eyes smouldered.

"It was shortly efter the quake. I trust he felt it necessary tae see tae her safety. She'd taken ill recently."

Grizel reached out and nudged his shoulder. "You must go back tae Comrie tae the house. I want tae know what mischief that ill-trickit orphant has been up tae."

"Mem, ye want me tae watch Ismay?"

"Aye and tell me what ye see."

"But you're marrying Mr. MacAllen. He's offered ye his hand."

"And nothing will stop that. You'll be paid well for your service."

"Oor family depends on it, Mem."

"If ye do, maybe that baurmie faither of yours can pay the senseless debt he owes."

Cael lowered his head. "I hope so. I'm doing it for my faither's sake and my family."

"I'm glad you see the benefits of helping me."

He nodded and slipped out the door closing it behind him.

*****

Grizel clenched her fist as she moved across the floor planks. Her gown swished back and forth in the empty room. "That clarty tinker believes she'll swee his mind, but I'll not have it. I'm not without my own tricks."

She tapped her fingers against her side as she stared out the window of her home. "Efter I've piped my tune he'll surely have nothing tae do wi' that schamin little tairt."

Grizel picked up a small, silver handbell that sat on her desk and shook it. An urgent sound chimed, and a young, nervous maid rushed in.

"You called, mem?" The small lass curtsied.

"Did ye hear the bell, ye daft girl?"

"I did. What is it you need?"

Grizel drummed her fingers against the folds of her silk skirt. "I want ye tae pack me a travel trunk wi' my best gowns. I plan tae make a trip tae Comrie again."

"Tae Mr. MacAllen's home?"

"Where else?"

"I'm sorry, mem. Do ye want the carriage, or the cart?"

"The carriage, of course. And see that ye pack for my faither. He'll accompany me."

"Yes, mem. I'll make the necessary arrangements." The maid cocked her head to the side. "I daena mean tae be troublesome, but when do ye plan tae leave?"

"Within the hour! Please!" Grizel waved her hand at the door impatiently. "Now go, and do it quickly! I want tae be on the road by daurk. I plan tae be at that fire festival with Mr. MacAllen afore it starts. Daena dawdle."

"Aye, mem." The young maid curtsied again. "I'll see that it's duin." She quickly exited while Grizel followed close behind.

*****

"They let ye out, Ailsa. I did not think they would."

Ailsa smiled. She pushed her thick hair from her eyes. "They're celebrating wi' Murdock. I suppose they want time alone wi' him. The whole town is out. We must go afore they change their minds."

Ismay grabbed hold of Ailsa's arm and pulled her outside. Darkness had fallen around them.

"Come, I need my good friend. I must hear the pipes. Let's pray for His good blessings and for the new year."

"Aye, there is much good in the world. May the blessing of the night be on us. May God watch over us, and may the dusk be as light tae us." Ailsa's cheeks glowed pink, and her smile widened as they walked down the path together.

*****

Ismay stared at the dark main street of Comrie. Her eyes widened at the animated voices blended as one around her.

The villagers raised their cups laughing.

"Are they comin'?" Ismay peered down the road outside of town toward the forest.

"Aye, it's them!" Ailsa took hold of Ismay's arm. She leaned closer. "I hear the pipes."

"The torches are lit. It must be midnight." Ismay straightened. "Oo aye! They're coming!"

Both young women eyed the dark forest path at the edge of town curiously as the pipe band came into the open.

The men marched in unison down the middle of the street behind twelve burly men carrying long, thick birch poles blazing with a fire at the top.

Villagers in costumes followed the band.

"Hogmanay!" Ailsa smiled. "Look! They're heading toward the bridge!"

Ismay smiled as the sound of the musical instruments blared. Musicians marched across the cobblestone street.

Both young women ran behind the procession to the bridge where the men took the torches and thrust them over the rails and down into the River Earn.

Ismay watched as the flames went out one by one while the poles floated down the river. She pulled her hooded cloak around her and watched the last of the dying embers ride down the stream like toppling stars in the night.

"The New Year's here, Ailsa. There's been much tae think about these last months."

"You've had a very difficult time of it. You've suffered much loss."

"Aye. I miss my mother and faither." She sighed. "Though I do have a roof over my head and good meals each day. I thank the Lord for his provisions." She drew her scarf tighter and looked down the street. "Maybe we should go back tae the square tae watch the dancers."

"I rather thought you'd want tae dance instead." Ailsa moved beside Ismay as they made their way back to the village square. She looked curious. "You're quieter than usual."

"There's news that Ian MacAllen and Miss Hawthorne are marrying."

"He told ye this?"

"Annag haird it this morn."

Ailsa squeezed Ismay's hand. They looked across the street to where Ian was.

Grizel was next to him. Her arm was linked to his.

"You care for him, don't ye?"

Dancers in the street blocked their view. Ismay turned back to Ailsa. "I suppose. I fear he'll regret his decision tae marry Grizel. I think he's doing it out of a sense of duty tae her faither. I daena know why he canna see her wickit ways. Though I doubt if he'd believe what I'd tell him."

"Maybe." Ailsa's brow wrinkled, and she spoke softly. "But ye might have told him ye loved him. I quite sure if ye did, things would be different."

"Ailsa! Hech Ay!" Ismay gasped and put her hand to her mouth. Her cheeks turned bright pink. "You must not repeat such things."

"When ye look the way ye do at him, he should know it too."

Ismay stared at her friend. "I admit, I find myself attracted to him, but ye must keep this to yourself. He's marrying Grizel soon."

"But I know ye well. We've been friends long. I know tis more than a passing attraction."

"Ye do know my thoughts, but it must remain as it is. I canna allow him to know the truth. There is too much to consider." Ismay sighed.

"If he marries, I believe you'll regret keeping this tae yourself." Ailsa sighed. "You must tell him your true feelings, Ismay. He must know how ye feel."

"But it's not possible. He understands the consequences of such a match and said so himself. He'd lose his position and place in society and be ruined if I were tae allow it. And I wouldn't."

Ailsa's hazel eyes turned a darker, solemn green. "I apologize. I shouldn't have said."

Ismay shook her head. "No, you did not mean harm."

She pointed to the dancers. "Look, they've changed the music. The night is young, and there's no reason tae be glum. It is a new year."

"There's hope in the pipe's song. I'll pray, my friend. God will do what He sees best."

"Aye, He will, and I will trust all is as it should be."

They listened and watched as the dancers on the street performed. There was no more talk of Ian MacAllen or Grizel.

When the festivities ended, Ismay turned. She gave Ailsa a quick hug and stepped back when her parent's wagon drove up next to them. "I'm happy we could have this time together. But I see it is time for you to go."

Ailsa nodded and then looked toward the wagon. "Aye, it was a good night. Daena hesitate tae visit."

"I'll will come again."

She watched as Ailsa got up into the wagon and sat in the back away from the others.

They both waved to each other as the wagon pulled away.

Ismay turned to look for a servant's wagon to ride back on. She drew a hand to her brow and let out a lengthy sigh.

The moon was high in the sky and full now. Night had come full swing.

As the servant's wagon stopped on the other side of the street, she made her way across. It was time to go. She needed to get on.

Morning would come soon enough. There would be wark tae be duin.

*****

A cock crowed as the sun's rays spread over the horizon and flooded the room through the window.

Ismay scooped porridge into three bowls and put them on a tray. She also placed a bun next to the bowls on a crockery plate. She sliced them revealing the colorful, jellied fruit inside.

She took the food into the dining room where Ian and Grizel's father sat talking.

She looked at the empty place at the end of the table. "Oh, I thought Miss Hawthorne planned tae join you. I brought breakfast for her also."

Ian turned in his seat and studied her. He said nothing.

Grizel's father motioned for Ismay to bring all three bowls and the fruitcake to the table. "Grizel will be here shortly." He smiled at the meal appraisingly. "New year's cake! Your maid's been busy."

Ian was interrupted from answering when the thick, wooden door opened.

Grizel came through the passage with Cael.

He trailed behind her.

Her satin dress swung from side to side as she entered. She walked across the room and sat at the end of the table next to Ian.

Cael stood at her side his eyes downcast.

"Good daughter." Her father nodded appreciatively.

Grizel took the tray from Ismay's hand and set it on the table. She shooed Ismay toward the kitchen entrance. "There's no need for you tae stay. I'll send back the rest wi' another servant." She took a bowl and placed it on the table, putting the tray aside.

When she noticed Ismay hadn't left and was at the doorway, she scowled. "Daena stand there gawking. Go!"

Ismay curtsied stiffly. The tone of her voice was short and clipped. "I will. I've other tasks tae attend tae and nothing more here worth staying for."

Before Ismay turned to go, her necklace slipped from beneath the neckline of her homespun, grey woolen dress.

Grizel stared at it curiously. She seemed to be contemplating something when a triumphant look suddenly entered her eyes.

She let out an injured sound and pointed at Ismay with a look on her face akin to shock. "Hech ay! What is this?"

Ian's brow deepened, and he sighed. "The lass has wark tae do, Grizel. Let her be. Gladys has need of her in the scullery."

"But, my jewelry." Grizel's voice rose an octave as she pointed to Ismay's neckline. "Where did she get it?"

The fire in the hearth snapped and sputtered as a quiet dread came over the room.

Ismay turned.

Ian's eyes went to the jewelry hanging from Ismay's neck. He looked puzzled.

Ismay put her hand to her chest. She straightened. "Tis mine. It's from my faither." Her eyes widened. "She's mistaken, sir."

"Not true! How would I not know my own necklace. It's mine I tell you." Grizel turned to Cael.

He looked away.

She grabbed his shoulder and pulled him back around. "I bought that very necklace from a tinker the other day! You remember it, don't you, Cael? You were there when we stopped." She stared directly at him and gave him a quick nod.

Cael swallowed drily. "Well, mem…"

"You saw all of it. Ye canna deny it."

"I…was wi' ye, mem." He looked down. "Aye, ye purchased it then."

Grizel jumped up and clicked across the floor to where Ismay stood. "I told ye it was true!" She grabbed Ismay's clenched fist. "Now, give it tae me!"

"No, you'll break it! Let go!" Ismay loosed her grasp to protect the chain from being torn in two. "It's mine, Cael? You know the truth!"

Grizel lifted the necklace over Ismay's head. She quickly turned it to the backside and studied it. "I told you! This is the inscription." She gripped the jewelry tightly. "She's a thief! She stole the horse, and now this, right under my nose!"

"No!" Ismay's cheeks flamed. "My faither gave it tae me. Ye canna take it!"

She reached for it, but Ian put his hand out to stop her. "Ismay." He stepped between them. "Efter what we've been through, what are ye thinking?" Tension formed in his jaw as he looked at her.

"But, it's mine!" Tears welled in her eyes. "It's not true. She's lying!" She attempted to push him aside.

"Cael was wi' her. I thought ye put this behind you, lass."

"My faither gave it tae me. It's not hers."

He reached out and took her arm giving her a dark look. "Ismay, you're not credible. Now, go. I'll speak tae you later concerning the matter."

Ismay's eyes widened as she looked up at him. "Truly! You believe I took my own faither's necklace? From her?" She shook off his arm and backed away. "I told ye, she's lying, like the diel! She's wickit!"

"Ismay!"

Ismay quelled the stinging tears that threatened to fall. Her cheeks flamed. "I'll go, sir, but I'll not confess tae what I did not do, and I daena wish tae speak of it again." She gave him an injured look, curtsied stiffly, then turned on her heel and walked out of the room.

She made quick steps to the kitchen and stood in the dark hallway. Her head throbbed, and her stomach stirred inside.

Ian believed Grizel over her. She saw it in his eyes. He believed the hatesome woman. Grizel had somehow convinced Cael tae lie for her.

Cael's hands had been shaking when he'd accused her, and it was plain tae see that he'd appeared pained by his own admission. There should have been no doubt that Grizel had taken her necklace from her.

Ismay's hand went to the empty spot against her chest.

Her heart sunk. Her most precious possession had been taken from her, and her word had been disparaged. Ian had believed Grizel over her, and now her treasured keepsake was in the hands of that wutch. What was she tae do?

She took hold of the rough stone arch that led into the small chamber of copper-bottomed cooking pots and steaming kettles over the coal grate. Then she went into the scullery.

Gladys turned and wiped her hands on her apron.

Ismay stopped and stared at the woman's grim face. "What? Why are you looking this way?" She put her hand to her chest. Something was clearly wrong.

Gladys swallowed and pushed back hair from her face. "Come, sit down. I've news for ye dearie." Gladys sighed.

"A kin of Robert stopped by and wanted ye tae know the latest news."

Ismay stayed where she was. She took hold of the back of a chair next to her. "Gladys? What is it?"

Gladys face was pained. "Your good friend, Barbara, is no longer wi' us. Her illness took her suddenly."

Ismay sat down and choked back a sob. "I wasn't aware she was so poorly. I thought she'd more time." She began to cry.

"I'm so very sorry, my dear girl. She took a sudden turn for the worse. They said she died peacefully. I could see how much ye loved her."

"But I did not tell her goodbye. I wasn't there when she went." Ismay stared at the dark, cold floor. She pulled her bare feet under her.

"She loved ye, but you'll see her again. Ye know this." She gave a slight nod.

Ismay didn't answer.

"It was clear that she was your good friend."

"She was." Ismay's head lowered. She wiped the tears on her cheeks and gulped back a sob. "I canna wark right now."

"I know, dearie."

"Can Maisie stay tae finish for me? I'd be obliged tae ye for it."

Gladys nodded. "I'll get her and tell Annag. Daena be anxious. Ye must take the rest you need."

Ismay spoke softly. "I'm sorry I'm not able tae do more. This is sudden. I did not expect it."

"Go now. Maisie will help. Ye should have time alone."

Ismay sighed. She curtsied and left through the back doorway.

As she walked down the path toward the servant quarters, she wiped away more tears.

Barbara. It did not seem possible she was gone. How could it be? Her friend had slipped away so suddenly. She held back another sob.

The sun had risen over the horizon, and a light, breathless chill lingered in the air. Fog hovered eerily over the bleak moor bogs in the distance. The dewy path under Ismay's bare feet was cold tae the touch in the early morning hours.

Barbara had been so kind and thoughtful toward her since the day they'd met. It'd been very much like her friend tae be so ill, and in need, yet praying for others and listening tae Ismay. How good she was.

Ismay shivered. If only she'd more time wi' Barbara. Though it wasn't possible now. If she'd have known.

She'd certainly go tae Barbara's folks efter she'd time tae think and grieve herself. It would be necessary.

But it would be best tae decide fairst which direction her own life would take. There were other considerations. Certainly she couldn't continue this way.

She recalled the earlier exchange between her and Ian MacAllen.

Ian had as much as accused her of theft again, yet this time there was no basis for it. He hadn't believed her and had taken Grizel's word over her own.

What was she tae do when her honor was challenged the way it had been, and her honest words had been taken as deceptions? It seemed she'd never be able tae establish trust wi' her employer while Grizel stood in the way.

The woman had outright lied and was glad of it. What Grizel had duin was cruel. Nothing she'd duin and said had been the truth.

Ismay lifted the edge of her skirt as she climbed the porch steps of the small stone cottage. She looked up the hill to the big house shadowed amongst the trees as she stepped inside her room in the servant's quarters.

She wondered if Grizel had left the home yet or spread other lies about her? Had Ian believed all that was said about her? Would he allow the wutch tae swee his thoughts?

Ismay reached for the knob and turned it pushing on the door.

She went into her room and lit the fire in the hearth taking a wool plaid coverlet from the arm of a chair. She lifted it around her shoulders and sat on the end of the feather tick bed staring at the waking embers in the fireplace.

She moved and looked down when she heard a gentle clinking sound, like a metal chain, next to her on the bed.

She moved again and stared closer at the bed.

Her mouth opened. Lying next to her against the folds of the quilted cover, was her necklace. She reached down and grasped it tenderly.

She lifted it to her chest. It had appeared so suddenly, and it was back in her care! Her faither's last gift tae her! She'd been heartbroken without it.

She looked up and stared at the door. But who had put it there? And why?

Certainly not Ian or Grizel. Cael and Grizel's faither were the only others in the room when it had been taken.

Ian hadn't believed her, and Grizel seemed to have derived pleasure over Ismay's distress at losing it.

Ismay held tightly to the piece of jewelry as she looked out the window. A couple of the servants were talking on the porch steps of the home.

Ismay blinked. Her mouth drew open. It must have been Cael who brought it back tae her. It had been returned tae her very quickly, and he'd been privy tae the matter. No one else would have had such access tae her room.

Though he hadn't defended her when Grizel had taken it, he had acted quite strangely. Could it be that there was more tae the matter than she suspected?

Ismay drew the blankets tighter around her. She stared into the fire watching the flames swirl and crackle in the stone hearth.

Whatever is was, she might never know, though the whole business disheartened her greatly.

She pushed a strand of hair over her shoulder. Efter all she'd duin tae prove herself tae Ian, it seemed all had been in vain. He'd not seen it, and was still condemning her for her fairst sin against him. He'd doubted Ismay's own honest words and had listened tae Grizel's ill-kindit rander not seeing the truth for what it was.

She pushed a tear from the corner of her eye and held back those threatening to fall. Though she couldn't have it right now. Instead she'd need tae put her mind tae better things.

At least she had her faither's keepsake, and it was back wi' her safe and sound. She did not know what she might have duin without it.

She grasped it tightly in her hands remembering her faither's last words tae her. "Keep it safe, dearie. He loved ye much. It's your heritage."

"But faither, you're confused," she'd said. She'd stared at him incredulously. "*He* loved ye? Who? What does this mean?"

He'd shaken his head slowly back and forth as his eyes had closed. "There are things ye daena know."

She'd taken him in her arms as he'd slumped against her. "What things, faither? What are ye saying?"

But he hadn't spoken, and she'd held him close and cried. She'd not thought of it again until this very moment.

She'd taken the words tae be the rander of a dying man who had not been thinking straight, as there was no other, and he was her heritage. It had tae be that he'd been confused on his deathbed.

She strung the necklace back around her neck and got up. She paced the dull, wooden-slatted floor as she tapped her fingers against her skirt.

For some time, she walked back and forth from one side of the room to the other as light rain made soft sounds on the rooftop above.

Efter mulling over what had happened that morning, and putting great thought to the matter, Ismay suddenly came to a realization of what she might do.

She'd no defense against Grizel's claims, and she'd not convince Ian MacAllen of her innocence. Nothing would be the same here when that woman became Ian's wife.

There'd be other accusations cast, and she wouldn't be believed.

Suddenly she stopped pacing and sat back down on the bed. She put her necklace safely in her pocket and bowed her head to pray. I must talk to the Lord. He'll tell me the answer, and if I'm goin' the right way.

Her voice was soft and quiet. She was direct and spoke plainly. "Lord, the very last time I went tae Crieff, there was no wark or shelter for me. I was as an orphant on the street, and I'd taken matters into my own hands. But now, Lord, I need tae know your will. This time, I want tae do as ye wish and not take my own path."

She wiped tears from her face and bowed lower. "I trust ye, Lord, tae guide my thoughts. Tell me, what is it you want me tae do? I'll wait and listen."

The rain quieted and silence permeated the tiny room as a small flame in the hearth flickered and waned. Only the sound of an occasional log repositioning itself in the hearth or a snap of a spark pervaded the space where she sat.

God knew her heart and the accusations that had been laid against her. He saw what had been duin, and he knew what was best for her.

Ismay breathed a sigh as His answer had come without hesitation. Something inside her lifted at the thought of goin' back tae Crieff. There was a quiet peace that filled her inside. She was sure of it.

It seemed suddenly very clear tae her what God's answer was, that she couldn't stay and that it would be best for her tae find wark elsewhere. She lifted her head from prayer almost as quickly as she'd begun tae pray.

She'd go back there as soon as she could. God would make it possible this time, and she'd trust in His goodness and blissin's.

She went to her wardrobe and took hold of her travel bag.

A tear escaped onto her cheek, and she wiped it away as she stuffed skirts, blouses, her hairbrush, and calfskin shoes into it.

Her heart raced as she collected more of her things and placed them into her bags glancing at the window as she worked. She wasn't sure how Ian would react tae her leaving.

Surely, it would be unwise tae stay and allow such mischief tae continue. Grizel's lies could only lead tae more trouble between her and the people there.

She layered her clothing and packed a second bag. She'd ask Tom if he would provide a ride for her tae Crieff. He made frequent trips tae town and most likely would be goin' there soon, maybe efter the funeral.

A few days prior, she'd been asked by Barbara's sister to visit and spend time there, so this is where she'd go fairst. She might be able tae offer her services in their time of need.

Ismay went to her desk and sat down, placing a sheet of stationery in front of her.

A letter to Ian was necessary, but it needed to be duin in a way that would deter him from comin' efter her. If she weren't tentie tae detail, Ian would surely try tae compel her tae stay. She'd need to make it clear that her debt would be paid in full and that there would be no reason for him tae keep her there.

She wrote with a feather ink pen in careful script.

*Dear Mr. MacAllen,*

*I've left your employ today tae obtain a position elsewhere. I believe it is in both oor best interests that I reside in Comrie no longer.*

*You must understand that though I am taking leave of my services here, I plan tae take full responsibility for the debt I owe you.*

*I bequeath not only my home and the servant's quarters tae ye, but I also submit my land, over and beyond my other properties, which will more than enough cover the losses I incurred tae ye. I've enclosed the deed.*

*I hope you will care for my place as ye would your own. My faither and mother would have desired it tae be well-tended.*

*I wish ye well in your future endeavors.*

*Respectfully,*
*Miss Ismay Innes*

Ismay slipped the post into an envelope and wrote Ian's name on the front as tears fell from her eyes.

She laid it on the desk then took one last look around the room. She went to the window and eyed Ian's home on the hill. She'd be leaving her town behind and the memories she held dear.

She picked up her bags and slung them over her shoulder. Her heels clicked across the floor as she strode to the door and went outside.

Tom's home was just over the hill.

\*\*\*\*\*

Ismay stayed to assist her friend's kin with the funeral arrangements and offer comfort to the sister. There'd been much to do, and time had gone by quickly.

After a few days following the funeral, she left and set off down the road to Tom's home. He waited at the gate with his horse and cart prepared to take her to Crieff this morn's morn.

If all went as planned, she'd leave Comrie within the hour and skirt away from Ian MacAllen and her home.

Shortly, the past would be put tae rest, and there'd be no more accusations cast against her, and she would have no more thoughts of either Grizel or Ian. God would guide her on the path of his chosing.

\*\*\*\*\*

# Chapter 18

When they reached Crieff, Ismay got down from the wagon seat.

She reached up and took Tom's hand. "I thank you dearly. I wasn't sure where tae turn, Tom, but I see now that God provided the answer tae my very prayers. You are a good friend."

"I'm glad ye came afore I left. I wish ye well."

"Tell Ailsa tae visit when she comes tae town. Tell her I'm sorry I couldn't see her afore I left."

"I will. She'll be happy tae know that you are safe and well. My sister will assist you and see to your safety until ye find a more permanent position."

"Wi' your help, all will be as it should."

Ismay waved as he turned his wagon around.

He smiled and then left in the direction of Comrie.

Ismay turned to his sister. She sighed.

Skye Kellie took Ismay by the crook of the arm. "Hallo, dearie, we've plenty of room. It's a good, big house where you will find yourself quite comfortable I'm sure."

"I hope I'm not a burden tae ye. I'll do what I can tae help while I'm here."

Skye smiled. "I will need assistance wi' the children until you find a place of permanent employment. Violet Mae and Ailbert are bright children though they are quite full of speeritie as you will see. They are a wee bit of a handful, but you'll meet them at oor evening meal and find this out for yourself. I'll show ye tae your room, and you can find your way to the main room for supper efter you've had time tae freshen up."

"I promise tae begin straightway looking for wark elsewhere."

"I surmise you'll be a blissin' tae us. Violet Mae and Ailbert have no nanny tae set them straight until the woman we hired arrives from Perth. She's staying wi' her dying mother, so it may be months afore she's able tae come. You're most walcome tae stay wi' us for as long as ye need."

Skye's hazel eyes sparkled, and her blonde curls bobbed up and down as she spoke. She smoothed out the folds of her blue and gold plaid dress. "I'm sure in no time you'll find a place for yourself. Crieff is not without its possibilities. If ye fare well wi' my children, I will surely recommend you tae others."

They turned to go through the iron gate which led to a wide, three-story picturesque home. Pretty peach-colored stone sided both the house and the short border fence along the road.

The sun spilled warm rays over the summit of the Knock, the steep, wooded hill that rose up, behind the home, in the distance as patches of yellow honeysuckle dotted the countryside. The scenery around them was breathtaking.

"Your property's charming." Ismay gave Skye a look of delight.

"Tis a very bonnie place tae live. Ross had the home constructed to accommodate both his mother and faither and oor wee bairns, though his folks both died, and it is less merry. But we walcome the lively chatter of guests."

Just inside the main door was a large, spacious music room on the ground floor.

Ismay's mouth drew open as they entered.

The rose-colored walls contrasted with a white fireplace and solid, white doors. Enormous gilt-framed portraits hung on the side walls of the room. Next to the fireplace there were two white sofas which faced each other in front of the warm, crackling fire.

A small, brown piano sat in the corner of the room with a tall candelabra perched on the end of it near a winding stairway with gold rails that led to an upper story.

A black cat with four white feet suddenly jumped off one of the sofas and came to Ismay. It curled itself around her legs.

"It appears you've made a friend already. Miss Cattie is very particular about who she goes tae."

Ismay leaned over to pet the young cat behind the ears. "She's very pretty."

Skye smiled. "It's the children's animal, although it stays quite a distance from them."

Then Skye turned and pointed down the hall. "There's a cloakroom, an office there, and a garden in the back."

Ismay nodded. "I see."

A butler came and took her bags.

"Chalmer will see that you're settled properly. He'll take ye tae your room."

Ismay put out her hand. "I'm glad tae make your acquaintance, Mr. Chalmer."

He reached out and took her hand tipping his head to her. "And I'm glad tae meet ye, miss. Please daena hesitate tae come tae me if you need anything."

Ismay bowed and smiled. "Thank you." Then she let go of his hand.

Skye pointed to the stairway. "Bedrooms are on the second floor. Efter you're finished readying yourself for supper, come tae the fairst floor where we've a parlor, oor breakfasting scullery, and oor dining room."

Skye and the butler started up the wide, winding stairway as Ismay followed.

They passed the first level where Ismay spied a sitting room with shelves of books and thick sofas in golds, rusts, and dark greens. Plaid throws and pillows were tossed on the ends of the settee, and a cozy fireplace crackled between the rows of books. There was a comfortable, warm feeling that radiated around the room.

"Ye mustn't be afeart tae borrow a book from oor library. Though if there isn't one that suits your particular interests, do feel free tae visit Innerpeffray Library in Crieff alongside a chapel."

"Oh, I look forward tae your own library here. You've a fine collection of books."

Skye nodded. "Aye, since Ross' parents died, it's rarely used." She pointed to the back of the hall. "We'll meet there shortly in the dining room. Ross will be home soon, and the cook will serve the meal around six."

"I'll be ready then."

Ismay followed Skye up another flight of stairs to a small bedroom at the end of the hall.

Chalmer opened the door for them. He set her bags next to a large, four-post bed with a canopy on top. A dark mahogany chest sat at the end of it.

"Here's where you'll be staying." Skye looked around the room. "Tis a wee bit smaw, but cozy. It hasn't been used in some time. We'll bring you hot stones efter the hearth is lit."

Ismay eyed the soft, dark green walls and patterned gold drapes that dropped to the floor in waves and a small lamp that sat on an ornate, wooden stand next to the bed.

A couple large paintings of women from the Medieval period were hung next to the bed on the adjacent wall, and a huge oriental rug lay flat alongside the bed. The colors of the bedroom were similar to that of the sitting room.

She curtsied and smiled warmly. "Tis a bonnie room. You and your husband are very hospitable. I thank ye kindly."

Skye smiled. "I'll have the maid bring ye water and a cake of soap for washing. There's a washstand and birch twigs for your teeth. We'll meet shortly."

"I thank ye, mem." She watched as both Skye and the butler left to go about their own business. She unpacked her bags and hung her clothing in the wardrobe.

Luckily, she'd been able tae stuff most of her dresses into bags and had layered them on her body. She'd have a few items to look presentable in.

\*\*\*\*\*

# Chapter 19

Roslyn turned to Lorna. "There's still been no sign of Callum. It isn't like him."

"I've not seen him either."

"I canna imagine where he's been. Something must have happened tae him." Roslyn paced the floor of the small, cottage home. She tapped her fingers against the folds of her skirt.

Lorna got up from the chair she'd been sitting on and put her hand on Roslyn's arm. "I've haird nothing, but will tell ye if I do."

Roslyn went to the window and looked out. "It's been weeks since he's been here. I pray that he's well and safe."

"His business has likely curtailed his visits. I'm quite positive there's no need for you tae fret."

"Maybe, but I daena understand it. He'd surely come if he could. I know it." Roslyn looked hopeful.

Then she sighed. "But while I wait, I suppose there's much tae be duin. There are chores which I can help ye wi' as things will not get duin on their own."

She brushed her hands on her apron and walked across the room to the kitchen.

Lorna followed. "I'll do what I can tae help. My arm is finally beginning tae heal. I may be able tae do a smaw task if ye can find one for me."

Roslyn motioned to the older woman. "There are things. Come, we'll finish what we started earlier."

\*\*\*\*\*

# Chapter 20

"I'm sorry I'm late. I hope you did not wait for me."

When Ismay took a place at the dinner table, the others were already seated. Dinner was ready at six o'clock.

A smile widened on Skye's face. "We're not formal at Stonegate. My husband came only a moment ago." She turned to a handsome middle-aged man at the end of the table. "Ross, this is Ismay, a friend of my brother, Tom. She'll be staying at oor home until she finds employment. She's a tae wark wi' the children."

Ross tipped his head in a friendly gesture. He had a warm look in his eyes. "We're glad tae have you as a guest, Ismay."

A young lass and lad with blonde-hair and dancing blue eyes, like their mother, watched as she lifted her napkin to lay it across her lap.

"Mama, is this the new governess?" The smallest child took a bite off a piece of bread after she'd dipped it into her bowl of barley broth.

Skye shook her head. "Ismay's oor guest, Violet Mae, but will see tae your care until the new nanny arrives."

Ismay smiled. "I will."

The young lad reached out and pinched his sister on the arm.

"Ailbert!" Violet Mae smacked his hand. "I'll set ye down if ye do that again!"

"Children," Skye scolded. "You must eat your meal or you'll not be given cake."

Ross stared blankly at his wife and children. He took a spoon of soup and said nothing.

Violet Mae gave Ismay a rascally smile and then stuck out her tongue.

Ismay was shocked at the children's behavior but said nothing. She turned to Skye as if she didn't notice the rude gesture. "It'll be my pleasure me tae wark wi' the wee ones, mem. I'll do my best tae support them anyway I can."

"I hope you're able tae deal wi' them properly." Ross' voice lowered. "As they're used tae having their way."

Skye nodded. "I fear at times I've given them too much leeberty for their own good. Daena be afeart tae discipline them as ye see fit."

They all turned when Chalmer came very slowly into the room and stopped at the foot of the table. "Mr. MacAllen is here tae see ye, Mr. Kellie. Should I have him wait in the sitting room?"

Ismay drew in a breath and a frown drew over her brow. Truly? Ian had come tae call on the Kellies? She sat up straighter.

Ross shook his head. "See him tae the table shortly, and have Wynda set a place for him. There's no need for formalities."

Chalmer nodded. "I'll send send him efter I've taken his cloak and gear from him. He rode through a soaking blaud. He'll need tae dry by the fire fairst."

Chalmer left the room, and it wasn't long before Wynda came in carrying another table setting. She set an empty pewter plate and polished silver on the table across from Ismay and poured another chalice of dark ale.

Ailbert stared at the door curiously as Skye shared a few brief pleasantries with her husband.

Ismay shifted in her seat and looked up when Chalmer returned.

"Mr. MacAllen, sir." The butler bowed formally to Ross. His voice was grave and low.

Ian appeared at the door. He looked around the room, and his face registered surprised when he saw Ismay. He looked puzzled though he didn't say anything.

Ross got up and shook Ian's hand. He gestured to the empty spot near the end of the table. "Sit and dine wi' us, Ian. You must be faimished efter your ride. We've moorfowl and dumplings and a spot of ale for you."

"I'd be very much obliged. Meals in my home have been a wee bit lacking the past week." He sat in the empty chair with a discontented arch of the brow as he directed another look at Ismay.

"And what brought you here on such a dreich efternoon might we ask?" Ross looked interested.

Ian ignored his question and gave Ismay a slight tip of his head. His hair was still slightly damp from the ride. "Miss Innes."

A blush formed on Ismay's cheeks as their eyes met. She returned the greeting. Her tone was indifferent. "Hullo, Mr. MacAllen."

"Ye know each other?" Ross took a seat next to his wife. He studied them both.

Ian nodded. "Aye, this young woman warked wi' my cook. She suddenly left my household, and I see has found a place at your table. So I'm not quite sure what tae think."

Ross eyed Ismay with a quizzical frown. "I was under the impression that you were without a position, lass."

Ismay cheeks colored again. She swallowed dryly. "I've taken leave of Mr. MacAllen's employ, sir, but I daena wish tae discuss the circumstances under which I departed. Tis my own private affair."

The two children stared at her and Ian. Their eyes grew large. They suddenly seemed interested apart from their meal.

An anxious frown drew over Skye's face. "Daena be concerned, dearie." She looked at Ismay. "Your place wi' us is secure, and ye owe us no explanation. My brother's a good man and has asked a favor I fully intend tae carry out."

Ross nodded. "Aye, we've already offered her oor home. Ismay's walcome here, if this is what she wants."

"Ye should have come tae me, afore ye left, lass. We might have talked fairst." Ian's jawline tightened as he stared at Ismay across the table.

Ismay looked Ian square in the eye. "I told ye, sir, I daena wish tae publically discuss why I chose tae leave. I've a good recommendation from Tom, who can affirm my worthy status tae others who might wish tae offer me a position."

Skye spoke quietly. "We're happy tae have Ismay tae help wi' the children until their governess arrives. By then I'm sure she'll have secured a new situation."

Ian gave Skye a disgruntled look. He turned back to Ismay. "The truth is that I want ye tae return. Gladys would like tae see ye back there also." Will ye think on it and maybe ride back wi' me?"

Ismay looked down at her figeting hands. As much as it pained her to tell him no, she was determined to trust God. She'd clearly haird his will that she leave Comrie. "I'm sorry, sir, but I canna. I'm quite certain Miss Hawthorne can find an adequate replacement for me once you're wed. I'm sure she'll not waste any time in it."

"Miss Hawthorne?" Skye stared at Ian. Her eyes suddenly turned a somber blue. "You've engaged yourself tae her?"

"Very recently, aye." Ian raked his hand through his hair. "Her faither's sick. He asked that I see tae her care."

"Out of duty." Skye looked disheartened. "You'll do such a thing? Did she put him up tae this?"

"Skye!" Ross interrupted her. "Ian knows his own mind. He'd not allow any woman tae swee him in such matters."

200

Skye put her hand to her mouth. "I'm sorry. I did not mean…"

"No, your apology is not necessary." Ian put out a hand. "But your husband is correct. Neither Miss Hawthorne, nor her faither, have influenced my decision."

He looked back at Ismay. "So you will stay here."

"I've a tae care for the wee ones until I find employment."

Both children turned to her. They looked displeased.

"But…" Ian sighed.

Violet Mae suddenly stamped her foot. "Wee ones? Tottie bairn!" Her face turned red.

Ailbert yanked a piece of his sister's hair. "Aye, ye are! Tottie dautie! Tottie dautie!"

"Children!" Skye gave them an exasperated look. "Please!"

They quieted. Ailbert smiled as he stabbed a dumpling with his fork and shoved the whole of it into his mouth. He chewed it with a pleased look.

Ismay ignored the young child and turned back to Ian. "It won't be long afore I secure a permanent position of my own." Her voice softened. "It wouldn't be proper tae stay on wi' ye, sir. You musn't ask me again."

Ian's look was one of surprise. He didn't seem to know what else to say.

Ross broke into the conversation changing the subject. "I overhaird you staked your claim in the cattle business wi' Miss Hawthorne's faither. Wi' the Highland property you've recently acquired it might bring you some worthy profits."

Ian didn't say much. "I believe it will." He gave a brief nod as he took a bite of the roasted moorfowl. He cleared the rest of his plate along with a slice of cake which had been added to the courses.

Ismay engaged Skye in their own private conversation about the children. She avoided Ian's steady gaze. She didn't say anymore to him throughout the meal while Ian talked business with Ross.

When most of the food was eaten, Chalmer motioned for one of the servants to take away the plates.

Ian got up from his seat. "I suppose I must be goin'. I thank you for the excellent meal, Mrs. Kellie. It was commendable."

Skye tipped her head to acknowledge his compliment.

Ross reached out and shook his hand. "Daena hesitate tae visit us when you're in Crieff. We enjoy your company."

"And I yours."

Chalmer entered with an embroidered blue waistcoat.

Ian took it from him and put it on. "I'm needed at the Highlands as there's a considerable amount of wark when I return."

He tipped his head to Ismay. "Miss Innes, I wish ye well. I hope ye find a favorable situation for yourself."

Ismay glanced briefly at him as she spoke. Her cheeks colored. "I have prayed and trusted God. I know he'll do what's best for both of us. Good day, sir."

"Good day." He seemed hesitant to leave, but turned when no one else said more and walked out the door.

*****

Later that evening, Ismay followed the children to their rooms. She'd promised to put them to bed.

Violet Mae tore after the cat which yowled and hissed at her and ran under the bed.

Ailbert pushed Violet Mae onto the floor. "You should let her be, ye eejit. The truth is the cat won't have your ill-kindit deeviltry."

Ismay sighed. The two of them surely were a handful.

Ismay went to Ailbert and took him by the arm. "You mustn't treat your sister the way ye do. You'll injure her."

"Hey! If ye daena let go, I'll scream right now." Ailbert attempted to pull away from her, but wasn't strong enough to remove himself from her grasp.

Ismay's voice was calm. "You decide what ye wish tae do, but if ye scream, you'll not go wi' us tae the loch on the morn's morn. Your sister and I will go there instead without you."

"Tell us what it is?" Ailbert stared at her.

Violet Mae sidled up to Ismay and grinned. "You'll go without him?" She tossed her head in her Ailbert's direction. "Tae do what?"

"I've a surprise for ye, but neither of ye will know what it is unless ye behave yourself and put yourself tae bed immediately."

"You should tell us." Ailbert eyed her curiously.

Ismay smiled. "It wouldn't be a surprise if I did. But I'm sure you'll find it quite tae your liking if ye do as your told." She loosened her hold on him. "Do ye promise tae treat your sister kindly efter this?"

"For tonight I will." Ailbert gave her a hesitant nod. He went to the wardrobe and got his nightclothes out. He put them on.

Miss Cattie came out from under the wooden stool and curled around Ismay's leg.

Ismay reached down and took the cat in her arms. The cat turned onto its back and nuzzled her neck.

"Och!" Violet Mae's blue eyes widened as Ismay stroked the animal behind the ears. "Miss Cattie won't allow anyone so close tae her."

"I did not chase her 'round the room and tease her. I allowed her tae make up her own mind as tae what she wanted. If ye let her be, she might lairn tae trust ye too."

Violet Mae and Ailbert came to stand beside her.

Violet Mae stared at her. "It's saicret powers, because I've never seen anyone tame that wickit cat. Miss Cattie is like the diel."

Ismay laughed. She put the cat on the floor. It sprung from her arms and leaped onto the fireplace mantle to lie down.

Ailbert went to the door that led into his room. "You're not goin' tae feed us tae the kelpie water demon, on the morn's morn, are you?" He stared at her as if he were unsure.

Violet Mae took a nightdress out of the wardrobe and put it on. She tiptoed across the floor past Ismay and got into bed. "She might if ye misbehave." She pulled the covers up to her chin. "Faither should've skelped your wee behind for the things ye did today."

Ismay crossed the room. She sat on the end of the bed and smiled. "You need not fear for the morn. I've other things in mind. Come, let's say oor prayers and get tae bed."

She tucked both children in, read them each a story, and slipped out quietly after they'd both fallen asleep.

*****

It took some convincing, but Ismay was able to persuade the cook to hand over a small basket of leftover bread crumbs from the kitchen. It swung on her arm as she led the children on a path toward the loch.

"You should have listened tae Ismay and wore a cloak, Ailbert." Violet Mae's blonde curls bobbed up and down as she spoke while taking quick steps behind Ismay. "It'll rain for sure afore we return. There's a gray mist."

Ismay eyed the heavy clouds that hung low in the sky. "A bit of rain never hurt anyone. Tis a warm day. He'll do fine as he is."

She pointed to some large, flat rocks at the edge of the loch. "Down there. We'll need tae go stand on those."

Ailbert looked interested. "What's in there, Ismay?" He pointed to the basket. 'What's it for?"

"You'll see. But ye must follow me fairst." Ismay pulled her hooded cloak around her shoulders and held tightly to the basket as she walked.

Both children hesitantly walked behind her.

When they reached the edge of the loch and stood on the rocks, Ismay looked up at the sky. "See now." She opened the basket and took out a handful of bread crumbs. She tossed them into the water. "Look."

Violet Mae and Ailbert sat down and watched the crumbs spread out over the surface of the loch and float in the current. They stared at it in anticipation as the bread bobbed on the water.

A lone gull screeched and glided across the water from the other side. Then they heard another cry.

Violet Mae's eyes widened as she watched the first bird circle and almost stop in mid-air above the food bobbing in the current. It flapped its wings and dropped downward. He took a bread crumb in his mouth and gulped it down, then he let out another cry.

"See, there's more!" Ailbert stood up and pointed to three gulls swooping in and grabbing crumbs.

"May I have one?" Ailbert went to Ismay looking at the basket. "Will ye let me feed them?"

"Here." Ismay lowered the basket for both children to reach in and take pieces of bread.

Violet Mae giggled as she threw a small piece into the water.

A large gull immediately glided to a stop over the top of the loch's surface and took it into his mouth.

"He ate it!" Violet Mae laughed.

Both children watched with fascination as the gulls multiplied, and a flock of upwards to fifty birds surrounded the rocks and water where they stood.

"Do ye have more, Ismay?" Violet Mae eyed the basket with a curious expression.

Ismay nodded. "A wee bit, but we'll need tae throw the rest in shortly." She looked at the sky. "It seems we have rain headed oor way, and we all know how that can be."

Violet Mae and Ailbert both took the rest of the bread scraps and threw them into the waters of the loch. They stared openmouthed as the seagulls attacked each other in attempts to get the last of the food.

Ailbert laughed. "Look at the bowsie one wi' the great big feet. He's wanting ivery last bite for himself!"

"Aye right! No one dares tae take it from that one." Ismay laughed with him. Then she put her hand up in the air and showed them drops of rain on it. "Oh, no! We've got tae run, or we'll be a collieshangle. The blaud's comin'!"

Violet Mae put up the hood of her cloak, and Ismay did the same.

They ran up the hill as water droplets fell, first in small spatters, and then pummeling them in torrents.

By the time they got tae the house and went inside, they were all soaked with rain. Ailbert shivered and giggled at the same time. "Let's all go tae the sitting room and warm oorselves by the fire."

Ismay a while she and Violet Mae took off their cloaks and hung them in the hall.

Ailbert sat closest to Ismay after they entered the room and took a place on the sofa. The fire crackled and sputtered as they warmed themselves rubbing their hands together in front of it.

"We'll be dry and warm again in no time." Ismay smiled at the children. "If it isn't misting or fogging in Scotland, it's raining, and we all know it."

The children giggled and nodded.

"Come next tae me, closer. I've tales you'll surely want tae hear. But they might scare ye some."

Ailbert and Violet Mae's eyes lit. "Ismay, please! Ye must tell us!" Their voices rang out together as they scrunched their bodies beside her.

They sat by the fire and warmed themselves while Ismay recounted stories of kelpies, trowes, and benshees, and all sorts of mystical creatures. She told them many wee tales her own mother and faither had passed down tae her as a child.

The children's behavior had improved greatly when they were given attention and their minds were kept busy. It seemed all that was needed, in their case, was a wee bit of time spent with them and some careful planning. Maybe she'd have a worthy impact on them afore their governess arrived.

\*\*\*\*\*

Each day, Ismay took long walks with the children through the forests, to rocky hillsides, and blue gray lochs for lessons in nature, picnics, dips in the water, and fishing from the shoreline. They read books, found games to play that interested both Ailbert and Violet Mae, and spent time divising plans for their daily outings.

Realizing that the two children were spiritee and full of vigor, Ismay kept them continually busy venturing out in merry escapades or active in their minds.

With so much to do, and so little time for ought else, both children seemed to have put the past behind and forgotten their own ill-deedie behavior and desire for mischief-making.

Their behavior had become greatly improved.

\*\*\*\*\*

On a Sunday afternoon, Ismay walked through the garden with Ailbert and Violet Mae. Each held tightly to her hand on either side of her.

Though the sky was overcast, the sun sent a few shards of light through the cloudy sky warming the small gathering.

Skye had orchestrated a quaint garden party with friends from Comrie and Crieff.

People milled about the old-fashioned walled cottage garden on the lovely paths that meandered through the courtyard.

Ismay breathed in the sweet scents of well-stocked garden flowers. The mix of charming plants, trees, and tall shrubs wove patterns through the stately, well-designed garden.

"Where's the food, Ismay?" Ailbert looked at her with mischievious, blue eyes. "Are there wee cakes or sugar treats?"

"Come wi' me, the both of you." Ismay led Ailbert and his sister to a table under an awning next to the house and dished a plate for each of them. They both sat on a blanket under a tree. Ismay stood to get herself a cup of tea.

Chairs were set out, and a couple elderly ladies were on cushions conversing quietly.

Skye came to Ismay. "Good lass, I must introduce ye tae my aunt and her friend. Come, bring your cup, and sit wi' us."

The children busily ate and played with Miss Cattie who finally allowed them to come near her. They were immersed in their own fun and games.

Ismay stood next to the women while Skye introduced them.

"This is the young woman, Ismay, the one I told ye about." She turned to the two women. "And this is my Aunt Rhona Dyce, and her neighbor, Mistress an Mair Morag Duffy. Mistress Duffy lives quite close tae my aunt. They've known each other for quite some time."

Ismay curtsied and drew up her skirt at the corners. "Hullo, Mistress Dyce and Mistress Duffy." She smiled at them.

Mistress Dyce received Ismay warmly. She reached out a hand and took Ismay's in her own. "Tis not difficult tae see that she's a braw lass, Skye. I'm glad the children will have her at their disposal until the governess arrives."

Morag squinted through thin-rimmed spectacles while quietly assessing Ismay. Her skin was wind-tarnished and creased with wrinkles, none of which crinkled upward around her eyes when she drew back her lips into a half-hearted smile. She tipped her head in a curt nod without a word.

Ismay extended her arm, but Morag only stared at her. When the old woman didn't return the gesture, Ismay withdrew her hand. Her cheeks burned with embarrassment at the rude woman's slight.

Skye stepped in to remedy the situation. "Please do have a seat, Ismay. Here, I'll put your tea on the table."

When Skye reached for the cup, Ismay stumbled and almost fell. Her father's necklace came loose from beneath her blouse. She accidentally pulled on the chain, and it snapped tumbling onto the table.

Morag let out a sound of disgust. "Hech ay!" She reached up and readjusted the wool bonnet placed strategically on the top of her braided gray hair. "Hold steady, lass. There's no need tae be so clumsy."

Morag suddenly cast a critical eye on the necklace lying on the table. She straightened drawing back with an odd look. Her face paled.

"I'm sorry, mem. I did not mean tae…"

The old woman put her hand to her chest and held it there. She choked on her next words. "Who gave ye that pendant. Come now, tell me at once, lass."

Ismay swallowed drily. Fairst Grizel, now this awful woman. She almost didn't answer the rude woman. "My faither, but ye wouldn't know him. He and my mother lived in the Highlands, Macalister and Lassie Innes."

"Is there an inscription on it?" Morag seemed almost unable to catch her breath as she spoke. Her voice was a whisper, and she suddenly appeared very feeble and small.

Ismay nodded hesitantly. "Aye, there are the words, Daughter of the King, on the back."

A hollow feeling stole over Ismay as a chill stole through her.

Morag twisted her hands in her lap and sat very still. She stared at the neckpiece with a haunted expression.

Mistress Dyce reached out and took her hand. "Are ye ill, An Mair Duffy? Do ye feel well?"

Morag sat straighter. She pulled her hand from Mistress Dyce's grasp. Her lips tightened. "I'm not unwell. My constitution at times isn't as hardy as it used tae be, but it is nothing tae fret over."

"Take a place here, Ismay." Skye pulled out a chair from under the table. "I'm sorry your necklace broke. It was my negligence that caused it. You're distraught on account of my own clumsiness."

"Please, daena be anguished by the way it came about. The jewelry can be easily repaired." Ismay took the broken chain and amulet and slipped it into her pocket.

Morag stared at Ismay oddly but said no more about the incident or the necklace.

Ismay took a seat next to the two elderly ladies.

"Ismay's been at oor employ wi' the children for a week. She's wi' us until she's able tae find other wark. Oor new governess is unable tae come straight ways, though the children have flourished under Ismay's instruction." Skye's blonde hair tumbled over her shoulder, and she pushed it behind her.

Morag leaned forward in her chair. She still hadn't taken her eyes from Ismay. "When is the youngster's governess returning?"

"Very soon. The wee ones and I will certainly suffer in Ismay's absence. She's lightened my burden considerably."

Morag's eyes fixed on her teacup, and her finger tapped the table. She seemed reticent to speak.

Ismay smoothed out the apron on her skirt. "I am glad I could be of help and am so very touched by your generosity. I hope tae find employment soon."

Morag looked up at her. Her voice shook. "I've a position I'm hiring for. It seems the right place for ye, lass." She stared a little too hard at Ismay. "When might you be available?"

Ismay let out a sound. A position wi' the diel herself? How could she consider it?

Morag sat up rigidly. "You *are* in need of wark, aren't ye?"

"I have asked around." Ismay's face paled. She reached down and scrunched the edge of her skirt in her hand.

"I'm sure you daena wish tae imposition Skye longer than ye should? The children seem settled enough without ye."

"Oh, but Ismay's not been an imposition tae us at all." Skye piped in. "On the contrary, she's been a blissin."

Morag let out a gruff sound. "She'll need wark when the governess comes, and you know as well as I that it'll be near impossible for her tae find a good fee these days for an honest day's wark."

Ismay sighed. Hech ay! The truth of it was almost more than she could bear. The auld woman was right. It would be wrong for her tae rely upon Skye's generosity forever. The woman was offering her a position, and she couldn't very well turn her down. It was better than taking her chances on the streets.

Ismay tugged on the sleeves of her blouse. She turned to Morag. "When will ye be in need of assistance, mem?"

"Ismay, ye must give some thought tae the matter." Skye gave her a wary look. "Ye should wait a bit more afore ye make a decision."

"But your governess will be here soon." Ismay attempted to appear nonplussed about the matter. "And truly, I wish tae be well set afore she comes."

Morag watched them both with a critical eye.

"Do ye mean it, lass?" Skye gave her a questioning look. "We've plenty of room here, and ye know it."

"I do, but I couldn't impose upon ye much longer as this was only tae be temporary. But I thank ye again for what you've duin for me."

Skye didn't answer. She stared at the old woman with an uncertain expression on her face.

Ismay turned back to Morag, ignoring Skye's skeptical glances. "Will ye need someone soon?"

"In time, lass." The old woman looked across the table. "When did ye say the governess planned tae come, Skye?"

Skye looked uncomfortable, but answered with a sigh. "Ismay would be available next week. But, is there a specific position in ye have in mind for her?"

Ismay pushed a strand of dark hair behind her ear and leaned closer. The blue in her eyes darkened.

Morag fingered the folds of her brown, woolen cloak. Her face was a mask. "I'm in need of a companion, one bright enough tae attend tae my town affairs and wark as my personal assistant. It seems the young woman has a good enough record."

Ismay drew in a breath. The position was lofty. It'd be wi' a wealthy woman, maybe not so bad.

Though the auld woman appeared quite difficult, Ismay didn't hesitate in giving Morag a quick nod. She lifted her chin a notch as she spoke. "I can do it, Mistress Duffy. Skye's given me a worthy recommendation if you'd like tae see it. I'll notify you when the governess arrives."

"Then I'll review the recommendation efter I obtain it from Skye which is iverything I need. If all is as it should be, I'll send the carriage for you when you're available." Morag nodded stiffly.

Ismay turned when a trill voice sounded from across the garden. Grizel came through the gate with Ian. She laughed and leaned close, to him, her hand crooked in his elbow. She fingered a piece of fiery hair that lay in soft waves over her shoulder while she looked around.

Ismay moaned inwardly. Oh no! What next?

Grizel locked eyes with Ismay. She leaned closer to Ian and whispered something in his ear.

He didn't respond, but turned in Ismay's direction.

They took the path through the garden to where Skye stood on the walk.

"Mistress Kellie, I'm so very happy that Ian and I were invited tae your pairty this efternoon." Grizel touched the lavender neckline of her blouse. "Your garden is quite lovely."

Skye smiled. "I'm glad you could both come. I hope you'll enjoy the refreshments and are able tae find my husband. I believe he went tae the loch."

A crooked smile wove its way across Grizel's face as she looked at Ismay. "Ian must inform him of the date of oor waddin nuptials. We're requesting the presence of half the town folk."

Ian tugged at the collar of his shirt. He turned and stared at the gate.

Ismay looked at the children who sat on a blanket in the grass near them. They'd finished their cakes while talking quietly.

She stood and took each of the elderly women's hands and curtsied. "Mistress Dyce and Mistress Duffy. I'm very happy tae have made your acquaintance."

She pointed to Violet Mae and Ailbert in the distance. "I must see tae the children, but will send word, Mistress Duffy, when I know that Skye's nanny arrives."

Skye's aunt smiled. "I'm glad you've been such a great help tae my niece. I can see that the children have duin very well under your care in the short time you've warked wi' them. It was a pleasure meeting you, Ismay."

Morag made a deep, guttural sound and cleared her throat but said nothing. She turned away.

Ismay politely tipped her head to Ian and Grizel. "I congratulate ye both on your upcoming waddin. I hope you'll both be happy. Now, I must go. I've wark tae do. I promised the wee ones a game of Horn cups."

Grizel brushed an imaginary piece of dust off her shoulder. Her voice was quiet with a hint of malice in it. "Ye shouldn't shirk your duties. A good servant knows her place."

214

Ismay didn't answer, but walked back toward the children.

"Ismay!" Both Ailbert and Violet Mae crawled into her lap. They smiled kindly at her. "We ate the cakes and sweets! And now look! Miss Cattie's come tae us. It's true what ye say. She's curled up and allows us tae pet her now."

Ismay smoothed out the children's blonde curls. She spoke quietly to them. "I'm glad she came tae you. You're sweet wee ones, and I'll miss ye both when I go."

"But you'll come tae visit us, won't you?"

"Aye, I'll be back again, because I'll want tae know that your behavin'." She tickled each of them and caused them to giggle.

Then she took each of their hands and walked away from the party.

As she left, her eyes briefly met Ian's. He watched her intently.

She tipped her head and gave him a solemn smile, then she walked away with the children.

*****

# Chapter 21

Roslyn pulled weeds from the flower bed outside Lorna's home. She stood when she heard the galloping sound of a horse's hooves. She straightened her work worn skirt. Her heart skipped a beat at the thought of Callum racing down the path toward her.

As the sound grew louder, she took a step forward when a horse came around the last bend in the road.

It was one of George Featherstone's servants.

She sighed and went to the gate. She opened it and waited at the roadside.

A young man got off the horse and took a piece of parchment out of his jacket. "It's a post for ye, miss. Mr. Featherstone has asked that I deliver it tae you and Madam Bissett."

Roslyn took the parchment into her hands and nodded. "I thank ye for it. I'll see that Lorna gets it."

"I've no more deliveries, so I willna stay longer." He got back onto the horse and turned it in the direction from where he'd come. "Good day tae ye!"

He didn't wait for her answer, but tore off down the road instead.

Roslyn watched him round the bend. After he was gone, she went into the house.

Lorna stood next to the fire poking at flames in the hearth with an iron tool. "I haird a horse. Who was it?"

"One of Mr. Featherstone's servants. He brought something."

She held the letter out to Lorna.

Lorna put down the fireplace poker and leaned it against the brick hearth. She reached out and took the letter into her hands. She laid it on the table opening the envelope and drawing out the parchment. Her eyes widened after she began to read. "It's an invitation tae a ball. He's having it at his country home."

Roslyn's brow rose. She spoke quietly. "I'm sorry, Lorna, but I've no wish tae go, nor tae dance. I've not felt festive as of late."

Lorna went to her and showed her the card. "Look, the invites have been sent tae iveryone in the countryside. Maybe Callum will be there. Ye might lairn why he's not come back tae ye."

"I would hope tae see him afore then." Roslyn looked toward the window. Then she shrugged. "But if I don't, I suppose I might see him there. He owes me an explanation why he hasn't come back."

"So we'll accept for this very reason." Lorna sat down at the table. She tipped her head to the side. "And I think it best that we not slight Mr. Featherstone, he being such a rich and powerful man. There's no cause tae offend any would-be suitor."

Roslyn lifted her chin and sniffed. "I've no interest in him, and ye know it, but I'll go. There's much tae consider."

"Good! I'll send oor measurements and have gowns ordered. We must give thought tae the matter."

"You've been kind, Lorna." Roslyn took an apron from a hook and the wall and slipped it on, tying it in the back. "I know you do have my best interests in mind."

"I do. You're a good lass. I want tae see ye well settled."

Roslyn picked up a large wooden spurtle and stirred the soup in a pot over the stove.

She sighed. There was still no sign of Callum. Had he changed his mind? Did he suddenly have doubts about marrying a traveler's daughter from such an uncivilized background? Or had he haird of Mr. Featherstone's visits and been angry wi' her for visiting wi' the dour auld man? What had he been thinking?

She moved back from the heat of the stove continuing to stir the contents of the pot. She looked toward the window and down the path from where Mr. Featherstone's servant had come.

Maybe the pairty would be a good way of finding out the truth of his feelings for her. She might be able tae set tae rights any confusion on Callum's pairt or straighten out any misconstrued thoughts. Surely Callum would attend, seeing that the whole county was invited. She might finally talk tae him again.

As the soup bubbled and popped, Roslyn hurriedly took the pot from the stove and covered it with a lid.

A thought stole deeply in her heart as she fueled the fire on the hearth with new logs. The flames flickered higher and took her back to the wagon trail at night.

She'd not wanted tae consider her parent's cautionary words afore she'd left, how they'd warned her of losing her heart over a man who wasn't a traveler.

What if she'd been wrong? What if what they'd said held merit.

She lifted her hand to her heart and held it there. It couldn't be a possibility. Callum had been so sure of his intent. If it weren't for him, she'd have never taken the position she did. The pain of her errant thoughts were almost more than she could bear.

Where might he have gone tae? Why hadn't he come tae see her? What might she find out about him at the pairty?

*****

# *Chapter 22*

Ismay rapped on the front door of Morag Duffy's stately home as she stood on the broad stone steps. If she'd thought highly of the Kellie's estate, this one could be said tae be ten times more grand, despite the fact that its upkeep had been badly rendered.

Untrimmed, heavy vines grew over the sides of the massive structure. The south-west wind and cool Scottish rain had torn the shutters and siding leaving melancholy bare spots. Hinges on the wooden-slatted doors showed tarnished wear, and faded curtains hung inside the deeply recessed windows.

An older gentleman came to the door and opened it. His eyes seemed almost too large for his face, and his chin appeared as if it was shrunken. Ismay envisioned an image quite like an upside-down pear when she looked at him.

"Hullo! I'm Scotty, the butler and the groundswarker!" He spoke with a toothless grin as strands of thin, wispy gray hair dangled in his face. "Good day tae ye, lass."

The wrinkles around his eyes deepened. "Ye must be the young missie, daft enough tae stay wi' that auld pensie scunner up there."

Ismay put her hand to her mouth. She whistled under her breath. "You shouldn't say such things about your employer. Do ye wish tae be let go?"

The old man laughed and slapped his knee. "Bless ye, child. You daena know a wee bit about this place." A twinkle caught his eye. "That speeritie grumpie has no hold over me. Rather, she'd suffer without my bonnie face about this wind-battered hoose. Who else would greet the guests wi' such a brawly grin?"

Ismay couldn't help but smile as he swung the door wide and made a large, stately sweep with his hand for her to enter.

He chuckled to himself again. "Come efter me, miss.
It's time ye meet your employer. May your chimney smoke
long and well."

\*\*\*\*\*

Morag Duffy clenched the arm of her chair with her
gnarled hand when the door of the room opened. She motioned
to a wide sofa next to her. "Stand over there, lass, in the light
of the fireplace where I can see ye." She had a hard look about
her eyes and a tightness around her mouth.

Ismay walked across the room. She stopped and eyed
the woman with a curious stare.

As before, Morag was elegantly put together. Her high-
collared shirt and lengthy buttoned cuffs covered half her
wrists. She sat straightbacked in the chair with her chin raised
slightly. Her hair was pulled upward out of her face in a tight
bun. Her well-pressed skirt fell neatly to the floor revealing
small laced leather boots.

Old Scotty left the room, closing the double entrance
behind him. The sound of the door slamming was periously
loud and made Ismay jump. Dust flew off the tops of the
frames as it jolted shut.

Morag scrutinized Ismay and made no sound other than
to tap her fingers on the ends of the chair's arm rest.

"What is it you want me tae do fairst, mem? I see a
basket of needlework, or I could do a bit of dusting." Ismay
pointed to a stand on which sat two half-finished collars and a
pair of scissors. "Or I could work on those lace pieces." She
smiled, though she was a bit unnerved beneath the old
woman's harsh gaze.

"You must address me as Mistress Duffy." Morag
pointed to a dark corner of the room. "Fairst of all, go and get
a piece of parchment from the desk, and bring an ink pot and

quill pen wi' you. Then ye might sit on the sofa next tae me here in front of the fire.

Then she tipped her head in the direction of the pile of work Ismay had referred to. "Disregard those things today. Instead, you must make a list for me. You are able tae read and write I presume?"

Ismay nodded. She went to the dresser and brought the items back. She set the ink pot on a stand next to her as she took a seat on the end of the sofa.

Morag's tone was clipped as she called out various sewing items, including fabric, lace, and a silver thimble.

"You'll go in the morn and bring these back tae me. I'll give you the coins you'll need."

She cleared her throat. "But for now you must put your own things in order. I've no more need of you today. Scotty will show ye tae your room."

Then, she vigorously shook the brass bell which she'd taken from the table next to her. "Scotty!" Her voice had a loud, gritty sound to it as if it were mimicking the blustery wind outside.

Scotty opened the doors wide and stood quietly. His face was a mask.

"Take the lass tae her room, and give her a bit of fish and chips tae get her through until the morn's morn. I'll see her back here then."

"Absolutely."

Ismay curtsied. "Good night, Mistress Duffy."

Morag had no answer.

*****

After another brief, curt meeting, the next morning, with the old woman, Ismay walked the path to town and went into the general store. She'd picked out the fabrics, laces, and tools that were on the list and went to the counter.

She asked the clerk for a small sack of sugar, a canister of black tea, and a fair price. She supposed it would be right to be thrifty. Her employer seemed the sort who might appreciate a bartered item.

She handed the clerk the money Morag had given her and placed the items in a basket on the counter. "Here, I suppose this will be a good amount for all of it."

The shopkeeper's mouth formed a grim line, but he took the coins and nodded. He eyed her curiously.

She crooked her arm under the handle and turned to leave when the door of the shop opened. She looked up and drew back when Ian MacAllen came into the room.

"Ismay." Ian closed the door behind him. He eyed the contents of her basket.

"Mr. MacAllen."

"What's this? A basket for Skye?"

"No, sir. Tis for a neighbor of Skye's aunt, Morag Duffy. Ismay lifted her chin slightly. "She was in need of an assistant, and I took the position."

"The auld widow on the hill? But why? Comrie's your home."

Ismay's cheeks colored. "I'm sorry, sir. You must understand why I thought it best I go. I've a position here wi' Morag and no daurk past tae contend wi' at her home."

"But that crabbit auld dame wi' the dour face? You would stay wi' her? I've not haird a kind word uttered from the woman's lips. Why would ye take a position there?"

"She's duin nothing tae bring me harm, and trusts my word. There are braw people there who wark for her." Her eyes turned a somber blue as she looked at him. "They trust me, too."

He glanced at her neckline and spoke quietly. "I see ye took back Miss Hawthorne's jewelry when ye left." His hand went to the chain around her neck, and he lifted up the necklace.

She took it from him and slipped it back under her shirt. "I did not take it, but ye wouldn't believe me. It was mine, and Cael knew it. He must have brought it tae my room." Ismay sighed. "I daena know why he said I took it."

Ian eyed her with a puzzled expression.

"It's been in my father's possession since I was a wee bairn. Ask Ailsa. Miss Hawthorne was mistaken." She put her hand on his arm, but then she took it away when he moved closer.

"Ismay."

"You daena trust my word, because you are unable see past my fairst misdeed against you. I suppose I might feel the same if you had duin likewise tae me."

"Stealing a horse is not a smaw thing. I've always held others tae certain standards."

"I understand this. What I did was very wrong, and I daena believe I iver will have paid the full price for the wrangous decision I made that day. I've lost iverything for the sake of it." Ismay readjusted the goods in her basket. "I often feel sorrow for causing you the discontent that I did."

Ian reached out, but she shook her head. "No, please, sir. You're tae be married soon. There need be no more trouble between us, and I've my own matters tae attend tae."

"So, you plan tae wark now for the auld woman and not come back."

She gave him a disheartened look. "I must do what's best for both of us. There's little else tae say. I suppose Morag will wonder where I am, and I've other business tae tend tae for her."

He moved aside for her to pass. "Ismay?"

"I told ye I must see tae Morag, sir. And I'm quite sure Grizel wouldn'tappreciate oor speaking tae each other as informally as we are. I canna stay longer."

She curtsied and walked across the room.

Ian didn't say anything as he watched her moved past him.

She opened the door and went outside. She expected him to follow, but was surprised when he did not.

She supposed it was best this way. Breaking all ties was what she felt was a right thing to do.

She walked down the street in the direction of Morag's home. She couldn't think about her own feelings and how much she suffered so far from her home and him. There was no time for it.

She put her shawl over her head and covered her basket when drops of rain fell. It wouldn't amount tae much, as the house wasn't far from town, but it was best the sewing supplies were protected.

*****

As Ismay skipped down the street in the rain, she heard a faint voice call out in the distance. She stopped and turned.

Ailsa waved to her from the top of the hill. She carried a satchel over her arm and was dressed in layers. "Ismay! I've been looking for you."

"Ailsa! Why are you here? You're alone."

Ailsa walked quickly down the hill. Her hair was wet and fell loosely over her shoulder. She pulled her hood up and tucked her hair into it. "I walked from Comrie." Her eyes were large. "I've left them."

"Your family? Truly? You walked away?"

"Aye, I have."

Ismay took her friend by the arm. Her eyes were large. "Ailsa, have you a place tae stay?"

Ailsa drew her cloak tighter. "Nay, I don't. I'm alone. I asked around tae see where you'd gone tae."

"So you'll not return?" Ismay put her hand on Ailsa's arm.

Ailsa shook her head. "I canna please her, and I've no wish tae. Few believe what I tell them, because she's different wi' me. She's charitable and kind tae others."

"Bless you, Ailsa! I know it too."

"I've no one, but you. I'm not sure where tae go. I thought ye might be able tae help."

"Dae not be anxious, Ailsa. You were right tae come tae me. I'll tell the auld woman, Morag. There must be something you can do for her. And if there isn't, you'll take my earnings as I've a roof over my head and a good meal."

"I couldn't!" Ailsa put her hands to her face. "I'll pray tae the good Lord that she'll take me in, then I'll have no need of your coins."

"We must both pray long and hard as you'll soon see that compassion is not Morag's strongest virtue. We must hope that there's a sufficient need for you in the home."

Ailsa looked at the path and sighed. "It's all I ask. I canna go back."

\*\*\*\*\*

Ismay led Ailsa into the dim candlelit room and left her at the door.

She approached Morag warily.

Morag's quick eyes snappily took in the young woman who stood meekly behind Ismay. "Who's the waif wi' the dripping cloak making a collieshangle of my floor?"

Ailsa shivered and looked at Ismay.

"She's my closest friend. I found her alone in the cold rain. Her name's Ailsa."

"Come tae visit ye, aye? Looking for a meal I presume." Morag's brow drew to a point above her sharp eyes.

Ismay curtsied and then drew back. "Ailsa's a braw warker, skilled in the needle, and cooking, and cleaning. She's dependable and able-bodied, and has never been ill a day in her life."

"Wheesht, lass! I'm not daft in the head. Enough!" Morag scowled. Her teeth grit together, and she rapped her fist on the arm of her chair. "There's no place for a clarty orphant making a hullabaloo of things here! Tell her tae go away!"

Ismay frowned. "But Ailsa's from a respectable home. She was caught in the blaud is all."

Morag stared at Ismay. The knuckles on her fingers tightened around the end of her chair arm. "Mud streaks down her face, a pretty mess I'd say. She won't be staying here tae clean herself up."

Ailsa's shoulders slumped, and she turned to go out the door. "I'm sorry, mem. I've caused ye distress, and I shouldn't have come. I daena wish tae impose on ye."

A tight smile formed a line across Morag's face. "Oo aye, it's a lass wi' a bit of sense. She understands that I've nothing for the likes of her."

"No!" Ismay pulled Ailsa back into the room. "I'll not have it. Ailsa's alone in the world, and you must help her! I'll not send her away when she's walked so far." Ismay's shoulders straightened.

"Hech ay, missy!" Morag hit the arm of her chair again, this time with greater force. Her pale cheeks streaked a dusty heated color. "You dare tae quarrel wi' me when I've told ye I will not have her. The lass will go, and I'll have no more talk of it again."

"What?" Ismay directed a hard stare at the woman. "Then I'll go wi' her, and I'll not set foot in this place again! I daena need your nae worth pennies!"

Morag suddenly coughed. A hacking sound came from her chest, and there was a sudden change in her expression. She loosed her hold on the chair and put her hand to her chest. Her skin paled.

"Mistress Duffy?" Ismay went to her and knelt by her side. "Are ye unweel? She took the old woman's hand in her own.

Ailsa came to stand beside Ismay. The color of her eyes deepened. "Is she all right?"

Morag cast them both a cautious glance.

She placed her hand back on the arm rest. "Haud your wheesht, the both of ye! Daena be ridiculous!" Her chin lifted as she spoke. "I'm very much indeed in good health!"

"Then we must hear what you were goin' tae say."

Morag sniffed. "I know my own mind, Ismay, and I can change them as quickly as I please. Do ye understand this, missy?"

Ismay shook her head. "I do Mistress Duffy. I serve you. Tis not the other way around. But, Ailsa…"

"I've my own plans concerning you, Ismay, and daena wish tae lose your service. There's too many a muddleheaded servant out there that I want no pairt of. I'll not send ye away."

"About Ailsa…" Ismay looked hopeful.

Morag's eyes narrowed.

Ismay tapped her foot on the floor. "I'll not stay without her. You can count on it as I must provide for my friend. Please consider her. I'll not ask for another thing. You can be sure of it."

"Haud your wheesht, lass! There's no need for beggin'. I've enough of that around here." Morag gave another snort. "She can stay as long as you will not up and leave me now.

But I won't tolerate dissention, and I canna take in ivery wayfarin orphan ye find along the way."

"I promise! I'll ask no more of you. Ailsa's my closest friend." Ismay's eyes lit! "Och! I couldn't have beared tae send her off alone. I wouldn't have duin it."

Morag scoffed at them both. Her voice lowered to something akin to a growl. "Spiritie, ill-deedie missy ye are, lass, speaking your mind so freely. Your either daft or daena know what risk ye take wi' such a forthright approach."

Ismay lowered her head. "I am willing tae lay down my life for Ailsa. I would've left this very instant if ye wouldn't have had us both."

Morag's eyes narrowed. "Then ye are daft." She let out a breath. "The world is not a kind place, and ye daena know what's out there. Give your friend a bowl of rose water so that she might clean herself, and tell Winifred tae find her a place in the scullery wi' the cook."

She waved her hand. "And hurry afore I change my mind."

Ismay breathed a sigh and curtsied. "I thank ye greatly, Mistress Duffy! You daena understand how grateful I am! God be thanked!" She took ahold of Ailsa's apron and tugged it.

Ailsa curtsied to Morag. Her cheeks pinkened as she spoke. "I am more grateful, Mistress Duffy. I've nothing, and you have duin a great thing for me."

Morag didn't answer. She made a slight tip of her head.

Something warm suddenly brewed subtly in Morag's eyes, but it was very faint and almost unnoticeable. Ismay caught a glimpse of it, but said nothing.

She tugged at Ailsa's hand. "Come, I'll introduce you tae Winifred and the others." She looked back at Morag. "I'll be back tae accompany you very soon, Mistress Duffy, once Ailsa is settled."

Morag didn't respond, but turned away staring out the window.

Ismay and Ailsa left the room, closing the door behind them.

*****

Outside the room, Ailsa hugged Ismay tightly. "Ismay! I did not believe that she'd change her mind! I thought we were both doomed!"

Ismay let go and laughed. "I thought the same, but I knew you couldn't go back. I wouldn't allow anything tae happen tae ye."

Ailsa's eyes widened. "Ismay, ye risked your bread and home for me. But why? I daena understand."

"Truly? I couldn't have it any ither way, and you'd have duin the same for me." Ismay spoke softly. She guided Ailsa down the hallway toward the curving stairway. She stopped at the top. "And though ye daena know it yet, the good Lord has been watching over you. He sees your worth and that there is no blemish in you, only beauty."

"When you say beauty, it's difficult for me tae see. I've not the long, daurk hair and sparkling blue eyes ye have. I'm pale and plain, and I've no voice tae speak my mind as ye do. God does love me, but canna see beauty as ye do."

"Pretty is changeable, Ailsa, so daena set your hopes on it. There's more tae it. There has tae be, or we'd grow auld, and it would be the end of us." She smiled.

"Yet ye say He sees beauty in me."

"Aye, in all who are His, like the kind, bonnie face of my friend, Barbara. Some might say she was plain and simple. She'd wrinkles and pale skin. She'd teeth missing. They might've walked directly past her without taking notice. But I daena believe oor God would've duin the same. He'd have seen the beauty in her heart, and all else matters naught tae Him."

Ismay sighed. "Grizel is tall and willowy with shining red locks and wide eyes. She's what the world would treasure above all else. But a hollow shell she is with a hardened heart. Indeed, I only feel pity for the likes of her. We've no need for any of that, Ailsa. God sees the heart and nothing more. Although I do believe ye underestimate your own fair looks."

Ailsa took Ismay's arm as they descended the stairs together. "He is good, Ismay, isn't he? I daena quite understand it, but I believe he cares very deeply for us both."

"He does. We've both lost oor homes and families, but he sees us, Ailsa, and he wants oor blissins tae be great. It's the broken-hearted who know the extent of his love."

"Ismay." Ailsa's eyes flooded with tears. "I'm grateful he's shown such tender care. Someday I might understand why he could do so much for me."

"I hope ye do, dearie. Tae see ye happy and whole, and for you tae know how deep and wide the Lord's love for you is, would be a true blissin."

Ailsa smiled. "It would please me greatly. Maybe someday I might understand it."

"I know you will." Ismay smiled. Then she turned, taking Ailsa by the arm. "Now, I must see ye tae the scullery tae meet Winifred. Morag will be waiting for me."

They took quick steps down the stairs and made their way to the cook's room. Ismay was sure that Winifred would be pleased with her newest assistant.

*****

Ismay worked on sewing tasks put out for her while she sat next to Morag on a small sofa.

Morag said little and slept in the chair frequently. When she was awake, she occasionally turned and watched Ismay with narrowed eyes.

Ismay sighed. "I've finished the dress. The lace collar's also ready. Where do ye plan tae wear such a grand design?"

Morag cleared her throat. She ignored Ismay's question. "Tell Winifred, or that new waif ye brought in, tae bring a cup of tea tae me. And use the patterned china."

"Her name's Ailsa." Ismay stopped what she was doing and looked up.

Morag's lips were tight, and gruff lines creased her face. Though Morag had hired Ismay as a companion, Ismay wasn't quite sure why. Morag had little tae say tae her in return and little tae offer.

"I will, Mistress Duffy." Ismay put the collar in the basket next to her and got up. She went to the door and walked down the long corridor taking the stairs to the main floor.

In the sitting room, Winifred dusted a small table placed in front of a brown stone fireplace.

"Mistress Duffy wants her tea now. She sent me tae tell you."

Winifred lifted a hand to her dark gray hair and attempted to smooth the pieces that had sprung upward and outward from the top of her head. "I just brought her cotton stockings. Sometimes it seems she has us all running from one end of the home tae the other."

Her face was flushed. She smoothed out her rumpled apron and tapped her shoe on the floor. "Tell her I'll brew her a pot and be up wi' the tea tray when I can."

Ismay nodded. "I'll bring it tae her if ye please."

Winifred's mouth drew open. "You're willing tae save my creeky knees from those long and steep stairs? Ye daena mind taking it there?"

"I'd be glad tae do it, mem. Tis no bother tae me." Ismay smiled. "I'm sure Ailsa would do the same if ye asked her, Winifred."

"Ye would?" The elderly woman eyes sparkled. She smiled widely. "I do believe the merry dancers have settled down upon us since the two of you have graced oor doorstep, and the auld woman has found herself a couple of true blissins!"

Ismay laughed. "Ailsa and I are glad tae have secured a position here. We're both young and can take the stairs wi' only a wee bit of effort."

Winifred gestured for Ismay to follow her to the kitchen. She spoke quietly as they went into the warm chamber filled with cooking utinsels. "Morag's not easy tae wark for, but she's fair enough."

Ailsa looked up from kneading bread and smiled. "It matters not tae me whether she's a difficult taskmaster or not. It's a blissin' tae have a place tae stay and warm food tae eat."

Ismay nodded. "Although I daena believe she's as tairible as I've haird others blether on about, though she's been aloof and cold most of the time and says little tae me."

"Tae be sure. Though some say she's hiding past saicrets and is paying for it, and I tend tae believe there's a bit of truth in their words." Winifred placed a kettle of water on top of the hot stove. "It might be a good thing for her tae spend time in another's company."

"Maybe it's why she kept Ailsa and I, for company." Ismay nodded.

Winifred loaded a wooden tray with cups and saucers, cubes of sugar, and a small plate of cookies. "I believe it's a fine thing tae have ye both here. God be thanked!" She looked at Ailsa and handed the sweets and tea to Ismay.

Ismay took the tray into her hands. She grasped it carefully. "Ailsa and I both want tae please both Morag and you. We're grateful for this home and the worthy meals." She tipped her head and turned to leave.

Winifred and Ailsa both smiled as they watched Ismay go back up the stairs.

\*\*\*\*\*

Ismay carried the tray back to Morag. She went into the room and put the tea on a small stand next to the old woman's chair.

Morag stared at it. "Winifred did not bring it."

"Her knees give her trouble. I told her that I'd do this from now on."

Ismay leaned closer. "Here." She took the pot into her hands and poured the steaming tea into a cup. She held the cup out for Morag.

Morag stiffened as she took it from Ismay. She lifted it to her lips and sipped slowly.

Ismay sat on a stool next to Morag and took out a pair of socks. She began to repair a hole in one of them. "I brought the listed items back from town, and I carried the food tae the scullery."

Morag took another sip of tea.

Her eyes went to the necklace hanging from Ismay's neck. "Ye say your parents gave ye this. She pointed to the chain."

Ismay nodded. "My faither, Macalister Innes." She eyed Morag curiously. "Why do you ask?"

"I daena believe it." Morag stared at her. She spoke quietly. "Take off your shoe."

"Mistress Duffy?"

Morag pointed and said it again. "Take it off, the one on your left foot."

Ismay colored. "But…"

"Ye know what's there. I want tae see it."

Ismay gave Morag a look of surprise. "But I've worn shoes since the day I met you. You couldn't know."

The old woman rapped her hand on the arm of her chair. Her eyes narrowed. "Show me now, lass!"

Ismay took her leather shoe from her foot and pulled off her sock. She stared at Morag in shock. "It's not a wutch's merk."

"I daena believe in those superstitions."

Morag didn't seem surprised by the cherry red mark that stained the top of Ismay's foot. The old woman nodded and reached for her cup of tea as if satisfied. She drew it to her mouth and took a sip.

"Someone told you about the birthmark. Who was it?"

Morag put her cup down and rested her hands on the arms of her chair. Her gnarled fingers tightened around the ends. "Was the man who raised you a tinker, Ismay?"

Ismay sat up with a start at the faint recollection of the tinker daughters she'd seen in Crieff which suddenly materialized again in her thoughts.

She shook her head. "No, he wasn't. My faither owned land in the Highlands in Comrie." A wary feeling ran through her.

The room suddenly became very quiet.

Morag clutched her teacup tighter and held it against her as if deep in thought. Her lips pressed firmly together.

"Why are ye asking me this? Why do ye want tae know?" Ismay sat up straighter. She leaned closer, studying Morag.

The look on the old woman's face was smug. Her eyes were watchful and shrewd. "No more questions, lass. I've no intention of answering anything. You're here tae wark for me and naught else. Please go back tae the tasks I set out for you. I'm duin in for the day. I must have my rest."

She placed her head against the back of her chair and closed her eyes. Her mouth tightened thinly. Her fingers were clasped around the arm rests.

Within minutes, Morag's breath deepened, and she tipped her head back further. It wasn't long before her mouth drew shut, and she drifted off to sleep.

Ismay watched as the lines in Morag's whole body grew less tense.

Ismay took out the sock she'd been repairing earlier and began working on it while she watched Morag's chest heave in and out.

Her eyes into a frown as she pondered all that had transpired between her and the old woman.

What could all the questions mean? And how had Morag known about her birthmark? There was no one but her mother and faither who'd iver set eyes on it. None of it made sense tae her.

There was much tae consider, more importantly, who was Morag, and what past did she have tae hide?

She'd spoken little to the elderly woman throughout the afternoon. There'd been no more questions or words about their earlier conversation. It was apparent to Ismay that the matter wasn't to be spoken of again, that Morag would have nothing more to say.

The old woman told Ismay what she wanted done the rest of the afternoon and throughout the evening. Ismay quietly finished the projects while occasionally leaving to bring meals and tea back to Morag.

Kara S. McKenzie, The Daughters of Crieff

*****

# *Chapter 23*

It had been more than a week since Ismay had left the Highlands.

Ian stalked back and forth in the dim-lit, starkly furnished room. He hadn't realized how many difficulties there'd be with her gone. She'd a profound effect on both the other servants and how the home had been run afore she'd off and went tae Crieff. Food had been better. Meals had been served in a more efficient manner, and the household staff had been more settled. He'd missed Ismay's Scotch pies and fancy puddings.

He pulled on his collar adjusting it around his throat. It seemed to be constricting his breath. He loosened the ties.

Och! It was more than the food he missed, and he knew it. He thought of her more often than not since she'd gone her way, and her bonnie face seemed tae be a permanent fixture in his mind as of late. Within the recesses of his heart, if he admitted it to himself, he realized he missed her greatly.

When Annag came into the room with a fretful frown, Ian couldn't help but notice her dismay.

She curtsied to him. "I'll need tae send someone tae town for messages. We've run low on supplies. I've a list tae give ye." She handed the parchment to him.

Ian took the note and nodded. "Tell Cael I'll tell him what we need. He can take the wagon tae Crieff."

\*\*\*\*\*

Cael came into the room. He stopped short at the door. "Ye wish tae see me, sir."

"I've a list for you tae take tae Crieff. Ye must bring back these supplies." Ian went to him and put the note into the boy's hand.

Cael took the parchment and gave a slight bow. "I'll be back by noon tae finish my chores."

Ian nodded, then gave the boy a hesitant look.

"Sir?"

"You did not…" Ian tapped his fingers against his side. "No."

"I did not what, sir?"

Ian took the boy by his arm. "Ismay told me that you put her necklace in her room. Is it true?" He stared at Cael intently.

Cael's face paled, and he suddenly fidgeted with his hands. He shook his head back and forth slowly. "Sir."

"Ye must speak tae me, lad. I must know the truth."

Cael winced. "I gave it back tae her, but I canna tell ye why."

Ian's eyes darkened. "You led me tae believe that Ismay stole it, but it appears it might not be true. I daena think you would have given it back, if it was. If there's a reason for what ye did, I want you tae tell me."

"No, sir. I can say no more about it. It's not possible."

"Not possible? What do ye mean?"

"Please." Cael winced again. "Daena ask me again, sir."

Ian stalked across the room to the young boy. The sound of his footsteps beat against the floor. He leaned closer. "Cael, your hiding something from me, and it concerns Ismay. What is it?"

Cael backed away. His eyes grew large. "I'm sorry, sir. I canna say."

Ian stared at him, studying him closely. "But, ye can, and ye will. You must be honest wi' me. I want tae know what's happened. You must tell me the truth."

"Sir, please. There'll be much trouble come tae my family and I, if I speak my mind."

238

"If, Cael? Come now. I'll not have pretense and dishonesty from my workers. Whatever is hidden must come out. If ye wish tae keep your position here, I must know what you're keeping from me."

"But sir! My family!"

Ian yanked his arm and pulled him closer. "You've been a braw warker, but you'll suffer for it if ye daena tell me all ye know."

Cael put his hands to his face and wiped tears away. He began to cry. His words came in gulps. "But she'll ruin my family. They're on the brink of starvation. Hence, I canna do it."

"Who? Ismay?"

"No, sir. I canna say."

Ian stared at the boy and then looked out the window at the cattle in the distant field. He turned back to the young lad and leaned closer. "It's Miss Hawthorne, isn't it?"

Cael swallowed and pulled away.

Ian held tightly to the boy's arm. He spoke less harshly. "She won't ruin anyone. I won't allow it, but I must know the truth. All of it. Do ye hear me?"

"But…"

"Cael, you will tell me."

Cael sighed. His voice came out in a whisper. He looked down. "Her extra coins have been feeding my family, sir. They canna make it without the money she's been giving us. They're poor and will starve."

"Wheest! I can provide for you and your family. There's no need tae take her coins. All ye would've had tae do was ask."

Cael's eyes widened. "She told me she'd say false things about me and that you'd believe her. And when I saw how ye did not believe Ismay, I knew it was true."

Ian let out a breath and raked a hand through his hair. "What's this? You should have said."

"Miss Hawthorne's very convincing, sir. I was afeart for my family."

"Tell me, please. I want tae know what she's kept from me. I must hear it all." Ian paced the floor. His face was pale. "And daena be anxious about your family. I'll make the necessary efforts tae care for them whether you've duin wrong or not."

"Sir!" Cael wiped more tears from his face. "I'm so sorry. I thought…"

"Grizel didn't tell the truth about the necklace, did she? Was it hers, or Ismay's?"

"She told me tae lie about it and about other things." Cael gulped. "I did not mean tae cause the trouble I did. Things weren't supposed tae happen the way they did."

"What things? What do ye mean?"

Cael put his hand on his stomach and almost doubled over. His voice broke. "The fire."

"Cael?" Ian stared at the young boy. "You must tell me what happened. Trust me. You'll not suffer for it."

The snap of sparks from the grate were the only sound in the room.

Cael gave Ian a mournful look. "Grizel wanted me tae make it seem as if Ismay had been careless. She wanted a smaw fire tae break out, but not for the house tae be burned down." Cael put his hands to his face again. "I did not mean for it tae happen as it did, but it was me who set the fire. Ismay had nothing tae do wi' it."

Ian stared at the boy as if at first he didn't know what to say. There was a shocked expression on his face. "Grizel asked you tae set the fire?"

Cael nodded between gulps.

Ian held his hand to his head and blinked. He looked distraught. "Hech ay, lad! What have ye duin?" He paced the room.

"She made me. I did not believe I had a choice." Tears ran freely down Cael's face. His eyes were large.

"But, ye did not come tae me instead. Ye did not trust me."

"She threatened my family. She told me they'd pay dearly for it in the end, if I did not do as she said. I did not want tae do it."

Ian grabbed hold of the end of his desk. "I've taken Ismay's home from her when I had no right tae. I've wronged her. I have treated her so poorly."

"Ye did not know, sir. I should've told ye afore this." Cael sobbed. "I won't blame ye, if ye send me out tae not return again. I've made a collieshangle of things."

"Ye have that." Ian brows furrowed above his dark eyes. Then he sighed deeply. "But ye did not orchestrate it. It was Grizel who made these threats against you, and ye had your family tae consider. Though you should have come tae me sooner. Ye should've trusted me."

Cael stared solemnly at Ian. "I'm sorry, sir. I never meant for any of it tae happen the way it did."

"To be sure, but there's no goin' back. What's duin is duin. You're a child, and I promised tae keep ye on and care for your family if ye told the truth."

Ian raked his hand through his hair. "Go, now. Get the things on the list. I've my own trip tae make tae Crieff, but I must set some things straight wi' Miss Hawthorne fairst."

Cael nodded while he wiped tears from his eyes. He got up and left quietly as he closed the door behind him.

*****

241

Ismay looked up when Winifred came into the room. "Mr. MacAllen's here tae see ye, Ismay. He says it canna wait."

"Ian MacAllen?" A suspicious look entered Morag's eye. She clutched the arm of her chair. "He's your former employer. What's he doing here?"

Ismay sighed. "I don't know. I've not seen him since my last trip tae Crieff." She lifted her hand to the chain around her neck and fingered the tiny golden links.

"You promised tae stay in my employ. You'll not go back tae him."

Ismay got up and paced the room. "No, I daena wish tae see him. Tell him this, Winifred."

Winifred's eyes widened. "But he says it's urgent and that the matter canna wait. I daena believe he'll keep things as they are. He was insistant."

"He'll have tae. I'll not see him." Ismay put her hands on her hips. "Too many things have been said and duin that canna be unduin. He's listened tae the blether spewing from a wutch's mouth rather than the truth. I'll have no more of it."

"But…" Winifred gave Ismay an anxious look.

Morag pounded on the end of her chair arm. "Tell Scotty tae send the scunner away! Ismay has no wish tae speak tae him!"

Winifred eyed them both nervously, but shook her head. "I'll tell him, Mistress Duffy, but I daena believe he'll want tae hear it."

\*\*\*\*\*

"You did not speak wi' him, Ismay?" Ailsa drew back the covers of her box bed and sat down in her white, linen nightgown.

Ismay took a place beside her friend. She left the candle on the stand between them lit. "He doesn't trust what I say or do, and I canna bear another accusation."

"But, it may not be as it seems. I do believe he cares for ye, Ismay."

"Even if he did, I'm merely an assistant of a great lady. I could be nothing tae him." Ismay lifted pieces of her hair and threaded them into a long braid. She sighed. "I'm quite sure it's best tae leave things as they are."

Ailsa slipped her feet under her wool coverlet and pulled it up to her chin. She lay down. "I daeno."

Then her expression grew solemn. "Sometimes it's best tae let go even when ye canna understand it. I've prayed for my mother, and faither, and Murdock. God spoke clearly tae me. I will not go back there."

Ismay lay on the hurlie bed next to Ailsa's. She turned on her side. "God wants you tae thrive and put away things that cause ye harm. Maybe someday you'll see that you are worth much more than ye know, Ailsa."

Ailsa breathed a sigh. "Thank ye, Ismay. God is good. His blissins are almost more than I can bear. He has given me much."

"And it's certain there's more in store for you, my friend, as you're His daughter, and He always gives abundantly tae His own." She smiled. "Good night. I hope your dreams are sweet."

"Good night, Ismay. God bless your thoughts and prayers."

Ismay leaned over and blew out the small flame on the candle in a heavy golden holder next to her bed. The room dimmed. Only a small glow from the coals in the fireplace and an occasional burst of withered flame remained.

Ailsa and Ismay withdrew themselves further under the covers as they closed their eyes and went to sleep.

Kara S. McKenzie, The Daughters of Crieff

*****

# *Chapter 24*

Ismay got up early for a brisk walk to town. She drew her scarf closer to her.

She stopped when she noticed a young woman, a little older than herself, in a plaid skirt and thick wool wrap coming toward her over the hill.

There was something distinctly familiar about the lass.

Ismay studied the young woman whose braids fell loosely over her shoulders and down her back. Dark brows tilted slightly inward over large, brown eyes. There was a wild sort of look tae her, yet her clothes were well-made as befitting a proper young lady.

Ismay couldn't quite decide where it was she'd seen the young woman afore, but she was sure she'd crossed paths wi' her sometime ago.

Ismay put up her hand to wave. "Hullo!"

The young woman waved back and half-skipped down the hill to where she stood. "Hullo! You're on your way tae town?"

Ismay nodded. "Where do ye come from? I feel as if I've seen ye afore."

"From Lorna Bissett's. I'm staying wi' her. She's broken her arm and is in need of assistance. She's a friend of my parents."

Ismay tipped her head to the side. "Who are you? What's your name?"

"Roslyn Day. My parents have known Madam Bissett for some time."

"I knew a lass named Roslyn once. I'm sure of it. Are you Madam Bissett's neighbors?"

"No." Roslyn gave her an odd look. Her voice quavered when she spoke again. "My parents are tinkers. They've known Lorna because of their travels."

Ismay suddenly recalled where she'd seen the young woman. "You were on the wagon wi' your sister when I was in Crieff. I saw you. Do I know ye from afore that? Something tells me I did."

Roslyn stared at Ismay blankly. "My sister, Shona, thought she remembered you." She looked confused.

"From where?" Something stirred in Ismay. "How could we have known each other?"

"From oor past. Your name's Ismay, is it not?"

Ismay's mouth dropped open. "How is it that you know my name?"

Roslyn smiled reaching out and touching Ismay's arm. "You were young. My parents told us about you, how we played together as lassies, and I remember it."

"You were traveling and came tae my home?"

"No, there was more."

"More?"

"Aye." Roslyn extended her hand and took Ismay's in her own. "You lived wi' us for a time on oor wagon, until we found proper parents for ye."

Ismay let go of Roslyn's hand. "Nay, ye must be mistaken. I had a mother and faither who were parents from birth."

Roslyn's eyes teared up suddenly. "I'm sorry. I thought ye knew." She stood awkwardly in the middle of the road.

Ismay put the basket she carried on her arm on the ground. Her heart thumped against her chest as she remembered her faither's last words to her. 'Tis your heritage. He loved ye very much.'

She put her hand to her chest. Her stomach clenched, and her heart thumped in her chest. "My mother and faither were Macalister and Lassie Innes, and I'm an Innes through and through. There's no more tae it. There canna be."

Roslyn didn't answer, her eyes large and gentle.

Ismay walked shakily over to a large rock that jutted out of the landscape on the side of the road. She sat on it. "He said things when he was dying. He made attempts tae tell me, but I wouldn't listen." She put her hand to her chest. "He wanted me tae know that he wasn't my blood faither." A sob escaped her.

Roslyn went to her and knelt beside the rock. "I'm so sorry, Ismay. I thought they would've told ye. A servant woman handed you tae us when you were a wee bairn. She told my mama and papa tae find ye a home, but she wouldn't say who your parents were, only that your mother died."

Ismay stared at Roslyn through her tears. "I've a birth faither who's alive."

Roslyn nodded. She spoke softly. "Most likely this is true. His servant left you wi' us, and you stayed on the wagon until we found you a new home. You played wi' my sister, Shona, and I for months."

Roslyn took a place beside her grasping her hand. "Macalister and Lassie took ye in as their own daughter. They'd been praying for a child but Lassie could not have bairns of her own. They believed ye tae be a gift from the Lord. They loved ye as their own."

"They did that." Ismay sighed. "They were kind tae me."

"Do ye remember any of your time wi' us?"

Ismay gave Roslyn an odd look. "When I saw ye on the street, the tinker's wagon struck a memory in me. I thought I knew ye, but I must have been a wee youngster at the time."

"About three or four as I recall. Shona and I were a few years older. We loved ye, Ismay. We were sad tae see ye leave us."

Ismay wiped a tear from her cheek. She squeezed Roslyn's hand. "Your family found me a proper home and kind parents. I loved my mother and faither dearly. You were decent people tae take me in like ye did. I thank ye for it, but it is difficult tae believe they were not my blood kin."

"My parents wanted you tae have a proper home. They are considerate and would want you tae value the life ye had."

"Someday I must thank them myself for what they did."

"I'm sorry you had tae hear about all this the way ye did. I suppose it was quite shocking."

"Very much so."

"But the way it happened, it seems tae be that God had a hand in it." Roslyn smiled.

Ismay drew in a breath of the cool, hillside air around her. "Aye, and now we have meet."

And then she was suddenly curious. "You say ye live wi' Madam Bissett. Why are ye not wi' your parents and your sister on the wagon?"

Roslyn tugged gently on Ismay's hand. "Let's walk together. You are goin' tae town, aren't you?"

"Aye."

"Then come wi' me, and I'll tell ye my story along the way and maybe recite ye a poem or two."

Ismay got up and wiped the rest of the tears from her face. "I will. It'll take my mind from what will require deeper thought in the future."

"Absolutely." Roslyn smiled.

Ismay picked up her basket from the road and walked beside the young woman listening as Roslyn recounted her own story. There was much tae tell about her family and Callum on their way to and from town.

*****

When Roslyn left Ismay at her doorstep, they both hugged.

248

"I suppose I must go now, but I look forward tae seeing you again." Roslyn smiled.

"Come tae visit wi' us, and bring Shona. I'd like tae meet her." Ismay tipped her head to the young woman.

"I will."

Then Roslyn's eyes suddenly lit. "Wait! Mr. Featherstone's ball! Did ye get an invitation?" She smiled wide.

Ismay laughed. "I believe iveryone in town has received his post. At least it's what I've been hearing. One was delivered tae oor doorstep a few days ago. I'm not sure there is anyone in the county who wasn't invited."

Roslyn laughed with her. "Then we will both be there."

"Aye, and we'll see each other again. I will take pleasure in it."

"Another day." Roslyn took one last wave and walked back to the road. "Fareweel, my friend."

Ismay waved back. "Fareweel."

*****

# *Chapter 25*

"But, I've no gown tae wear. How can I go wi' ye?"

"I'll ask Morag for it, Ailsa. She's very rich, and you've came tae her wi' nothing." Ismay ran her hands along the shiny rail of the staircase.

"I'm not sure I could ask for such a thing."

Ismay giggled. "But ye must come wi' me, and ye willna go in your wool skirt. You must have something proper for the occasion. Morag willna care a whit if I ask her. She'll likely clothe the whole household for such a grand affair."

"I had a beautiful gown once." Ailsa sighed.

Ismay frowned. "Once?"

"Mother gave it tae me for a special confirmation in the kirk. I wore it at the pairty, and thought I'd up and went tae heaven. It was lovely, white with patterned lace and sleeves that came tae points, covered in shining pearls. It was hers when she herself was confirmed, and I was so proud tae have have such a beautiful dress. I would've kept it on all that night as she'd never given me anything so dear tae my heart."

"I daena understand? Where is it?" Ismay stared at Ailsa.

"It seems she wanted me tae look appropriate for the occasion but had not truly given it tae me, though I thought I might pass it down tae my own youngster someday." Ailsa shrugged. "When the pairty ended, she asked for it back, in the event Murdock might someday have a youngster who could keep it as their own."

"Ailsa, she'd given it tae ye. She raised your hopes. I'm sorry she hurt you like she did."

"I wouldn't want it now. Mother loves Murdock very much. It was meant for his kin. But I've no beautiful gown of my own. I never did."

Ismay reached out and pushed a golden strand of hair from her friend's face. "The Lord will see that your gown is the most beautiful at the ball, one of embroidered silk that will draw ivery eye." She smiled. "And Morag will do His wark whether she knows it or not. It'll be yours tae keep."

Ailsa's dark, hazel eyes stood out against her pale skin and rippled hair. She seemed afraid to smile back, but did. "I thank ye, Ismay. God has provided for me in ivery way. He is good."

She spoke quietly. "Now, Ismay, I must get back tae the scullery. They'll be wondering where I am. And you should see tae Morag afore she's asleep in the chair."

Ismay rolled her eyes and smiled. "Aye, I'll go tae her now." She held the stair railing again and took quick steps to the top.

*****

Ailsa went into the kitchen. Winifred was working on the meal for the evening.

"Hullo. What can I do?"

Winifred smiled. "See tae those on the table, and I'll get the kettle on."

Ailsa nodded and put on her apron. She washed vegetables, chopping them for a soup. As she worked, she recalled the verses she'd been memorizing from her Bible. 'Be strong in the Lord and in his mighty power…' The Lord had impressed upon her the necessity of knowing the chapter. Would there be a 'day of evil', or would she be spared from it?

Both she and Winifred looked up when a knock sounded at the kitchen door that led to a small meadow in the back of the home.

"I'll answer it." Ailsa rose quickly and went to the door to open it. Her eyes widened when she realized it was her mother who stood just outside the door.

"The groundskeeper told me I'd find ye here, Ailsa. I must speak wi' you."

Ailsa gave Winifred a hesitant look.

Winifred tipped her head. "I'll finish. The meal's almost ready."

"Come, Ailsa," her mother directed. "I've things I must say."

Ailsa grabbed her wrap. She stood outside the doorway under the eves. Rain dripped along the edges as they stood facing each other. "Why are you here?" Ailsa studied her mother.

"You've left home. I must know why you've taken leave so suddenly."

Ailsa's heart pounded as the words of the Bible verses she'd memorized ran through her mind. '…you will be able tae stand your ground.'

She spoke quietly. "I no longer wish tae suffer ill-treatment there or take the blame for what I've not duin, mother. I've found a good position here. I wark wi' very kind people."

"Come now, Ailsa. We've duin nothing tae wrong you. You must know that you deserved any treatment you were given. No one can say they're without blame."

"I've never told ye that I have not sinned, mother, as we all do." Ailsa drew back. "I've repented many times, in earnest, for my own waywardness. But, you must know that you're not without sin either. I speak the truth, but I'm certain you daena wish tae hear it."

"Are ye saying that I've hurt you and caused *you* pain?" Her mother stared at her icily. "What an addled thing tae say, Ailsa."

"No, we've all sinned, mother, I as well as you. But there'll be no admitting tae it on your pairt, and I know that."

"Ailsa, you've lost your head? How could ye be so hurtful? Why would ye blame me as ye do?"

"Mother, please, I daena believe you've come tae heal oor wounds, or make amends, but tae condemn, and I'll not have it. I can stand for no more of this."

"Ai-l-sa. Come now, lass. You're confused. Ye must know you've been a willful child. Not one thing duin in oor home has caused ye harm. All has been duin for your own good. You must see this."

Ailsa put her hands over her ears. No! She couldn't listen tae her mother's cunning words. They rolled off her tongue wi' such ease. "No, mother. I tell ye, it'll not do, tae continually cast the blame but claim no wrongs. Your words are like sweet poison, and they seek tae draw me in."

"Truly!" Her mother scowled. "Tell me a time you were treated badly. When! Out wi' it!" Her voice was threaded with anger. "Speak up, lassie, and allow me tae be the judge of my own wrangeous actions."

A tear slid down Ailsa's cheek. "You hope that I might reduce a lifetime of sorrow tae an instant or two. Your demeaning words and actions have wounded and torn down, when they should've built up."

Ailsa pleaded with her mother. "The Bible says that love is patient and kind, not jealous and envious or boastful, proud or rude. It forgives and is not hurtful and doesna insist on its own way. What you've expressed tae me has not been love. You've twisted what is right and good, therefore I canna continue in this dishonest way any longer. I'll not have it."

Her mother stared at her with darkened eyes. Her lips tightened as she spoke. "You're an ungrateful girl and care nothing for others! Ye canna see the wrongs ye do."

Ailsa groaned. "Ach! I'll not hear it, mother. Not one word iver again!" She covered her ears with her hands. "If you want healing, mother, then go tae the cross. The Lord did not mean for me tae pay for iveryone else's sin. I'll have no more of it."

Her mother's eyes suddenly filled with tears, and she lowered her head. "My own daughter speaking in such ways against me. And a good, Christian lass at that. I canna understand any of it." She began to weep and then looked up.

Ailsa almost reached out to soothe her but then realized the tears which the older woman had displayed had suddenly ended abruptly. It was as if her mother had the ability to turn her emotions on and off at will. She played upon Ailsa's soft nature.

Ailsa backed away, tears in her own eyes. "Your flattery is insincere, mother. You wish tae get back into my good graces, for whatever reason, but I've suffered too long on account of your changeable moods and will listen no more tae it. There have been times where I have failed you as a daughter, but I've been willing tae admit the wrongs I've committed against you and have been quick tae apologize. Unless your willing tae do the same, I see no reason tae continue in this way."

"But the family? What about your brother, and faither, and I? What will we do?"

"Go home and salvage the remnants of what remains of it. You have each other. You should be thankful for that."

Ailsa sighed. She looked away. "Good day, mother. You're forgiven, but I daena wish tae listen tae more of the same."

Before her mother spoke again, Ailsa turned and went inside. She closed the door behind her.

She lowered the clasp and turned the lock. She spoke quietly to Winifred. "Please daena allow her entrance again. I'll not see her efter this."

Winifred nodded without saying anything.

Ailsa went back to her work, and for the fairst time in her life, the condemnation that constantly tormented her was gone. She breathed a sigh. Her Lord had fought for her, and she was free.

She lifted her hand to her chest and held it there. Was she finally deserving of His love? Could she accept God's grace in full without blame?

She'd left family, home, and her auld life behind and had mourned the loss of what might have been. She'd accepted the honest truth that, sometimes, the starry-eyed dreams of a youngster were not always possible, and her own idea of a happy ending might not be what God had planned for her.

She breathed a sigh of relief knowing what she knew about her Heavenly Faither and all the things he'd duin for her since she was a wee youngster. He'd accepted her long ago into His family. He'd protected her, listened tae her prayers, cared deeply for her, and saved her. He'd called her His own. He'd never forsaken her. He'd been her strength.

His blissins were more than she could imagine, and His love was all that His Word claimed it tae be. He'd never fail her. He only lifted her, and never tore down. He cherished her, defended her, nurtured and preserved her. There was nothing bad about Him. He was very, very good.

*****

Ismay opened the door and went inside Morag's room. The old woman was asleep on the chair.

Ismay took a seat beside her and took her embroidery into her hands. She worked quietly while she watched the gentle rise and fall of Morag's chest.

The woman seemed regal even when she slept. Not a hair was out of place. Her clothes were without crease or wrinkle, and her hands were clasped carefully on her lap.

Though still gruff and cantankerous in manner and speech, as of late, the auld woman seemed tae have softened when she looked at Ismay or spoke tae her. Something had changed.

Morag suddenly cleared her throat. Her eyes fluttered open, and she made a quiet noise when she turned and saw Ismay watching her. Her knuckles clasped the chair tightly, and her breath turned shallow.

"Water, lass. Bring me some," Morag choked out. "Come now."

Ismay got up and brought the old woman the water pitcher. She poured Morag a glass of the crystal clear liquid from the spring. She gave it to her. "Here, take it and sip slowly."

Morag tipped her head. She attempted to clasp the container with her hand, but her fingers weren't able to tighten around it.

"I have it." Ismay lifted the glass to the old woman's lips while Morag took a drink.

Their eyes met.

Morag's gray eyes were distant and wearied. "I must tell ye something, lass. Come closer." There was a harsh gurgle sound coming from her throat. "Be quick. You must hear it."

"Are you unwell, Mistress Duffy? I'll fetch the doctor."

Morag's hand was like a claw. It slipped over Ismay's wrist and held it fast. "Necklace." Her eyelids fluttered, and her breath labored.

"This one?" Ismay pointed to her chain.

Morag nodded. "Aye." Another gurgle sounded in her throat again. "It was mine once."

Ismay stared at Morag uneasily. "What do ye mean?" She clutched her chest.

Morag's eyes closed again, but she managed to draw them open for an instant.

"I wronged ye. I wronged your faither. Your mother, she was dying." Her voice shook. It was barely a breath.

"Mistress Duffy?" Ismay whispered in her ear. "Lie still. I'll get the doctor." She pulled away.

Morag wouldn't let go of her hand. "No, ye must hear this. There's no time." The gurgling was louder. Morag shuddered. "I wronged ye, and I want tae make amends afore I die. I sent you away." She coughed and couldn't speak for a moment.

Ismay moved closer. "I must go and get someone. Please."

Morag shook her head. "No, I'm your grandmother, Ismay, and I've wronged ye and your faither."

Ismay took a step back. She made a wounded sound, then took Morag's hand in her own. "Grandmother?"

"My daughter, she'd been talking nonsense. She'd an illness, and I blamed it on your faither. I had ye sent away wi' the tinkers when she died. Your faither did not know. Ye must forgive me, lassie. I must know this afore I die."

"I grew up wi' a worthy faither and mother. I wasn't without kin who loved me."

"But, I stole you from your own, Ismay, your own good birth faither. I'd no right, but I need your forgiveness. I've had no peace." She gurgled again with a panicked look in her eye. "He loved ye so, and searched the land tae find you."

"But I forgive ye, Mistress Duffy, and you'll not die." Ismay gulped back a tear. "I must go. The doctor must see ye."

Ismay attempted to shake her hand free from Morag who gripped it tightly.

She reached with her free hand and grabbed Morag's brass bell. She shook it wildly and put it down when Morag spoke again.

A huge raspy sound struck Morag's throat. She put her hand to her chest. "God will not take me. I'm condemned tae Hell. I've duin wrong."

"No, grandmother, you're wrong! He will. Remember how He took the condemned man on the cross, the one who'd murdered and stole. He'll take you too. The man was sorry for what he'd duin, and he made things right wi' God in the end. You can do this too!"

Morag was fearful, but hopeful at the same time. The wrinkles around her face consumed her. "But, how? I daena know what tae say."

Ismay quickly put her hand on Morag's arm. "Ye tell Him your sorry. Ask Him tae save ye, and tae take ye home wi' Him! Daena delay. Tell Him now."

Morag closed her eyes as she mumbled a prayer under her breath.

Afterward, Ismay heard the auld woman whisper. "Your beloved daughter? Surely not I, Lord?" There was a puzzled look on her face. Then the frown in her brow softened.

A shuddering sigh overtook her, and she opened her eyes one last time. She said in a soft voice not quite her own. "My Faither. My King." And then she was gone.

Ismay breathed a sigh. A grandmother she'd barely known was now safely in heaven wi' her own dear parents.

And she'd lairned that her birth faither was alive. How was she tae comprehend it? What was she tae think?

*****

The door opened, and Winifred came bursting into the room. When she saw Morag dead in the chair, she let out an eerie scream and gathered her skirts. She ran back into the hallway.

"Scotty! Come quickly! Scotty!" Her screams echoed down the corridor, despite there'd be no bringing the old woman back.

*****

"She's left ye the estate, her income, and the deed tae the property. A note has been written in her own handwriting explaining the particulars. She made it clear that you were her granddaughter and only heir." The banker handed Ismay the parchment while the others in the room eyed her in shocked silence. "It's all yours."

Ismay blinked. She stared at the note's contents while her eyes filled with tears. She said nothing.

"She gave you her heirship." Ailsa put her hand on Ismay's shoulder. "She cared for ye all along."

Ismay looked up at her friend and the others in the room.

Scotty nodded to her.

Winifred took his hand in hers and tipped her head in unison. "I believe she cared for you in her own way."

Ismay folded the letter gently and placed it in the pocket of her apron. She wiped away new tears that had fallen onto her cheeks. "I only wish she would've told me the truth afore the day she died. I would've like tae have known her in this way."

Ailsa patted her arm. "It is good that she told ye about your faither, and she is at peace now."

Ismay shook her head. "Aye, she was repentant in the end, and I'm glad for it. On the morn's morn, I'll hire someone tae find him for me."

She tipped her head to the banker and took hold of the doorknob. "Thank you, sir. I'll be on my way tae my place now. Scotty and Winifred, if ye wish tae retain your employment at my estate, you may return wi' me."

"Aye!" Both of them replied in unison. "We'll be happy tae serve you."

Ismay smiled at Ailsa. "And you, my friend and confidant, will live wi' me as a sister. We'll find an assistant for Winifred tae replace you."

Ailsa followed Ismay out the door. "I've never had a sister." She smiled widely. "Thank ye, Ismay. God has blessed me two-fold on account of you. It's impossible tae describe the joy in my heart. I thank ye heartily."

Ismay took her hand, and they walked together with Scotty and Winifred to their carriage.

*****

Ismay eyed her drab housekeeper skirt and shirt as she stood at the foot of the headstone behind the home. She'd call on the dressmakers in time tae measure her and Ailsa. She'd already purchased a colorful array of expensive fabrics and laces, threads and patterns. Soon they would both have beautiful gowns for every occasion.

But for now, they would be content wi' their plain, simple wools fit for maids and cooks.

She sighed when she eyed the stark, cold headstone with the dark, deep lettering on it. Here lies Mistress an Mair Morag Duffy who claimed her stake at the foot of the cross. RIP. 1740-1811.

It sounded so final, yet Ismay read it again, emphasizing the word, 'cross'. She reached out and fingered the etched letters. Though cool tae the touch, a warmth struck her heart. She remembered Morag's last words. The auld woman was His daughter now, and eternity was forever.

She heard a sound behind her and turned.

Ian had walked up the path.

Ismay drew in a breath at the sight of him. His braw looks never failed tae cause her heart tae skip a beat. Would he be married by this time? Why had he come?

"I haird the auld woman died, Ismay. I'm sorry for you."

Ismay nodded. She planned to speak until he interrupted.

"I suppose you'll be advertising for wark again." He eyed her woolen skirt and the frayed edges of her apron.

He wasn't aware of her situation. She was about tae tell him the truth, but decided against it.

He spoke quietly. "Ismay, Cael told me the truth about the jewelry. He told me other things. I've treated ye wrongly and wish tae make amends."

She eyed him suspiciously. Amends? Maybe he had lairned of her heirship. Was it the money and estate he was efter? "What are ye here for? Why have ye come?" She took a step back.

"I told ye that I've come tae apologize. I've been wrong and wanted tae set things tae rights. I owe ye much."

"What do ye mean? Owe me?"

Ian raked his hand nervously through his hair. "I've come tae return your property and beg your forgiveness. I've no right tae it and canna keep it."

Ismay stared at him puzzled. "But why?" She didn't know what to say.

"I came here several times, but have been turned away. I wanted tae make amends for what I've duin. Cael started the fire."

"Cael? But…"

"Grizel threatened his family. It wasn't meant tae burn my house down, only tae cause you tae look careless." Ian shook his head. "Ismay, since ye stole the horse, I'd lost trust in you. But Cael confessed that it was her all along. Grizel lied about the jewelry, and I took her word for it. I've been a fool. I should have listened tae you."

Ismay put her hand over her mouth. "Ye married her afore you knew?"

"No, Cael told me, and I ended the engagement. I've been making attempts tae see you, but have been turned away."

Ismay's cheeks heated as she looked up at him. "But you asked her tae marry ye."

"Aye, though I never should have engaged myself tae the woman. I listened tae her lies but never loved her." He went to Ismay and took her hand. "Ye must believe that the engagement was short-lived. Talk tae Cael. When you left, I was terribly distraught. I couldn't bear the thought of losing you. I knew it then."

Ismay pulled her hand away. Her eyes widened. "You were in town. You want tae benefit from my situation. I've haird none of this afore."

Ian looked surprised. "I've no intention of taking ye back as my cook again. I mean it. I know you've lost your position in this home, but it's not what I've come for. I'm willing tae give ye back your home and your property wi' the intention that we could live there as husband and wife. I've a spread of cattle. I've an income wi' the herd and my horses. I'm able tae care for you."

"But…"

Ian put a finger to her lips. "That ye lack a title or a position matters little tae me. I wouldn'thave ye on account of the trials you'd face if we iver did. Though I realize now that you'd have been hearty enough tae bear it."

"What are you saying?" Ismay stared at him breathlessly.

"That I've come tae love ye, Ismay, and I'd marry you if ye were an orphant off the streets. I've always thought you were beautiful in heart and looks. Though you're a wee bit like a selkie, difficult tae catch."

Ismay's eyes suddenly sparkled. "Ye liken me tae a seal, sir?" She moved closer to him, and her lips drew into a pout.

"Maybe." He leaned over and took her in his arms and kissed her tenderly.

Ismay's eyes widened in amazement as she held him close to her. She whispered in his ear. "I wanted ye tae come back, and I'm very happy that ye did."

"I've come iveryday since I spoke tae Cael, but that scoonrel of a butler of Morag's wouldn't let me near you."

"I suppose it is justice for your lack of faith in me." Her eyes lit as she said it.

Then she tipped her chin upward, and she spoke in a cross tone. "Though I canna have my husband doubting my word or accusing me of theft again. This will not do. You must trust what I say efter this. Do ye understand?"

Ian laughed and held her around the waist again. "My wee horsethief. I promise I'll tae take your word fairst, if ye say you'll marry me."

Ismay smiled. "I'll marry you, Ian, but there is one smaw confession I must make afore we both agree."

"A confession?" Ian eyed her curiously.

At that moment, Scotty came out the front door and down the steps. "Mistress Innes! I'm sorry I allowed this Pensie deil tae get past me!"

He rushed at Ian as he waved his arms at him. "Ye schamin scoonrel, finding your way tae the Mistress. You'll be causing the auld woman tae chitter in her grave."

Ismay stepped in front of Ian. She put out her hand. "Scotty! Wheesht! Can't ye see I'm having a ceevil discourse wi' this gentleman. He's mended his ways and has come tae set things straight."

"But, mistress, I thought ye did not wish tae speak tae him again."

Ismay slipped her hand into the crook of Ian's arm and looked up at him with a smile. "We've warked out oor differences. He's walcome here now."

Ian patted her hand and drew her closer. "I'm glad of it, love. I've missed your bonnie smile and speeritie ways. I'd be pleased tae see more of you again."

Scotty stopped on the path. He looked from Ismay to Ian. "But..."

"Scotty, please." Ismay laughed. "We're friends."

Ian drew her closer to him and brushed his lips against her hair. "I believe we're more than that, Ismay."

Her cheeks pinkened as she nodded to him.

Scotty pushed a thin strand of gray hair behind his ear. He smiled with his toothless grin as he looked between the two of them. "Hech ay! It appears the world's suddenly gone tapsalteerie!" He laughed aloud as he studied them both. "I believe I've seen that look afore, the one that sets off the waddin bells. I be thinking I'll be calling on the meesionar at the kirk in time. Isn't that right, Mistress? Have I judged the situation rightly?"

Ismay laughed as she observed his antics. "You've an observant eye, Scotty, as Mr. MacAllen and I have only this very day made oor intentions known tae each other."

Scotty reached out and shook both their hands. He turned to Ismay. "I believe your granny would be happy tae see ye settled. She did rander on about ye in a gruff way, but I could see that the auld woman favored you."

"Granny?" Ian stared at Ismay with a puzzled look on his face. "But I thought ye had no living relations."

Ismay dusted off her skirt with her hands. She smoothed out the folds of the fabric, then she cleared her throat. "Well, afore Scotty came out, I told ye I had one more confession tae make. I've not been altogether honest wi' you again." She pushed back a strand of hair that had fallen into her eyes and took a breath.

Ian's brow rose. He turned to her. "Ismay, please daena tell me you've duin something else. What is it ye need tae confess tae?"

Ismay shuffled her feet and looked up at him. Her large, blue eyes twinkled, and she grinned at him playfully. "I thought ye promised tae trust my word from this day forward, sir. Are you believing me to be errant in my ways again?"

"I do not know." His voice was soft like a caress. He eyed her curiously. "Ye did steal my horse once, lassie, a worthy one at that. I'm not quite sure what tae think."

"Ye need not be anxious about your prize horses as I've lairned my lesson from my last venture. You found me out rather quickly, and I saw you were not tae be reckoned with."

She knelt next to the tombstone and touched a petal on one of the roses she'd laid across the grave. "Though I do not believe my grandmother would appreciate my dishonoring the family name the way I did. Horsethieving might not be the type profession I'd wish tae tie tae the ancestral records."

Scotty laughed. "I daena believe it would, Mistress Innes-Duffy. You'd do well tae set the past tae rest, if ye did such a thing."

"Mistress Innes-Duffy?" Ian stared at the grave and then back at her. "It seems you've acquired a title, lass, since I've last seen you."

Ismay smiled. "I have. I've recently lairned that Macalister and Lassie Innes were my adoptive parents given tae them by a tinker's family. I was taken from my faither without his knowledge. My grandmother, on my birth mother's side, was Morag Duffy, but I was unaware of it until the day she died."

Ian looked interested. "But how did she know? I thought ye met at Skye and Ross's garden pairty."

"I did. She recognized my jewelry." She slipped the necklace out from beneath her shirt. "She was acquainted wi' the piece that was given tae me by my birth faither. She asked tae see my foot which has a distinctive merk on it. She waited tae reveal the truth of it tae me until the day she died."

"But, your faither? Is he alive? Have ye met him?"

"Winifred told me he'd estreenged himself from Morag when he found out that she'd given me away. She wouldn't reveal where I was tae him. My mother died of an illness, and my grandmother blamed my faither for it, though Winifred said it was no fault of his own that she died. There was no medicine hardy enough tae save her."

"I'm sorry, Ismay. All this must have been difficult for you." Ian's face was grim. He eyed the chain around her neck. "I wasn't there for you, and I almost allowed Grizel tae take your faither's jewelry. I'm glad Cael saw fit tae give it back tae you."

Ismay held the engraved metal piece in her hand. "I'm grateful he did as it was the key tae lairning the saicrets of my past. But daena torment yourself over the ordeal as you were deceived and not tae blame while Cael knew the truth. In the end, Morag discovered oor connection because of it, and it was a blissin that she revealed it tae me."

Winifred came out the door. She motioned to Scotty. "Come! Ailsa needs you. The knob on her wardrobe door needs fixing."

Scotty turned. "Tell Ailsa I'm comin'." He looked back at Ismay. "If ye need assistance, Mistress Innes, daena hesitate tae call. I'm happy tae serve such a kind lady as yourself."

Ismay smiled. "You've been kind, Scotty. I appreciate it, but I've no more need for you at this moment. It seems Ailsa could use your help."

Scotty tipped his head, then he walked up the path to the house.

Ian studied Ismay with a curious look. "You're the owner of Morag's home? Was this your confession, Ismay?"

"I've been attempting tae tell you." Ismay's cheeks brightened. "Efter Morag passed away, she named me the sole heir of her estate and all her monies. I did not expect anything of the sort. I've been quite conflummixed by the whole situation."

She put her hands on her hips and paced in front of him. "So, ye see my position in society is much changed, and I'm not sure what tae think of it."

Ian caught her arm and tugged on it. He drew her closer. "It matters not tae me whether you're a housemaid or a grand lady. I have loved you, Ismay, because of your kind heart. You're hard-warking, prayerful, and care for others. I've seen it and know your worth, wi' or without a title."

"You were willing tae marry me without a shullin tae my name, and I knew the criticism you'd face for it." She smiled. "I'm glad you'll not suffer such censure for my sake. I wouldn'twish tae injure ye in that way."

"And you will be accepted. I'm glad of it also."

It suddenly rained, and they both looked up at the sky.

"Och!" Ismay laughed. "It seems a blaud has come upon us! We must not didder here, or we'll be soaked! Come to oor house."

He smiled and took to her side.

They ran hand in hand to beat the sudden downpour.

Ian slipped inside behind Ismay.

Both couldn't contain their laughter after they closed the door behind them.

Inside the home, Ian turned and pulled her into his arms and kissed her again.

Ismay returned his affection, suddenly joy-filled with the thought of it. Changes had come quickly but were well worth it in the end.

*****

When the storm quieted, Ian got up from the chair he'd been sitting on in the parlor while talking to Ismay. "We'll meet at the upcoming ball and discuss the date for oor waddin. I believe invitations for the dance were sent out all over the countryside."

Ismay nodded. "Aye, Ailsa and I have plans tae be there. We're waiting on proper gowns and clothes for the staff."

"Then I'll meet you in the main room efter my own town business is settled." He leaned down to kiss her again.

Ismay smiled. "Will ye dance wi' me then?"

"Ivery dance of the night. I daena intend tae let ye out of my sight." He reached up and touched her cheek.

"I'm glad of it, and that Grizel will no longer be at your side."

"Only you, my love. No one else."

After he stepped out the door, Ismay took to the stairs two steps at a time to the top. Her cheeks warmed at the thought of his tender kisses and declarations of love. Never afore had she felt such happiness.

When she reached the door to Ailsa's room, she put her fist to it and rapped. "Ailsa! Are ye there? Where are ye, dearie!"

"Come in, Ismay! I am. Tell me your news."

Ismay opened the door and went inside. "You'll not believe what has happened."

"Quick! Tell me! Ye have that sparkle in your eye so I know what ye have tae say is sure tae be good!"

Ismay smiled at the thought of all that had happened that afternoon. All that had come tae pass had surely been eventful. Her heart burst with joy.

She couldn't wait tae tell tae Ailsa all about Ian.

\*\*\*\*\*

# Chapter 26

"Which gown should I wear? God has blessed us wi' so much, Ailsa! I've never afore felt such joy."

"There are more riches than I can comprehend. It doesn't seem right for me tae wear such fine clothes. I feel unworthy of it."

Ismay went to Ailsa and shook her head. "You must not, Ailsa, as the Lord sees ye differently than ye see yourself. He loves ye more than you know. Someday I might persuade you tae see how precious ye are tae others."

Ailsa sighed. "So much is wrong. How had I not known it? Why could I not see what they were doing?"

"When the whole town speaks highly of them, and ye see good deeds duin in the name of the church, tis difficult tae see things straight. How could ye not want tae believe your own mother and faither whom ye trusted?"

"I thought I had no right tae love or joy. I couldn't question right from wrong."

Ailsa's eyes pooled with tears. "Ismay, I lairned truth when God revealed tae me His gracious love, otherwise I wouldn't have known the beauty of His purpose. He doesn't condemn us, and neither will He allow others tae."

"I'm glad ye see this, Ailsa, as there's truth in your words. I sense you've a new freedom tae accept God's blissins." Ismay held up a royal green skirt with a white blouse and plaid scarf. "Accept the gifts He gives ye, and lairn tae love the person He made you tae be, a daughter of the King."

Ailsa took the clothing in her hands. She smiled as she spoke in a whisper. "I'm glad for the hardships I've faced, for they've made His gifts that much sweeter. He is a good, good Faither."

"He is very good. He's comforted me as I've grieved of the loss of my own faither and mother. He's been my Rock and the strength of my salvation."

Ismay took a dark blue and green plaid from the wardrobe and held it in front of her. "I'll also accept his blissins and joy in my life along wi' my sufferings."

"Tis a beautiful gown, Ismay. Ian will not be able tae take his eyes from you."

Ismay laid the gown on a chair and clasped her friend's hands in her own. "I suppose we should end oor chittering and ready oorselves for the ball. Scotty told me he'd have the carriage ready within the hour. I daena wish for him tae have tae wait on us."

Ailsa laughed. "And I daena want tae be late for such a grand affair. The dance will begin soon! Let's up and away!"

They closed the door to dress and finish preparations in the excitement of the moment.

*****

Roslyn stepped into the carriage and sat next to Lorna. She clasped her gloved hands in her lap and looked out the window.

"Mr. Featherstone will be happy tae see ye, Roslyn. You should be honored he thinks so highly of ye tae have invited you."

Roslyn gave Lorna a quick nod. "I'm honored, but not inclined tae feel the same as he does." The carriage jolted and rumbled over a slippery path. "He has a large estate and money, but I find it very troublesome when he speaks tae others in the high-handed way he does. It is very unpleasant."

"But despite this unbecoming manner, he's a man who could raise your status. Though ye might find his behavior impertinent, I'm inclined tae think that you should consider the attention he's paid you. I know ye desire tae take leave of the traveling path. Sometimes you must make concessions if ye wish tae see your dreams come tae fruitation."

Roslyn let out light laughter. "I'd rather find my own way out than settle wi' such an unceevil scoonrel as that man."

"Callum's disappeared and not come calling for at least a month soon efter he engaged himself tae you. You might speak unkindly of him as well."

"I daena understand why Callum has deserted me, but I intend tae find out. He's abandoned oor property, and I've not seen him in the town. No one seems tae know where he's gone tae."

Lorna spoke firmly. "It seems his undying devotion has been lacking. It would be commendable if he were tae come this evening so ye might lairn why he's deserted ye and be duin wi' him."

Roslyn didn't answer but smoothed out the folds of her dark, rose-colored gown. Callum would certainly have some explaining tae do, though she would wait tae see him afore making any judgement against him.

*****

# *Chapter 27*

Ismay descended the wide, cascading stairway with Ailsa at her side. She caught her breath at the sight of the crowded ballroom trimmed without restraint in glittering silver and blue décor. Dark cerulean curtains swooped skillfully over tall windows that encircled an octagonal-shaped room. An opulent, diamond, chrystal chandelier glowed elegantly over the center of the room.

Her eyes widened at the brightly colored gowns in plaids and deep, rich hues that blended like flowers in a field while lilting Celtic instruments unveiled a lively tune.

"Tis more than I expected." Ismay put her gloved hand to her chest and grasped the rail with her other. "I've never seen such extravagance."

Ailsa nodded. "Nor I. I must say that I'm astounded at the magnificence displayed by Mr. Featherstone in his grand home. He's a man of great means."

"Aye."

Ismay looked for Ian, but spotted Roslyn instead in the corner of the room. "Come, it's the tinker's daughter. I'll introduce you."

Ailsa smiled. "The one you lived with! I must meet her."

Ismay took Ailsa's arm as they made their way across the crowded dance floor. "Roslyn!" Ismay called out.

Roslyn turned. "Ismay! How beautiful you look. I haird of your heirship and am so very happy for you."

"There's much tae be thankful for, and I may someday find my birth faither on account of Morag." She pulled Ailsa beside her. "This is my friend, Ailsa. She lives wi' me at the estate. She and I are close like sisters."

Roslyn extended a hand and took Ailsa's in her own. "I know we'll be good friends in time. I'm pleased that introductions have been made. Ismay holds a special place in my heart from my own youth."

Ailsa smiled widely. "Oo aye! She's told me about you! We must not hesitate tae call on each other in the future."

Roslyn nodded. "I look forward tae it."

She let go of Ailsa's hand and then looked around the room.

Ailsa turned. "It's Mr. Featherstone coming this way." She smiled. "Imagine the grand owner of the home chittering wi' the likes of us."

Ismay breathed a sigh. "It seems acquiring an inheritance and title has raised my status in polite society."

Roslyn's demeanor suddenly changed. She spoke quietly. "Please daena be offended by my hasty retreat, but I must go. I'll find ye both later. There are matters I must attend tae at this time."

Ismay tipped her head. "Neither Ailsa nor I are offended, but if there's anything we might do…"

"Not now, but I thank ye kindly. She curtsied to them both and then slipped into the crowd disappearing.

Ismay was curious. "I wonder why she scurried off so quickly."

"I daeno," Ailsa looked across the dance floor. "But I suspect it has something tae do wi' Mr. Featherstone."

"I believe you're right."

When Mr. Featherstone appeared with an older woman on his arm, Ismay smiled.

There was a look of displeasure on his face when he saw them, but he stopped to make introductions.

Mistress Innes, this is Lorna Bissett."

Ismay and Ailsa both curtsied. "Ailsa and I live in Morag Duffy's estate now. Morag was my grandmother."

Lorna nodded. "Roslyn has spoken highly of you. I'm glad we've met."

Ismay smiled. "Aye."

Mr. Featherstone looked around the room. "You've not seen Miss Day, have you? I thought a moment ago she was wi' you."

Ismay sighed. "She was, but it seemed she had other matters tae attend tae. She plans tae join us later."

"I've been waiting the evening tae talk tae her." His brow dipped low, and he scowled. "I would have thought she'd have something tae say about the ballroom and my grand home."

Ismay didn't answer but listened as he randered on about his ungainly fortune and magnificent estate.

"I've another spacious room in the east wing, but it's too smaw for an important affair such as this. Half the countryside is comfortable in this room as it's quite lavish." He tipped his nose into the air and sniffed. "The décor was duin in the French fashion which has a most walcome feel tae it."

Ismay sighed as Mr. Featherstone lifted his chin higher blethering on further in reference tae the opulence of his estate and the abundance of his possessions.

When he was finished, he spoke unendingly about his family history and how he'd come to attain such personal wealth.

The man was certainly an unpleasant sort, pompous and arrogant, thinkin' mostly of himself and only a wee bit of others.

Ismay could understand why Roslyn ran off.

She eyed Ailsa who appeared bored by the man. She drew in a breath hoping the night wouldn't prove tae be a very long, disagreeable sort of affair. Wi' this man at their side, time wouldn't prove tae be their ally.

Maybe Ian would seek them out soon and save both her and Ailsa from this most difficult situation.

\*\*\*\*\*

Roslyn caught ahold of the balcony outside one of the many doors and stood looking over the grounds. She drew in a breath of cool night air.

She'd escaped that dreadful man, Mr. Featherstone, at least for a time. The ballroom was large and full of people meandering about. She might be able to sidestep him while looking for Callum. She'd no intention of spending the evening wi' that self-centered, boorish man.

The moon was bright and full overhead. It's light cast a glow on the fields behind the grand home. Crickets chirped in unison almost tae the very tune of the violins inside the great room. She smiled solemnly.

She missed the quiet sounds of the trail and her mother and faither. Shauna might be dancing this very moment afore a great fire. If it weren't for Callum, she would have gone back tae them quite some time ago.

The stables in the distance were hushed and dark save for the steps of a couple stable hands. One was bent over the rail talking to the horses. His gentle voice calmed the jittery animals. He worked quietly intent on the horses.

The other carried a bucket and set it down near one of the stalls. He went back inside the building.

A young lad, in servant's attire, ran to the sleeping quarters of the staff. He went inside, closing the door behind him. A candle was lit in the window. He scurried past it.

Rosyln's voice was a whisper as she breathed quiet words.

My love, where have ye gone
aneath the patterned stars?
My heart it dies

without ye
while I wait in the
silence of the night.

Roslyn couldn't think of anymore. She stood a moment gripping the rail.

Maybe she should go back inside. If Callum was anywhere, he'd be amidst the crowd. But where would she find him.

She stared into the night sky. Surely, the Lord would lead her tae him.

She bowed her head. Tell me what I should do, where I should go. I've no plan, Lord, but let Your will be duin. Tell me where tae find him."

She opened her eyes and looked across the field again to where the stablehands were tending the horses in the stables. Something in the way the man moved caught Roslyn's attention as he tugged on the reins of the great horse and led it into a partitioned area.

The man resembled Callum and was certainly similar in bearing and posture. But what would he be doing at Mr. Featherstone's residence warking as a stablehand?

She blinked as she watched him disappear into the barn. Was it him? Could it be? No, it couldn't.

She turned when she heard a noise behind her.

One of the estate's staff, an elderly woman, dressed in a wool skirt and plain blouse, came out the door. "What are ye doing here, mem? You'll get the chill."

Roslyn pointed to the stables. "Do ye know him?" She peered into the darkness as the man came back outside of the stables. He drew water from the well to fill the troughs.

"Tis Robb, or what we call him. Mr. Featherstone took him in when he fell from his horse. Never saw oor maister do a good deed in his whole life, but it was a credit tae see how helpful he's been tae this man."

The woman gave a quick nod in the direction of the animals. "Robb's a might fine warker, and if he weren't habbled in the head about his past he'd be a fine gent."

"He lost his memory?"

"Aye, he recalls little about where he came from and who he was afore the accident. Mr. Featherstone was gracious enough give him a position at the estate until he could find him employment. And now the young man has been commissioned tae wark on a ship. Mr. Featherstone's friend owns it."

A sound escaped Roslyn, and her hand went to her throat. "It has tae be Callum." This was the explanation for why he hadn't come and why she'd not seen him. "It's him." And now, Mr. Featherstone planned tae send him off!

"What, mem? Ye know the man." The woman looked surprised.

"I believe I dae." Roslyn didn't say more, but took the steps leading to the patio. She gathered her skirts and ran across the yard as fast as she could to the stables. "Callum!"

The man turned when he heard her voice and watched as she went to where he stood. He dropped the bucket in his hand and waited for her to reach the stables.

He stared at her with an odd look as if he were trying to recall who she was. He raked a hand through his hair.

Roslyn breathlessly stopped in front of him and took his hand. "It is you. Callum. I did not know what happened. Do you remember me?"

He gave her a slight nod, though it seemed as if he were trying to fit together the pieces of a puzzle in his mind. "Roslyn?" His voice suddenly choked with emotion. "Hech ay!"

She flew into his arms and wept. "You did not leave me. You've been injured. I couldn't understand where you'd gone."

Callum's eyes filled with tears, and he wiped them away. "You were staying wi' a woman wi' a broken arm. You were caring for her."

"Lorna…Bissett."

"Aye! The one who did not care for me so much." His eyes sparkled when he said it. "I know it, and I know you, my love. My wee songbird and Locksley lass! I've not been able to recall anything until now."

Roslyn took his hand and held the back of it against her mouth. She kissed it and then looked up at him. "Do ye remember your promises, the ones ye made tae me? The last time you left?"

He drew her to him, and his words were thick with tears. "I'd plans tae marry you. I've a home outside of Crieff. I know it now, but couldn't remember any of it afore I saw you. Mr. Featherstone's home was foreign tae me and the people too. I must've needed tae see something or someone from my past tae recall it."

Then he put his hand on his forehead and held it there with a sudden painful expression.

Roslyn took a step closer. "Are ye unweel? I've said too much. I've hurt ye." She looked concerned.

He grasped her hand. "No, but I'm so sorry, Roslyn. You'd no way of knowing why I hadn't come tae see you. I never meant tae harm you."

"But ye couldn't know, Callum, and it's of no account. You remember now, and we're together. I've found you, and now will see tae it that all will be put tae rights very soon."

She turned to the manor house as a frown drew over her brow. "Though Mr. Featherstone's plans were tae take ye from me. He wanted you out of his way."

Callum drew himself up to his full height. His smile waned. "He wronged ye, Roslyn. He had it in the warks tae conveniently send me off on his friend's ship. Then you'd be free tae marry him. He spoke quite frequently of marrying a young woman soon."

"I've rejected Mr. Featherstone's advances more than once and refused his offer of marriage. I would've gone back tae my parents on the traveling wagon, if it weren't for you. And now I want nothing more tae do wi' that wickit man."

Callum smiled and touched her cheek. "He'll know it in time." He gestured to the home. "Go in Roslyn. Find your friends and wait there, but make no mention of what you've seen. I must wash and put on clean clothes. Then I'll find you."

"But…"

"My thoughts are intact, and it's my desire tae set the record straight, but I plan tae do it in the proper way wi' you at my side. I canna very well go in there in workman's clothing."

Roslyn nodded hesitantly. She took a step back and smiled. "I'll wait for you, Callum, but not long. Come back tae me afore the ball has ended, or I'll be looking for you."

He laughed. "I'll be there for sure. You can surely count on it."

She turned and skipped back up the path toward the home. She looked back once along the way and then continued into Mr. Featherstone's home.

Callum was already headed to the servant's quarters.

Roslyn's heart fluttered with excitement at seeing him again.

\*\*\*\*\*

Mr. Featherstone had disappeared somewhere into the crowd with Lorna.

Ismay and Ailsa hop-stepped on the dance floor to the quick, lively music, their hands crooked on their hips. They swung round in wide circles. Neither could contain their merriment and laughter.

The meesionar had joined Ailsa and laughed along with both of them as he swung her around.

Ailsa's cheeks glowed, and her smile widened at the look of surprise on Ismay's face.

Ismay moved close to Ailsa and whispered in her ear. "He's a good man. I do believe he likes you, enough tae dance wi' you. A meesionar!"

Ailsa smiled shyly and only nodded as she twirled away to finish the dance.

*****

Roslyn stood in the shadows awaiting Callum. She scanned the room, occasionally taking a sip of punch. Anticipation grew in her, like the billowing of the ladie's skirts on the floor, as she envisioned her reunion with the one she loved.

*****

# Chapter 28

Ian laughed as he swung Ismay around taking both her hands in his. "The Scottish lass, I've come tae know so well. Ye dance a bonnie jig, Ismay, and make the night a happy one."

Ismay's cheeks brightened. "I'm fond of the pipes and the lively pairty. And when I've a brawly partner, tae share the day, I find it all the more tae my liking."

"You find me respectable then, do you?"

"Aye, ye clean up quite well for such an occasion."

He laughed again. "And I will for oor waddin soon. I plan tae marry you afore ye change your mind."

"Then you're not afeart of losing your horse again? Do ye believe me tae be honest now?" Her eyes twinkled with a speeritie look.

"Aye, Ismay. Good Lillias is yours afore ye ask and any others ye wish tae have. Although I've less tae offer you than ye have tae offer me." He winked and grinned at her.

Ismay took his hand and twirled around once. "I am a very rich woman. So we'll share oor fortunes and oor horses."

He smiled when the song and dance slowed and ended. Ismay took his side as they left the floor to join the others.

They walked passed Grizel who stood eying them both with a look of distaste.

She was near a tall, extravagantly dressed older man with a pinched expression and an unusually small mouth. He lifted an eyeglass in his hand to his face to peer at the people around him.

When Ismay and Ian were within an arm's length of Grizel, she spoke loudly enough for those around them to hear. "I recall a time when this ill-fashioned orphant stood in the street like a common hissy, and now she believes she can don a gown of lace and hide what she truly is, a low-born kitchie-dame."

Ian moved in front of Ismay. His eyes darkened, and the tone of his voice was low and gritty. "I'll have ye know, Mistress Hawthorne, ye bring yourself down when ye attempt tae discredit another. Tis quite unbecoming of you. Though Ismay's heritage is one of great consequence, it doesn't matter tae me what title she holds."

His tone softened as he turned back to Ismay. "I've loved Ismay afore I iver knew her tae be the granddaughter of Mistress an Mair Morag Duffy."

"Morag Duffy?" Grizel stared at them both in surprise. Her lips tightened. "It isn't true. Morag's granddaughter?"

"Tis true, Grizel! And what's more, she owns the whole estate and retains the title." He squeezed Ismay's hand. "Though her speeritee, merry heart, and graci presence is what drew me tae her, not her grandmother's name. My humble proposal was made at a time when I presumed Ismay tae be an honest housemaid wi' a bonnie heart. I realized then that I could never be tied tae a woman wi' a perpetual scowl and an endless bitter countenance for propriety's sake."

Grizel drew her shoulders back and lifted her chin. "Well! I've haird quite enough of this foolish rander."

She turned to the pinched-faced man next to her. "Get my cloak, Broden. I believe it's time we leave this dull affair. I can no longer tolerate these impertinent guests."

Ismay and Ian both tipped their heads to her and left to look for others in their party.

*****

# *Chapter 29*

"Roslyn! She's back." Ismay pointed to a dark corner of the room. "But in the shadows."

Ian turned to look.

Ismay took his hand and tugged at it. "Come, we must save her from Mr. Featherstone!"

Ismay pulled Ian across the room as Ailsa followed. They went to where Roslyn stood.

Ismay sighed as she took Roslyn's hands in her own. "Oh, dearie, ye did not find Callum. And you thought ye might." She let go taking Ian's arm.

Then her eyes met Roslyn's twinkling ones.

"Wait, what's this?"

Roslyn smiled.

"Ye saw him? Where? What's happened?"

Roslyn eyes brightened when she looked across the room. "There." She spoke quietly.

Ismay, Ian, and Ailsa all turned.

Under a massive, arched doorway that led into the ballroom, Callum entered wearing gentleman's attire. He looked around the room.

Roslyn stepped out of the shadows as a wide smile spread over her face. "There's a reason he hasn't contacted me. I know it now, but things will be set straight soon enough."

Ismay gave her a curious look. Then she smiled. "I believe he sees you."

Callum started across the floor but suddenly stopped when Mr. Featherstone jumped into his path.

"Robb, you understand you were needed in the stables this evening. Ye must go back." He grabbed hold of Callum's arm and looked around nervously, attempting to redirect the younger man to the door.

Callum shook his head. "Tis no use, George. I remember it. I know all of it and am fair scunnered about it."

"No, you're my stablehand, Robb. You're leaving shortly tae go tae sea." George tugged at the collar around his neck. "You'll be leaving soon. Ye have a good position wi' my friend."

A muscle in Callum's jaw tightened. His voice lowered. "Ye knew all along, didn't you? You knew who I was and planned tae keep me from Roslyn."

George took a step back. "I'd met ye once. I did not know your name. I took ye from that horse and provided for you."

Roslyn ran across the floor and went to Callum's side. "You used the situation tae your advantage. Callum could remember nothing because of what happened. It was wrong what ye did tae him, Mr. Featherstone."

She took hold of Callum's arm. Tears shone in her eyes. "Ye separated two people who loved each other, and you were about tae send Callum away so that I would never see him again."

The people in the ball room gasped.

Lorna moved nearer to Ismay. On her face was a look of shock.

Mr. Featherstone reached and tugged at his collar making a choking sound. "He had so little tae give ye, Roslyn. You deserve a grand estate, a worthy home wi' many pretty gowns and great riches. I could give ye so much more than he could."

He stretched his hand out for Roslyn to take it, but she pushed it away. "My intentions were tae protect you. You must believe me."

"You think your grand home and promises can swee my heart when I've lived my childhood on a traveling wagon selling wares?" Roslyn put her hands on her hips. "Tae be wi' the husband I love in a wee cottage in the hills wi' a flock of skittish lambs is fine enough for me. Nothing is more bounteous than the unmatched stars awash in the night sky, or the great expanse of an ice blue loch. None of your riches can compare tae what God has laid out iveryday."

She sighed. "And I say this not tae discourage those who the Lord has seen fit tae bless in the way of material possessions." She smiled at Ismay across the room. "I know my friend would likely oblige me if I iver had need of a spot of Scottish tea from a silver cup."

Ismay smiled from the edge of the crowd. "You'd be very walcome tae it." She curtsied to Roslyn after she spoke. "The good Lord's country is always oor bonniest possession, yet a silver teacup's not always without it's charm and appeal. God blissins extend tae us in many ways."

Ian laughed. He leaned over and kissed her on the cheek.

A few of the ladies in the room nodded their approval while others drew their hands over their mouths in shock.

Roslyn smiled at Ismay then turned to Mr. Featherstone again. "The Lord didna allow your ill-faured plot tae come tae fruitation. I've prayed ivery day that I'd see Callum again. I'm thankful He has listened tae my humble requests. Now, we must go, sir. I hope that you will someday see the error of your ways."

Mr. Featherstone's brow contorted sideways. He tipped his head for the sake of propriety and spoke quietly. "I wish ye well, Miss Day. From this moment on, I will set my sights on a lady who appreciates the finer things."

Roslyn curtsied to him and nodded. "Good day, Mr. Featherstone. I wish the best tae you." She turned and waved to Lorna, Ismay, Ailsa, and Ian. "I'll see you soon, my good friends!"

Callum spoke quietly to Mr. Featherstone. "I plan tae take my horse back wi' us, the gray. It's name is Kurrie. There's little I daena remember now."

"Tis yours. I've no reason tae claim it."

Callum nodded stiffly as he took Roslyn's hand in his own.

The ball suddenly came to an abrupt end as the reunited couple exited the room.

*****

Under the moonlit night, Callum tugged his horse's rein and pulled it off the path. "Come, Kurrie."

"Where are ye goin'?" Roslyn followed him.

"Here." Callum tied the leather strap to a post that jutted from the ground near a fence row.

"But it's almost dark. Lorna will be expecting me."

Callum nodded. "I know, and I'll take ye there shortly. But I thought about what ye said." He took her hand and led her into the field. "I wasn't able tae dance wi' you, Roslyn."

She smiled.

He took her hand in his and drew her close. He spoke quietly. "I daena have a grand ballroom wi' a chandelier, nor servants, nor carriages such as George Featherstone…"

She put her hand near his lips. "Shh…please, Callum."

He lowered her hand. His expression was solemn. "I've none of those fineries, not one."

"But, Callum…"

He touched a length of her hair and ran his fingers through it. He swallowed drily, yet his voice was raw with emotion. "I have none of those things, but I'm happy Roslyn, because I have you."

His voice was a whisper in her ear. "Dance wi' me, lass. Wi' oor love, and oor cozy home, we've iverything we need." He kissed her then took her hand.

Out of the stars, a chandelier emerged. Scotch pine trees stood straight like servants awaiting their command, and a hovering wind became their pipes. And they danced to the song of the robin's trill while the blooming heather encircled them like a bonnie wreath.

Roslyn's heart soared at the thought of being with Callum again. All would be well in time.

\*\*\*\*\*

# *Chapter 30*

Ismay came out the door of her home and cocked her head to the side. She raced down the path to open the gate as Ailsa followed.

"The bagpipes! Do ye hear them, Ailsa? Who's comin' down the road?"

"I do not know, but the sound is clear and beautiful throughout the countryside."

Ismay waited near a rosebed at the gate as her heart lifted at the strong, brave melody surging round the bend. "There couldn't be a bonnier sound than this tae warm my day! And not a spot of rain!"

She was dancing by the time the band of merry villagers came into sight around a curve in the road. "Tis Ian in a kilt! He's playing the pipes in the front!"

She squealed and clapped her hands. "And there's Callum and Roslyn, Roslyn's family, Ross and Skye, the meesionar and the children, and half the village folk all dressed in their finest clothes! What's this?"

Ailsa laughed with knowing eyes.

Ismay looked surprised. "You knew about it, too!"

"Aye! And now I'll leave ye tae them." Ailsa smiled and went to stand next to the meesionar who immediately made room for her.

Ismay gave a pleased look then turned when Scotty and Winifred came out of the gate.

Winifred wiped her hands on her apron. She adjusted the starched cap on her head. "They've beat the blaud. He said they would even though a little rain never hurt anything." She smiled.

Ismay gave her a shocked look. "The whole knew this."

She turned and watched as Ian led the way on the path with the town following behind.

He finished playing the song and stopped standing at the end of the drive.

Ismay lifted her hand to her chest to still her beating heart. "What a beautiful sound tae wake tae!" She went to Ian and looked at him with smiling eyes.

Ian handed his instrument to one of his friends and took her hands in his. "I've a present for ye, love. Oor waddin shouldn't lack for it, and I know how much you've been desiring this." He let go and turned.

Ismay studied him curiously. "I'm not sure what tae think."

The other folk were silent as Ian stepped aside for an older gentleman with a weathered face to move to the front of the procession. "Your faither, Ismay. I found him."

Ismay stared at the man in surprise as tears filled her eyes. She wiped them away as the salty gentleman came closer to her.

The man eyed her necklace with a look of shock. "Tis you." His voice broke, and he wept openly. "I searched the countryside, Ismay. I looked all over for you. Though I did not find you, I hadn't given up. Och! My bairn, my blood."

She reached out and took his hands in hers, then she hugged him gently. "Morag told me she'd duin wrong. She told me I'd a faither I'd not known and that ye searched for me. I did not know where tae look efter all these years."

She turned to Ian. "My love! You did this!" She tugged on his arm and brought her faither and him together. "A faither who'll walk me down the aisle. Ye canna know what it means tae me."

Then she reached out and flipped the medalian around her neck over. The letters, ye know them? What do they mean?"

"P.L.P.D. I had no room for the words, but I wanted you tae know what ye are…priceless, loved, and a precious daughter. You were dedicated a daughter of the King. I knew He was looking out for you."

Ismay smiled. "When I lost my adoptive parents, these words, they gave me hope. I knew I had a Faither and a home and security wi' Him."

Ailsa nodded. "I've lairned tae rely upon Him also. When Ismay read your words tae me, I was comforted and lairned oor heavenly Faither loved me and gave me peace."

Roslyn eyed the jewery with a look of interest. "How beautiful it is tae know He's there for us."

Ismay motioned to her. "Come, look." She tipped the necklace over for Roslyn to read the back of it. "Your parents, they canna always be wi' ye, but your heavenly Faither watches over you."

Roslyn's eyes misted as she sang a pretty song.

He gave me rubies and gold.
He restored my soul.
He gave me peace and love
like I never felt afore.

He's my reason for living,
and my life I owe tae Him.
I am priceless and precious,
a daughter of the King.

I am priceless and precious,
a daughter of the King.

Roslyn smiled. "I haird this once along the trail. I never forget a song."

Ismay's faither smiled. "It's beautiful. God does look out for His people, His daughters and sons."

"Aye, He does." Ismay took Ian's hand in hers. "God be thanked for all of this, for friends and God's family, and for Scotland."

Ian nodded and then turned to the others. "Come, join us in dance and more song. We've a wedding tae attend."

Cheers went up all around as everyone made their way to the garden in front of the home dancing amidst the sound of laughter and the music of the pipes.

Ian bent down and kissed Ismay on the cheek. "Is it a good day for ye, love?"

Ismay nodded with sparkling blue eyes. "Better than I could have imagined. We've much tae be thankful for."

"Aye, we do." He tugged gently on her hand. "Let's go now, lass. It is oor day, and I've a mind tae marry you if you'll have me."

"Nothing would please me more."

Her eyes brightened as they headed in the direction of the meesionar to say their vows and join in the celebration.

*****

# Kara S. McKenzie, The Daughters of Crieff

Scottish - English

A Skelpin' - thrashing
Acause – because
A face like a bulldog chewin' a wasp – not very happy
Afeart – fearful
Aff the fair streenger – stranger
Afore - before
Often – often
Aff the fair – off the straight
Either - either
All – aw
An awfy pie-faced lassie – a plain girl
Another – another
Around - around
Auld – old
Aye – yes
Aw, Hullo, you'll have had your tea. – welcome to the home
Away ye go – You're talking rubbish
Bairn - child
Bairn- baby or young child
Baloo - used to hush a child to sleep
Bauld-bold
Baurmie - foolish
Bethankit! - God be thanked!
Biden - biding
Binkie – dent
Bittie - small piece
Blaud - rain, Heavy downpour
Blether – gossip
Bletheration – nonsense
Blissin - blessing
Blythesome – cheerful
Blythesome - merry
Bonnie - beautiful
Bonnie - good or nice
Bowsie – big, puffed up
Bowsome - obedient
Braisant - shameless
Braw - fine
Braw - handsome
Brawly - fine, brawly
Brither - brother
Broth - soup
Canna - can't
Carfuffle – mess
Cold - cold
Chitter - shiver
Clarty – dirty
Clood - cloud
Collieshangle – disturbance
Couldn't - couldn't
Crabbit - crabby
Daena - don't
Does – does
Dafferie - foolishness
Daft - mad, insane, silly
Dame - woman
Daunder - stroll
Daurk - dark
Dautie - darling
Deeviltry – deviltry
Different - different
Dead - dead
Deil – devil
Denner – dinner
Didder – take time
Did not - didn't
Diskivered – discovered
Dochter – daughter
Down – down
Downwith – downward
Dout – doubt
Dowie - sad
Dreich – dismal
Duin - done
Efter - after
Eejit - idiot
Efternoon - afternoon
Faither – father
Fair scunnered – fed up
Fairst – first
Fareweel - farewell
Farin - traveling
Fee – hire
Flink – frolic, to flirt, walk jauntily
Fullish – foolish
Furr beast, staig (young) - horse-horse
Gairden – garden
Gaein – going
Gentrice - gentry
Glen – valley
Goin' - going
Gracie - devout
Gree-agree
Great -great
Greatly - greatly
Gruel - porridge stick
Grumpie - pig
Grumpie-grumpy
Gustie - tasty
Haird – heard
Hatesome - hateful
Haud yer wheesht- Hold your tongue!
Hardships – hardships
Hech ay! - Indeed!
Heidy - headstrong
Heifer - cow
Heirship – inheritance
Hertie - hearty
Hillock - hill
Hissy-hussy
Hooch ay! - Yes!
Hoose - house
Hullo - hello
Ill-aft - crazy
Ill Trickit - tricky
Ill-deedie – wicked, mischievous
Ill-fashioned - ill-mannered
Ill-faured - ugly
Ill-kindit - cruel
Irksome - bored
Ither - other
Itherwise - otherwise
Iver – ever

293

Ivery - every
Iveryday - everyday
Iverything – everything
Jimpy - jumpy
Joskin - country bumpkin
Jyle – jail
Kampie - brave
Kelpie - water demon
Kiver – cover
Knitchie – a bundle
Kyndness - kindness
Lang – long
Lairn - learn
Lauboured - labored
Leeberty - liberty
Look see – look see
Linky – sly, roguish
Loch – lake
Loss of the heid – temper
Lowed up – on fire
Mad - hot tempered
Maister - master
Maister - teacher
Meesionar – preacher
Meesterious – mysterious
Mem – madam
Merry dancers - Northern lights
Mine ain folk – my own folk
Misbehauden - rude
Mischance – dangerous
Missie – Miss (young girl)
Mither - mother-mither
Morn's morn – tomorrow morning
Mind - mind
Naither - neither
Och! - Oh!
Oo aye! - Yes!

Oor - our
Orphant – orphan
Ouf – oaf
Overhaird – overheard
Pairt – part
Pairty - party
Pensie – pompous
Pilking - stealing
Puggled – tired
Raither - quite
Rander - talk nonsense
Ratton - rat
Rideeculous – ridiculous
Saicret - secret
Sairly - sorely
Sauld - sold
Schamin - scheming
Scoonrel - scoundrel
Scunner – nuisance
Sample - simple
Shullin – shilling
Skirt away - leave
Smaw - small
Speeritie - energetic
Speeritie – spirited
Spurtle - spoon
Stairt – start
Stairvin - starving
Stealt – stole
Straight oot the gate - honest
Streenge - strange
Streenger – stranger
Swee - sway
Sweetie - sweetheart
Swick - cheat
Swick – swindler
Swickery - cheating
Tae-to
Taigle - tangle
Tairible - terrible
Tairt - tart
Tapsalteerie - topsy-turvy
Tenti - attentive

Tattie - potato
Thaim – them
Tottie – small between - between
Unceevil - rude-unceevil,
Unchancie – dangerous
Unchancy – unlucky
Unnaitural - unnatural
Unweel - ill-ill
Unweel - sick
Unweel - unwell
Very - very
Waddin – wedding
World - world
Walcome - welcome
Walthie - wealthy
Watherful – stormy
Wayfarin - wayfaring
Wee - small
Wee-ane - child
Weel - well
Wheesht! - Hush!
Wi' – with
Wickit - wicked
Withoot – without
Wrangous - wrong
Wutch-witch
Yammer - cry
Ye - you
Yestermorn – yesterday morn
Yestreen – yesterday
You're doin' my heid in – Please stop talking.
You're talkin' mince – You're talking rubbish.
You're the wee hen that never laid away – You're pretending innocence

*All quotes taken from the King James's Version of the Holy Scripture

*****

Dear Reader,

If HEIRESS OF COMRIE, was a book you enjoyed and learned from I'd love it if you could tell your friends and family about them. My other women's fiction books and children's books are listed on-line on Amazon which you might also be interested in. I would also appreciate it if you would let me know your thoughts of my book on Amazon in the comment and star section or on your Facebook page, website or blog.

Thank you! In Christ's love,

Kara